Thomas Archer

Our sovereign Lady, Queen Victoria

Her Life and Jubilee

Thomas Archer

Our sovereign Lady, Queen Victoria
Her Life and Jubilee

ISBN/EAN: 9783337110901

Printed in Europe, USA, Canada, Australia, Japan

Cover: Foto ©Raphael Reischuk / pixelio.de

More available books at **www.hansebooks.com**

OUR SOVEREIGN LADY

QUEEN VICTORIA:

HER LIFE AND JUBILEE.

BY

THOMAS ARCHER, F.R.H.S.,

Author of " Pictures and Royal Portraits, illustrative of English and Scottish History," " Fifty Years
of Social and Political Progress," " The War in Egypt and the Soudan," &c.

ILLUSTRATED BY AN ORIGINAL SERIES OF HIGHLY-FINISHED ETCHINGS.

The present year, 1887, will mark an epoch in the social
and domestic as well as in the imperial History of Britain,
as being the Jubilee Year of the reign of Queen Victoria.

Everywhere in the United Kingdom, and throughout the
British Empire, there is an earnest desire among all classes
of the community to join in celebrating what is regarded
as a real occasion for public rejoicing, not only because Our
Gracious Queen and Governor has reigned for fifty years, not
solely because that reign has been marked in a high degree by
national progress and prosperity,—but also for the reason that
the Sovereign has displayed those personal and household
virtues which are dear to her people, with whom she has
ever manifested sincere, and it may even be said, familiar
sympathy.

While many of the celebrations of the Jubilee of Her Majesty's reign will be marked by all the pomp and splendour which properly belong to great national demonstrations, and while institutions of various kinds will be formed in honour of the occasion, it is believed that for the multitudes of men and women who regard the Queen with a sentiment that may be spoken of as that of personal regard and affection, no more fitting memorial can be provided than a complete and worthy Life of our Sovereign Lady – a " Life," such as that which is here announced.

The forthcoming narrative will present a biographical rather than a historical record: a record, faithful, interesting, and well illustrated, of the Royal Family and of the Queen as Sovereign Lady rather than as Sovereign Ruler. It is designed to be a complete and consecutive account, derived from the most trustworthy sources, of the life story of the revered and beloved Lady to whom we owe more than ordinary allegiance; and it will also be a permanent record of the celebrations by which the year will be distinguished. This will of itself constitute a distinguishing feature of the Work, and materially add to its historical value.

To narrate such a story as will be presented would, of course, be impossible without taking into important account the many great events and public occasions with which the Queen and the Royal Family have been personally and intimately associated; but the chief endeavour of the author will be directed to bringing before the reader in a bright and attractive form the chronicle of more than fifty years of the real life, the pure womanly, and therefore truly Royal life of our gracious Queen. For though Her Majesty as a constitutional sovereign has always taken a direct and personal part

—a larger part than is frequently supposed—in the government of the country, it is less the political or imperial aspect of her sovereignty, than the still higher recognition of it by the will and affection of the nation, that leads our thoughts towards emphatic and significant demonstrations of reverence and regard, now that we seek to celebrate the jubilee of her reign.

The life of Queen Victoria has been in perfect accord with the real life of the nation, for with the "people," their hopes and efforts, their aspirations and their troubles, the highest Lady in the land has ever been in sympathy. For cottagers and peasants—workers in factory and mine, at loom and forge — for soldiers in the ranks, sailors in the forecastle, toilers by sea and land—for all who strive to do their duty--she has on countless occasions manifested true and gentle interest, and in their times of rejoicing or of sorrowing has sought to convey to them assurances of her constant desire to be at one with them in the sentiments that rule the heart and support the spirit of a nation.

"Let my people see me," said the youthful Queen on one of the earliest occasions on which she chose an open carriage, that she might more freely respond to the loyal demonstrations of welcome from the crowds that filled the streets. The words were significant. For many succeeding years, and until the shadow of a great sorrow had fallen upon her, and more than the weight of passing days had impaired her strength, the Queen may be said to have lived in the sight of her people. The story of her life from year to year, even to the present hour, is one that will deeply interest loyal and truthful souls, to whom she has been ever true and loyal.

The publishers, therefore, have reason to believe that this work will be received with hearty welcome as a complete and timely memorial of Her Majesty's Jubilee, and they will spare no pains to make it worthy of the occasion by producing it in an elegant and attractive form.

The work will be in form small 4to, printed in the best manner on a fine paper specially manufactured for the purpose. The illustrations will consist of a series of twenty-eight highly-finished etchings, including portraits of Her Majesty, the late Prince Consort, and all the members of their Family; also scenes and events, public and private, in which the Queen has personally taken part.

*** The work will be published exclusively by subscription, and will be issued in 4 volumes, cloth extra, gilt edges, price 9s. each. No subscriber's name will be received for less than the entire work. Any subscriber who through change of address or otherwise is not regularly supplied, will please notify the Publishers.

LONDON: BLACKIE & SON, PUBLISHERS,
GLASGOW, EDINBURGH, AND DUBLIN.

(Vol.)

QUEEN VICTORIA:

HER LIFE AND JUBILEE.

OUR SOVEREIGN LADY

QUEEN VICTORIA:

HER LIFE AND JUBILEE.

BY

THOMAS ARCHER, F.R.H.S.

AUTHOR OF "FIFTY YEARS OF SOCIAL AND POLITICAL PROGRESS;"
"THE WAR IN EGYPT AND THE SOUDAN," ETC.

ILLUSTRATED BY A SERIES OF HIGHLY-FINISHED ETCHINGS.

VOL. I.

LONDON:

BLACKIE & SON, PUBLISHERS,

GLASGOW, EDINBURGH, & DUBLIN.

1887.

CONTENTS.

ILLUSTRATIONS.

CHAPTER I.

CONTENTS.

QUEEN VICTORIA:

HER LIFE AND JUBILEE.

CHAPTER I.

Birth of the Princess Alexandrina Victoria. The Opening of a New National Prospect. Kensington Palace and Gardens. The Queen's Predecessors. A Retrospect of the House of Hanover. The Georges. Family of George III. The Prince Regent and the Royal Dukes. Princess Charlotte and Prince Leopold. The Duke of Kent. His Marriage and Return to England. The Duchess of Kent. The Future Queen. Her Sponsors and Teachers. Early Training and Education. On the First Step to the Throne.

ON the morning of the twenty-fourth of May, in the year eighteen hundred and nineteen, an event, destined to be a blessing to this country and to the great colonies and dependencies included in the British Empire, was made known in the brief announcement:- "At a quarter past four o'clock this morning, at Kensington Palace, Her Royal Highness the Duchess of Kent, of a daughter."

There were neither electric telegraphs to flash the message to remote regions of the world, nor railways to carry it swiftly to distant provincial towns and villages in the United Kingdom: but as quickly as the news spread, it awakened deep interest among thoughtful people not only in England but on the Continent of Europe. There appeared to be little immediate probability of the infant princess succeeding to the throne, but peculiar circumstances had placed the royal authority in the hands of the Prince Regent, who was fifty-seven years old. His daughter the Princess Charlotte had died two years before, and as only the Duke of York and the Duke of Cumberland had been married previous to that event and were still childless, the announcement from Kensington Palace gave to the nation an impression, which soon became a lively hope, that the infant daughter of the Duke of Kent might become Queen.

An impartial retrospect of the history of social and political progress in England during the past fifty years will show how great has been the influence exercised,— at first perhaps almost unconsciously,—but always honestly and directly,—by a sovereign who in her earliest days won the hearts of the people by the happy characteristics of fearlessness, simplicity, and truthfulness, no less than by a personal charm which was altogether different and superior to the artificial mannerism of mere etiquette. The early training and the native disposition of the Princess Victoria had made it impossible to her to endure the sickening atmosphere of court intrigue, and she appeared to a multitude of loyal souls as a gracious, pure, and childlike presence, coming forth unsullied by old evil traditions, low aims, and narrow selfish interests; to represent from the throne a genuine sympathy with the higher aspirations and brighter hopes which had begun to stir even the masses of the people.

Considering the period of turbulent political demonstration that had preceded and followed the passing of the Reform Bill, and the rumbling of the storm which wrought such changes in France and Belgium, it may well be believed that by the accession of the young princess, and the sentiments of loyalty evoked by her youth and the frank confidence with which she trusted her subjects—serious social and political dangers were averted. It is quite certain that the pure womanly, sincere, and affectionate nature of the Queen had the effect of at once promoting all legislation and all social movements designed to strengthen family ties and enhance the sweetness and dignity of domestic life; and at the same time, the sentiments with which the sovereign continued to be regarded, were immediately associated with the best endeavours to attain to a higher standard of national morality, to improve the condition of the poorest, to promote social purity, and to advance the claims of mental and physical education.

In a word, it was universally understood and taken to the heart of the people that (to use the common phrase) the " bringing up " of the youthful sovereign had been that of a healthy English child—untainted by heartless ceremonial observances, and though subjected to rather more than usual responsibility in pursuing those studies which made her one of the most accomplished girls to be found even amidst the cultured aristocracy, enjoying the freedom and docile independence that comes of wise maternal influence and companionship.

The suite of rooms in Kensington Palace was a home which, though often dull, and always secluded, as the home of a widow and a fatherless child must too frequently seem to be, was the abode of loving care and assiduous attention. The mother, even in the first hour of her bereavement, had chosen to devote herself to the nurture of the infant before whom lay the probability of having to fulfil a great destiny at a time when the relations between the sovereign and the people would undergo a marked and significant change.

The public interest which was still manifested in the palace at Kensington was almost entirely associated with the knowledge that the Duchess of Kent and her infant daughter dwelt there. The queer composite building, distinguished neither by antiquity nor by architectural beauty, would, but for its being the birth-place of her Majesty, claim little really historical importance, for though the courts of William and Mary, of Anne and of the two first Georges were held there, its history scarcely takes us further back than

> " The tea-cup days of hoop and hood,
> And when the patch was worn."

It is desirable, however, in the interests of those among us who may not have a clear apprehension of the relationships which governed the accession of Queen Victoria to the throne by direct succession, to make a brief retrospective reference to the former courts and royal occupants of Kensington Palace, and this will enable us also to appreciate more distinctly the remarkable contrast presented by the court and reign of our Queen.

Speaking of Kensington Palace itself, it may be remarked, as Leigh Hunt says, that "it possesses a Dutch solidity; it can be imagined full of English comfort; it is quiet, in a good air, and though it is a palace, no tragical history is connected with it: all which considerations give it a sort of homely fireside character, which seems to represent the domestic side of royalty itself, and thus renders an interesting service to what is not always so well recommended by cost and splendour. Windsor Castle is a place to receive monarchs in, Buckingham Palace to see fashion in, Kensington Palace seems a place to drink tea in.   .   The reigns that flourished here, appositely enough to the nature of the building, were all tea-drinking reigns."

There had previously been royal residences, as well as those of the nobility and gentry, in Kensington, for the whole district was delightfully open and distinguished for the purity of the air; but there had been no palace till William the Third bought the mansion of Daniel Finch, second Earl of Nottingham and son of the first earl, Heneage Finch, the famous Lord Chancellor, who had risen to that office after having been Solicitor-general at the restoration of Charles the Second.

The garden belonging to the house included fifteen acres, a pleasant and ample breathing space even for a hard-worked official of such distinction; but Sir Heneage, who, though above reproach, prudently took care of himself, increased it by a grant from the adjoining land of Hyde Park. These gardens consisted principally of the ground squaring with the south side of the building, laid out in the formal and rather dreary style which existed in England before Charles the Second had invited Le Notre, the famous French gardener, to come to England and make a new fashion in some of the royal parterres. Clipped yew-trees and other sombre accessories were also in accordance with the fashion when the ground was first laid out, and some of these features remained till quite recently.

William, having designed to live at Kensington, and there to hold such court as suited his reserved and somewhat repellent temper, converted the country-seat of the Finches into a palace, not so much by architectural improvement as by making it the nucleus for a more extensive building; for which purpose he added to the lower portion an upper story designed by Wren, who also designed the Orangery, an accessory which was perhaps the most attractive feature of the palace.

Queen Anne, when she succeeded to the throne and to Kensington Palace, added about thirty acres to the gardens, which, it would appear, did not previously to 1705 extend further to the north than the conservatory, a narrow building then used for its original purpose of a banqueting-house. The palace itself was little altered, and was even at that time regarded as having no great claim to admiration; but the famous gardeners, Wise and

Loudon, carried out the picturesque improvements, and Addison in the *Spectator* says, " If as a critic I may single out any passage of their work to commend, I shall take notice of that part in the upper garden of Kensington, which was at first nothing but a gravel pit."

George the First succeeded to both palace and gardens, but he cared little about either, or about England for that matter, in comparison with his native Herrenhausen and his own countrymen. He could not speak English; he had left his queen, Sophia Dorothea of Zell, in Germany, imprisoned for life on an accusation never really proved to be true, so far as history has made known; and he was on no good terms with his son the heir to the throne. The government here was in the hands of Sir Robert Walpole, and the king seldom appeared abroad, even in the comparative seclusion of Kensington Gardens, where, however, persons of fashion who obtained admission had begun to meet and promenade, on certain days, to see and be seen. Caroline of Anspach, the consort of the Prince of Wales, of course attended the court with her maids of honour, and as the gardens were at first open to a few favoured visitors, and afterwards to a considerable number of persons who had claims to gentility, the promenades became famous. Caroline was a handsome or at all events an attractive looking princess, and though the king used to express dislike to her, presumably because she was the wife of his son (whom he disliked still more), and used to speak of her as "Cette diablesse, Madame la Princesse," there can be little doubt that she did much to popularize not only the promenade and the assembly at Kensington, but the dull and splenetic King also.

At anyrate, when her husband came to the throne, Caroline of Anspach obtained the respect and even the admiration of

those who knew her best, and though her assumption of a kind
of encyclopædic knowledge, or of the love of it, gave a curious
air to the court at Kensington, she succeeded in making the
palace and the gardens the resort of a great number of distinguished as well as of undistinguished people, and contrived to
let her conceited, narrow-minded, and tyrannical little husband
imagine that he had by far the largest share in attracting
attention, even though the royal train was composed of famous
wits and beauties, who, whether their claims to eulogium were
well founded or not, are celebrated by name in the published
poems or letters of Pope, Gray, and other writers of immortal
verse or polite and amusing letters.

To Caroline, Queen of George the Second, is due the
inclusion—perhaps the preservation as a fine open space—of
the present Kensington Gardens, for which she obtained about
three hundred additional acres, and practically commenced that
free admission of visitors and promenaders which has resulted
in this now delightful resort becoming a public haunt, where
innumerable Londoners go to "breathe in sunshine and see
azure skies,"—amidst the pure air of verdant open spaces, the
shade of pleasant groves, and beds, plantations, and borders,
where the best old characteristics of the gardens are preserved
in numerous trees and shrubs which are still marked by labels
showing their botanical designation, and in the beautiful flower-
ing trees that make the north walk so delightful by their spring
bloom or summer burgeon.

The gardens are now so thickly wooded that the only large
open space is that in which the "round pond" is situated, and
the vista which leads from that spot to the park. The "Ser-
pentine River," as it is called, was also formed under the scheme
of improvements ordered by Queen Caroline—a series of ponds

being so connected as to unite them in one sheet of water, which instead of being straight like a Dutch canal was irregular in its course.

Though William of Orange made a palace of the house at Kensington, it can scarcely be said that he formed a court there as a court was understood by the previous frequenters of Whitehall. There was little society, though there were many important councils. Not well used to the manners or the language adopted by the nobility of France or of England, he was characterized by a bluntness of speech and a reserved and saturnine demeanour, which, to the superficial observer, appeared to indicate a cold and unfeeling heart, though it is evident that beneath that impassive manner and expression there existed the capacity for sincere regard and intense feeling, as may be proved by the long and unbroken affection which, in his own undemonstrative way, he manifested for his sincere friend Bentinck, the companion who, with quiet and unselfish solicitude, had served him so faithfully and so well. But the plots and snares that had encompassed his youth had made William wary and reticent; the peculiar circumstances under which he came to the throne, and the rivalry of parties which he had to encounter, increased his caution, and there were few in whom he could confide. At the council of war or of state he was congenially employed, and still more so in forming plans for attaining the ends to which he devoted himself—a strong confederation for the purpose of resisting and ultimately breaking the power of France. He cared little or nothing for dramatic performances such as were then common; and during a youth, one might almost say a childhood, absorbed in the study of state affairs he had acquired neither the knowledge of nor the taste for poetry and general literature. Science was of little interest to him, except as far as it related to politics or to the improvement of the art of war; but he had acquired sufficient knowledge to speak and write in Latin, Spanish, French, Italian, and German, and he was acquainted with English as well as with Dutch, so that he was under no such disadvantages as those that beset the Hanoverian successor to Queen Anne.

The delight of the small, frail, "asthmatic skeleton," as Macaulay has called him, was in action. Neither stage-plays, court concerts, cards, dice, assemblies, nor the small observances of society had any charm for him. He had little leisure for amusements, and his chief recreation was hunting, which he followed with a violent and almost reckless ardour.

But little as William loved England, and few as his sympathies were for the English ways and people, he always made his own pleasure and ease, and even his supposed prejudices, completely subservient to the duties he had undertaken. He visited Hampton Court once a week, on Saturdays, and made his home at Kensington; and though his domestic and even his moral character was not a type of perfection, it cannot be doubted that the presence of his devoted and amiable Mary—Queen in name though she yielded all authority to her husband— made Kensington Palace more attractive than even the old house at the Hague would have been without her. It was at Kensington, when she died, that he was carried from her bedside fainting and overwhelmed with grief. It was to Kensington that he was carried after the accident that threw him from his horse while he was riding at Hampton Court, and occasioned the injury which hastened his death and left the succession to Anne.[1]

---

[1] According to the generally received story the King was riding at his usual gallop when the horse stumbled on a mole-hill and the rider was thrown to the ground, breaking his collar-bone. The Jacobites used afterwards to drink "to the little gentleman in black," meaning the mole which had caused the King's death.

In her reign Kensington Palace was no more lively than it
had been in the time of her predecessors; the Queen was dull,
her husband was duller, and probably as a consequence the
company was dullest, though several of the letters and annals of
the time indicate some "high jinks at Saint James'" amongst
the court ladies and gentlemen. In fact there was often little
company to speak of except on particular occasions, for the
Queen was "wrapped up" in Sarah Jennings Duchess of Marlborough, a passionate friendship for whom had begun at an
earlier date, and but for the intrigues of political parties and the
insatiable greed and ambition of the favourite herself, might
have continued till Anne's death. We all know how the
difference of rank was abolished between them in the confidential sense of equality insisted on by the Queen. How, as
Mrs. Morley and Mrs. Freeman, they lived as two idle and
rather self-indulgent gossips impatient of the ceremonial occasionally to be observed before strangers until the companion
and confederate became a dictatorial tyrant, and Anne suffered
under the constant domination of her unscrupulous termagant,
and the political opponents of Marlborough induced her to
abandon her former dearest friend and to adopt Mrs. Abigail
Hill as her confidante, with the new appellation of Mrs. Masham.

Kensington Palace, dull as it was, must have been the very
centre of intrigue at that time—a time, however, which has
been called the Augustan age of literature. We can indeed
scarcely refer to Kensington Palace and the court of Anne,
without thinking of Pope, Addison, Swift, Steele, Prior, and
the galaxy of dramatists, wits, poets, and philosophers, in
whose writings political allusions, descriptions of society, and
satires upon the court and the fashions are to be found.

There is no need to dwell upon the domestic life of Queen

Anne at the palace at Kensington. Her husband, who was too insignificant even to raise the ire of James the Second at his desertion, was neither ambitious to take any prominent part in public affairs nor capable of doing so if he had been permitted to assert himself.

In a reign during which the union with Scotland was effected, and the power and prestige of England was restored by the victories gained by the army of the Duke of Marlborough and his generals, the court was perhaps the "dowdiest" in Europe. The Queen had been on no good terms either with her sister Mary or with William of Orange, though her determination to support the Protestant succession—and, therefore, her own claims —had caused her to desert her father, who had not scrupled to desert her, and by her presence she had encouraged a meeting of the adherents of the Prince of Orange. During his reign, however, she had been tolerated rather than cherished, and, having married the kind of man who would do little to discourage her own indolent disposition, she fell into that kind of easy, self-indulgent way of living which is commonly called "coddling," a tendency which was obvious enough in Mary, but in Anne's case had been fostered by her having remained in retirement at Campden House in Kensington, with the permission to spend a month or two of the year at Windsor. It should be remembered, too, that she had a very large family of children, none of whom survived the days of early infancy except one, the unhappy little Duke of Gloucester, who died at the age of eleven, two years before his mother came to the throne—died, it was alleged, of the arduous studies set him by Bishop Burnet, appointed as the child's tutor and governor by the order of William, who, of course, recognized the boy as heir to the crown. It is on record that the little fellow had command of a regiment of boy soldiers, who

wore a special uniform, and with their band used to parade
before him as he sat on his pony in full regimentals of a general
or colonel, and that they would occasionally have a field-day on
Wormwood Scrubs or a review in Kensington Gardens, where
William the Third would himself be present to see how the
mannikin commander managed his Lilliputian force.[1] But the
little prince was already suffering from water on the brain,
though neither his parents nor others seemed to be aware of
the cause of his lethargy and physical feebleness. It is even
said that he was cruelly punished for ill-temper, laziness, and
obstinacy, while his apparent sullenness and indisposition to
exertion were the results of the disease of which he died.

It is not to be wondered at, perhaps, that the new régime in
Kensington Palace did not promise much court gaiety. The
husband of the Queen was a cipher, not devoid of a certain
undemonstrative regard, but caring little for anything that
disturbed his enjoyment of a good dinner, and with neither taste
nor talent for literature or art. There can be little doubt that
he exercised his dull persistent influence to aid the Duke and
Duchess of Marlborough in neutralizing any practical expression
of a sentiment which had arisen in the mind of the Queen in
favour of forgiving the injuries she had formerly believed she had
suffered by the marriage of her father with Mary of Modena, and
the birth of the son who was now known as the "Pretender."
With a weak but kindly and generous nature she had repented of
the complaints and invectives that she had so often indulged in
against Mr. and Mrs. Mansel, as she called her father and his
wife when writing to her sister Mary, and her penitence seemed
likely to take the form of acknowledging her half-brother as her

---

[1] The late Emperor Napoleon III. caused a regiment of boy soldiers to be drilled and placed
with their juvenile officers under the command of his son, the late " Prince Imperial," at a very
early age.

successor. This disposition was seized upon by the adherents of James and by the more violent opponents of the influence of Marlborough and the Whigs, and the result was continual plotting to bring the prince to England, and mutual vehement denunciations between the two parties, in which the clergy of the English Church took a prominent part. It was to the clergy that Anne in a great measure owed the title of "Good Queen Anne," for she consistently supported the Church not by empty patronage but by relinquishing the "first fruits" and "tenths" of ecclesiastical benefices to augment the small livings, so that "Queen Anne's Bounty" represented substantial relief to many who were in need. The Queen was not wanting in dignity of manner, combined with an attractive presence and a kindly pleasant aspect which made her popular, but her nature was generous and confiding— qualities which her weakness of purpose allowed self-seeking statesmen to turn to their own advantage. The whole atmosphere of the court at Kensington was that of political intrigue, and public opinion was in a tumult of divided interests, in which fierce animosity was stimulated by songs, caricatures, satires, and pasquinades which the rival factions printed and distributed broadcast.

The reign of Queen Anne has been called "glorious" because of the victories gained in the long wars, of which the nation at last grew tired; and doubtless the advances made in literature and the drama contributed to make it appear like the commencement of a new era. There were Tory and Whig writers, wits, panegyrists, and satirists, and many of them were to be seen at the levées or receptions at Kensington Palace; but Anne herself was often too depressed or too indolent to hold a brilliant court, and though she demanded the observance of strict etiquette on such occasions, she was apparently relieved

when, after a reception, she could get away from her ceremonious visitors and go to dinner, and to the card-tables which
were set out for the evening.

There was no startling breach of morality, no coarse or
disagreeable diversion in the court circle, but it was often
almost insufferably dismal, and no wonder, for the poor Queen
had no children, her health was failing, her former intimate
associate had been dismissed in disgrace when the Tory influence triumphed, and Marlborough and his duchess had been
abandoned. She had outlived her husband, her increasing bulk
and her infirmities prevented her from taking her former exercise of following the hounds and the stag in a light carriage
built on purpose that she might "hunt" at Windsor, and she
was now wheeled about the gardens at Kensington in a chair.
She suffered from what appear to have been epileptic fits, and
while she lay dying after the last of these seizures, the Jacobite
party in power had nearly succeeded in proclaiming the Pretender; but their plans were frustrated by the Dukes of Argyle
and Somerset, who presented themselves at the council sitting
at Kensington Palace, while Argyle's regiment was marched
from Westminster to take the place of the soldiers who were on
guard at Kensington. The queen was then dying —it was on a
Friday evening. A little after daybreak on the Sunday morning
there was a commotion in front of the gate leading to the
palace, where a large crowd had already assembled, and the
guards stood waiting for something. There was a blast of
trumpets, and presently the heralds came forth to proclaim
George Lewis, Elector of Hanover, King of England.

The succession had changed, and the throne was waiting for
the son of Ernest Augustus Duke of Brunswick Luneburg and
Elector of Hanover, and of Sophia the youngest child of

Frederick Elector Palatine and Elizabeth daughter of James the First. Bolingbroke and Ormond, the Tory leaders, had fled, Marlborough was on his way back, but was detained at Ostend. There would soon be new inmates, and the language of the court at Kensington Palace would be a foreign one, for the king could speak no English, and was not very likely to acquire a complete knowledge of the language, for he was fifty-four years old. His son George Augustus, now to be created Prince of Wales, was thirty, was already married to Caroline of Anspach, and their little son Frederick was seven, so that the new dynasty already seemed to be secured, while there was an additional advantage in the fact that George Augustus had served with the British under Marlborough, and had distinguished himself at Oudenarde.

The change of dynasty involved important changes in many other respects. William the Third had maintained the claims of personal government, but the conditions on which he had been accepted as King of England were in accordance with his own political professions and secured the authority and privilege of parliament. The restoration of the Stuart rule would have been impossible without a reactionary revolution, and those who had formed the new government were too strong for the conspirators who were in constant communication with the late king, whom the nation had never loved. It might have been said:

> " Pricked by the Papal spur we reared
> And flung the Second James;"

and this would have expressed the general sentiment, though men like Atterbury and other less distinguished representatives of the English Church were among those who took an eager part in the endeavour to bring over the Pretender, that he might be ready to mount the throne at the moment of Anne's death.

They might have succeeded in inducing the Queen to nominate her half-brother as her successor, which would at once have provoked a storm of opposition that could scarcely have stopped short of civil war, but Anne had become more infirm of purpose as her bodily infirmities increased, and the fury of the rival parties had driven her into a condition of constant timidity, which, while it made her subservient to the faction which was using every effort to keep in office, drove her to seek seclusion, at Hampton Court or Windsor, from the turbulent assemblies at St. James's. Yet in earlier days the Queen had been more than a mere lay-figure. She represented to the English people some very definite sentiments. She was an English queen, she made no demands that conflicted with the liberties secured by the constitution, and she was of a kindly and liberal nature, finding pleasure in acts of benevolence. Her coming to the throne was in a very popular sense a "restoration," and her name was "a name to conjure with." It seemed, to some, to open the door for James Francis Edward from St. Germains. But James the Second had alienated the English people, and his son was more French than English in character, manners, and language. His mother, Mary of Modena, was a foreigner; he had been educated in the Roman Catholic religion under the patronage of the French king, the arch-enemy of England and of political freedom; and if report spoke truly he had inherited or acquired the family vices and the family weakness and duplicity, even though he some-times displayed an engaging courtesy, which belonged rather to his uncle Charles than to his father James the Second.

So much of wealth and liberty had been squandered in the attempt to make James accessible to reason, so much had been sacrificed to regain the rights which he had endeavoured to annul, that men, looking at the young Chevalier de St. George as he was called—and at the middle-aged George Louis, Elector of Hanover, saw in the latter an heir to the British throne, who, by religion, education, and experience in constitutional government, was most likely to leave the administration of the state in the hands of English ministers, and to refrain from attempting to reinforce that personal sovereignty which in either case would have been unbearable.

Nor were these conclusions ill founded. George the First was not a candidate for the throne of England. He received the intimation that he had been proclaimed with a reservation that was next to disappointment. He prepared to grasp the situation with the cool and assiduous determination which distinguished him, and set off as soon as he could to present himself to his new subjects; but he did so rather from a sense of the responsibility which had fallen upon him than with elation. George represented a branch of the great Guelph family, which on both his father's and mother's side was related to the Norman and the Saxon kings of England, by the marriage of Henry the Lion with Matilda, daughter of Henry the Second. Not only his son but his daughter, Sophia Dorothy, was already married when he came to England. He accepted the succession not with avidity but with reluctance, and never afterwards scrupled to show that Hanover stood far before England in his regard; and that he left his adopted country with satisfaction whenever his duties there permitted him to visit the land of his birth. It would, perhaps, be too much to say that he disliked England and the English people,—but he was not at home here, and he was too old to learn to sympathize with English manners, to assimilate himself to the peculiarities of English character, or even to acquire the language. "He could speak no English, and was past the learning of it." Only two or three of the ministers of his council spoke French,—none of them German— and it is on record that Walpole, to whom he continued to intrust the control of affairs, had to manage the best way he could with conversation in Latin.

The court life at Kensington Palace and St. James's was of a quiet sort. The evening parties must have been dull enough for the few English peers or gentlemen and ladies who met the German friends of the King, including the repulsively gaunt and the monstrously corpulent ladies who had been respectively made Duchess of Kendal and Countess of Darlington, and of whom the least said here the better, as their rapacity was the theme of numberless satires and pasquinades; and their relations to the King, who brought them with him to England, were such as to have offended a truly moral court—if a truly moral court had been in existence at that period in England or elsewhere. Not that society at the palace was conspicuously immoral. It was dreary though occasionally there were episodes of rather forced merriment. The King was somewhat lazy in his recreations. The evening party mostly went to cards: if his Majesty visited the play-house or the opera he was carried in a sedan-chair, and sat like any private gentleman in the corner of a lady's box, "with a couple of Turks in waiting, instead of lords or grooms of the bedchamber." So Lady Townley—the wife of one of his ministers—wrote; and the couple of Turks appear, or once appeared, in the wall paintings at Kensington House. They seem to have been two faithful pages, named Mahomet and Mustapha, who had been taken prisoners by Prince Charles, brother to George the First, in the Austrian war against the Turks.

If George had exhibited no alacrity in assuming the English throne, he was not wanting in tenacity when he had once occupied it. This was a part of his character, but it was also a part of his character to endeavour honourably to fulfil such duties as his rather narrow judgment and limited education enabled him to undertake. Doubtless he was always ready to promote any measure which appeared to be to the advantage of his Hanoverian kingdom, and much of the revenue which he personally derived from this country went there; but his character contrasted favourably with that of the Stuarts. His word could be depended on. In a dogged narrow kind of way he was anxious to do strict justice without much tinge of generosity, and on the other side with a persistence in punishing offenders which was often brutal in its want of sensibility. A dull, unsusceptible, hard man, with undeniable courage and firmness, and not much humour. On the whole meaning well, and so far as England was concerned, doing well, by leaving the government in the hands of ministers whom he had found could best carry on the work.

It is only necessary to touch lightly the story of the courts of the Georges at Kensington, St. James's, or Buckingham Palace. In the letters and other writings of Swift, Horace Walpole, of Lady Mary Wortley Montague, Pope, Steele, Addison, will be found pictures of the coarseness as well as of the polished courtesy of the society of that period; the society that met at Ranelagh, at Vauxhall, and sometimes in taverns, where titled dames would entertain their friends—as well as at those masked and costume balls where the license of the time and the merely conventional decency of some of the leaders of fashion permitted such scandals that public opinion rose against them.

It must be noted that the whole country teemed with political squibs, satirical songs and lampoons, skits upon the fashions and bitter sarcastic letters, social and political libels, and furious, defamatory denunciations.   Nothing was safe from the wild torrent of imputation which teemed from the press, and many of the songs, stories, and anonymous broadsides were either impious or obscene, though numbers of them were distinguished by genuine wit and literary ability.   The political and other caricatures, too, became powerful factors in directing public opinion, and the best of them were, and are still, distinguished for marvellous faculty of art as well as for trenchant humour.   Hogarth, Gillray, Rowlandson — how the three names stand forth, and what a power the men represented; though among the amazing number of pictures that Gillray and Rowlandson issued, especially among those of Rowlandson, are many that shock modern sensibilities because of their uncompromising coarseness.   But they only somewhat exaggerated the actual coarseness of the day, and the dress, habits, and manners of the people whom they portrayed.   The country, and of course more especially the town, was, so to speak, pelted with caricatures, pictorial and literary; and coarse and violent as many of these productions were, it can scarcely be denied that the caricaturists were sometimes among the most powerful of the moralists.   Down to a date within living memory lampoon and caricature remained, if they do not still remain, a powerful factor in public life; as *The Caricature History of the Georges*, that able work compiled by the late Mr. Thomas Wright, abundantly testifies.

The dislike of George the First for his son had been so marked that, though it was afterwards concealed by an external compromise which enabled the Princess Caroline to attend the court at Kensington House and St. James's, there was no cordial regard.   It has been stated that the determination of the Prince to defend the reputation of his mother against the charges brought against her, and the endeavours made by his grandfather and the King to compel her to agree to a formal divorce, was the cause of the mutual animosity, but it was also alleged that the King resented the independent action of the Prince who was left as regent during his Majesty's visits to Hanover. However this may have been, it was certain that there was no love lost between father and son; and though the daughter of George the First (Sophia Dorothy) had, in 1706, married Frederick William, afterwards King of Prussia, and the chief place at court was therefore left to the Princess of Wales, we have seen that there was also no love lost between the King and his son's wife. But Caroline had a rare if somewhat a motley following of wits, poets, divines, and men of science, as well as of beauties, and she herself, of tall and commanding presence, and with no small pretensions to beauty, was well able to hold her own, even when the King and her husband were on the worst of terms, and while the Prince was in political opposition at a time when the efforts of the Jacobites added to the embarrassment of the government.

It is so difficult as to be almost impossible to make a trustworthy estimate of the real character and disposition of the eminent personages of that time. The whole atmosphere of the court and of society was one of detraction and those disparaging slanders that belong to the meanest and most spiteful exhibitions of party spirit. From the time that we have already glanced at, and of which we may read in Horace Walpole's letters, down to this later period—and even to the time of the French Revolution, to which his flighty, heartless records extend—levity, scandal-mongering, and misrepresentation seem to pervade the successive circles that moved in the precincts of the palace. Lord Chesterfield, Selwyn, Hanbury Williams, and Beau Nash King of Bath, were the contemporaries of Walpole, who saw out many fashions and many successive beauties: the Bellendens and Lepells, who were followed by Miss Chudleigh—the maid of honour who married first the Earl of Bristol and then a duke; and the Misses Gunning—those famous beauties who were mobbed by an admiring crowd whenever they appeared in public, and who received offers of marriage from the highest noblemen of England, till one of them became Countess of Coventry and the other the Duchess of Hamilton. So determined was the Duke of Hamilton to marry the younger of these two sisters, that he insisted on an extempore wedding; and having met the lady at Lord Chesterfield's sent for a parson, who, refusing to perform the ceremony without license or ring, at last agreed to use the ring of a curtain and married them in Mayfair Chapel. There was nothing very unusual in this, for the Fleet marriages, as they were called, were not only permitted, but had grown to be fashionable, and any couple could get a parson to perform the ceremony in a few minutes for a fee that sometimes did not amount to more than a bottle of wine or half a guinea. Society in these days was riotous, dissipated, and apparently reckless. Vauxhall and Ranelagh were by no means the worst examples of the manners of high life; and it may be declared that there was a degree of brutality, ignorance, and gross indifference to morality among some of those who belonged to the ranks of title and fashion, which is not now commonly found in any class, and may be illustrated by reference to the plays and novels of the time, and emphasized by the accounts of the "Mohocks," the "Scowrers," and the bands of fashionable bullies and drunkards, who made the streets of London terrible to timid and decent people compelled to be abroad after nightfall. Foot-pads in the thoroughfares and purlieus of town, and highway-men no further off than Kensington itself, added to the dangers that beset those who went out, even for a short distance, unprotected, but a section of the fashionable world had little more to boast of on the score of morals than the heroes of Gay's *Beggar's Opera*. When a waiter at Arthur's Coffee-house was arrested for robbery George Selwyn said, "What a horrid idea he will give of us to the people in Newgate!" and the sarcasm had a deep truth in it. But they were marvellous times for all that. When George the First, dying of an apoplectic fit in his carriage on the way to Osnaburg, left the throne vacant for his already middle-aged successor, the country was prosperous and rising in power among nations; and though George the Second was an obstinate, self-sufficient, and conceited little sovereign, he was not altogether without the qualities that were needed for holding his own and taking a prominent part in the affairs of the world. At all events he possessed that personal courage which is always a valuable quality, as he showed when he led his men, sword in hand, at Dettingen, and though he had the egregious vanity, which could not rest without his prowess and accomplishments being made conspicuous by the compliments of his courtiers, he was not otherwise devoid of the sturdy common-sense that had distinguished his father.

The fashions of dress during the greater part of the reign of George the Second were as preposterous as the manners, though artificially courteous, were wanting in real decorum. Enormous hoops, paniers, and sacks or loose robes over vast expanses of whaleboned petticoats were succeeded by towering head-dresses, constructed of horse-hair, grease, and flour, finished off with lace, bows, flowers, and feathers. Some of these "heads," as they were called, were designed to represent cabriolets (a fashion brought from France), post-chaises, and even wagons, and mingled with the natural hair as a foundation and plastered

into a solid edifice, were worn for weeks without being opened
and the monstrous rows of curls combed out. The dresses of
some of the men who aspired to be beaux were absurd; the
wigs being of stupendous size, the coat either artificially spread
out in the skirts or reduced to a mere jacket, and the stockings
"clocked" in various devices. There was no end to the
vagaries of the fops who were called, or called themselves,
macaronis, and wore an immense knot of artificial hair at the
back of the head, a very small cocked hat, and jacket, waistcoat,
and breeches cut down to the closest dimensions, the costume
being completed by a tremendous knotted walking-stick furnished with huge tassels. The lives of people of fashion were
passed in trivial pursuits, and there appeared to be little delicacy
or propriety as there was scarcely any privacy. The fashion
of receiving company at the *levée* or morning toilette was
common. A set of verses entitled "A Modern Morning,"
written in 1757, is little exaggerated. The lady, after taking
her chocolate, has risen from bed.

> "Then Celia to her toilet goes,
> Attended by some fav'rite beaux,
> Who fribble it around the room,
> And curl her hair and clean the comb,
> And do a thousand monkey tricks
> That you would think disgraced the sex."

The *Spectator* and other periodicals of that day frequently
refer to these morning receptions, and they are sufficiently
indicative of the manners of the time when in fashionable society
there was little modest reserve, and when people with any pretensions to "ton" lived in a kind of publicity which led to their
flaunting vices and foibles as though they were evidences of
good breeding.

It need scarcely be said that the conversation and some of the amusements at the levées and assemblies of Caroline of Anspach would not be tolerated now even among people of lower rank, but Caroline was superior in delicacy and in other respects to many of the "ladies of quality" who assisted in her boudoir. Lord Hervey (the vice-chamberlain), who wrote a kind of satirical comedy representing a supposed scene on the intelligence of his own death, gives us the impression that the conversation was vapid enough, that the Queen was a good-natured soul, with capacity for the smallest of small talk. But Queen Caroline was watchful and sagacious under a slightly skittish assumption of a desire to engage in conversation with clever people, and to listen to theological controversies, about doctrines to which, as far as can be known, she was indifferent, except as they may have afforded intellectual diversion, or even the lower kind of amusement derived from setting dogmatists by the ears. Lord Hervey's not very pleasant "skit" is as wanting in taste as its author was in honour, but the fact that it was read in the royal circle and afforded much amusement shows what could be tolerated there.

In the first part of this comedy the Queen is represented at the toilette in her dressing-room with the princesses and the ladies of the bed-chamber, Lady Stanhope, Lady Burlington, and Lady Sundon. Morning prayers are being said in the next room, of which the door is partly open; and the Queen says, "I pray, my good Lady Sundon, shut a little that door, those creatures pray so loud we cannot hear one's self speak [Lady Sundon goes to shut the door]. So, so; not quite so much; leave it open enough for these parsons to think we may hear, and enough shut that we may not hear quite so much."

It has been explained that this satirical passage does not

honestly represent the Queen's attitude towards religious offices, to which, though she was in general indifferent, she accorded reverence when they were supported by men of learning and of religious sincerity; but what strikes us is that a chief official of the court in constant attendance should have written a drama in which this and other professed reproductions of the scenes at a morning levée and reception should have been accepted, and have caused, not offence, but amusement.

It was not altogether a pleasant society at Kensington Palace at that time. George the Second with his high-heeled shoes, his swagger and assumption of dignity, his boasting of a courage which nobody could deny, his conceited airs, intended to carry a notion of gallantry, appeared to be artificial even when his intentions were honest. He was nearly as brusque as George the First; but he, of course, spoke English fluently, though with an accent, and this gave him a greater advantage. He was as avaricious and more meanly parsimonious than his father, but yet he was ready to disburse large sums on occasions, and never went from his word if he had promised to give or to pay. Happily for him and for the nation the Queen exercised great and constant influence over him, which she had acquired without his knowing it, and maintained because he scarcely suspected it. She was a woman of great tact, and was able to manage him without his perceiving that she did so, because she was his confidante. He consulted her about everything that concerned him. Even his faults and more than frailties she condoned, humoured, and to some extent controlled. That he loved her as deeply as he could love anybody was not to be doubted, and she deserved it, for she sacrificed what most women would have considered to be self-respect rather than alienate his confidence; and she may be said to have shortened her life for the sake of her dutiful attendance on him, plunging her rheumatic feet into cold water that she might, with whatever difficulty, walk with him in Kensington Gardens or ride in her hunting chaise at Hampton Court.

In the promenade at Kensington the King and Queen were in early days surrounded by a bevy of princesses, for, beside Frederick Prince of Wales, and William Augustus Duke of Cumberland, there were five girls, two of whom never married, while the eldest and the two youngest married, respectively, the Prince of Orange, the Landgrave of Hesse, and Frederick the Fifth, King of Denmark. Neither Frederick, Prince of Wales, nor his wife made long visits to Kensington: for if there had been dislike and disagreement between George the First and his son, the feeling of George the Second towards his son Frederick amounted to detestation. Nor was this profound aversion confined to the King. Neither his mother nor his sisters could long endure the society of the Prince of Wales, who never seemed to lose an opportunity of opposing his father, either by supporting the adverse faction in parliament, or by demands for money at the very time that he was acting with shameless animosity.

Whatever were his faults of manners and of violent temper George the Second was honest and true to his word; he was so regular in his engagements that it was said of him that "the fact of his having done a thing to-day was a reason why he should do the same thing to-morrow;" and he was undoubtedly brave, temperate, and honourable in fulfilling his promises. Frederick was, in many respects, the reverse; and his tastes were low; his conduct marked by want of feeling and a falseness and irresolution which caused unmistakable dislike and an expression of contempt to be applied to him by his parents, his sisters, and even by ministers and politicians, except those who had something to gain by a temporary adhesion to his interests. He had been a trouble and an anxiety to his mother from boyhood, and in manhood he traduced and insulted her even after he was married to the Princess Augusta of Saxe-Gotha, and made occasional visits to Kensington, where he would annoy the Queen by going late to the chapel, and making his wife, instead of entering by another door, squeeze to her seat between the Queen and her Majesty's prayer-book.

William Augustus, the Duke of Cumberland, was not often at court either. He was with his father at Dettingen, and was afterwards, as everybody knows, engaged in the suppression of the rebellion which greeted the arrival of the Pretender in Scotland. In his case, as in that of every prominent personage of the time, it is difficult to estimate the popular opinion, for on one hand enthusiasm for his signal success and the victory at Culloden led to his being spoken of in terms of adulation, while the bright and fragrant flower known as Sweet William is said to have been named after him; on the other hand, the cruelties which under his authority were needlessly and indiscriminately inflicted on the wretched people of the Highlands after the suppression of the rebellion, gained for him the appellation of "the Butcher," and this with his corpulence gave the cue for numberless caricatures and lampoons. The duke never married. In the latter part of his father's reign he was driven from Hanover by the French and returned to England, where he lived but little noticed till 1765, five years after his father's death, when he died after a stroke of palsy.

The Queen had died in 1737, but the event did not take place at Kensington Palace. George was deeply affected at his wife's death, declaring that he had never seen another woman

who was worthy to buckle her shoe, and perhaps he then awoke
to the consciousness of all that she had borne for his sake,
including the knowledge of his immoralities and the uncon-
tradicted aspersions that had attributed his parsimony and
avarice to her influence. His sense of her loss did not, however,
prevent him from bringing Madame Walmoden from Hanover
and making her Duchess of Yarmouth.

Caroline had on her death-bed recommended the King to
the minister in whose sagacity she had so long confided, and
Walpole continued for some time to maintain his pre-eminent
influence, but other times and other complications were at hand:
the new alliance against France, the war which drained the
King's private resources for the protection of Hanover, the
political situation, which, after Walpole had been made a peer,
led to the administration of the elder Pitt, and the subsequent
stirring period in which England recovered and triumphed over
threatened adversity, closed the reign of the second sovereign
of the house of Brunswick-Hanover.

The Prince of Wales was still a thorn in the side of the
King—still had his party, which was ready to push the tactics
of faction almost to rebellion—but there had been a tacit toler-
ance on the part of his Majesty, and a more decent regard for
appearances on the part of the prince, for some time before the
death of the latter, which occurred after a short illness in 1751,
when he was forty-five years old. The cold self-contained
King was greatly affected when Lord North was sent to him
with the intelligence. The King, who was playing at cards—
for it was in the evening immediately went down to Lady
Yarmouth, looking extremely pale and shocked, and only said,
"Il est mort;" but brief as the remark may appear, and little
as it might have implied, the conduct, kind and even gentle,

of the King to the widow was a proof that he was not destitute of a feeling of deep regret and of compassion for her and her children. George the Second was, so far as we can judge, a better man and a more kindly one, than his reserved nature and disdain of pretending to an interest in pursuits and conversation for which he did not really care, led people to imagine.

At the death of Queen Caroline the court at Kensington Palace underwent considerable changes. On the death of George the Second it ceased to be held there; for his grandson, George the Third, abandoned it as a royal residence. George the Second had survived his troublesome son for above eight years. Early in the morning of the 25th of October, 1760, he had risen as usual, had taken his chocolate according to rule, and was about to go down for a walk, when his valet, hearing a heavy fall, ran into the room. The King was either dead before he could be raised from the floor or died immediately afterwards; one account being that he had said, "Call Amelia," referring to his daughter, who, coming presently, but because of her deafness being unable at once to understand what had occurred, did not perceive that he was dead till she went to look at him lying on the bed or couch where he had been placed. The cause of his death was the bursting of the right ventricle of the heart. He was seventy-eight years old.

Frederick, his son, had left six children, George William Frederick, who, as George the Third, succeeded his grandfather; Edward Augustus, Duke of York, who was never married; William Henry, Duke of Gloucester, who married the Countess Waldegrave, and whose son Frederick William married the Princess Mary, daughter of George the Third; Henry Frederick, Duke of Cumberland, who married Lady Luttrell, but left no children; the Princess Augusta who married the Duke of

Brunswick-Wolfenbuttel and was mother of the Duke of Brunswick who fell at Quatre Bras, of Charlotte who married the Duke of Wurtemburg, and of Caroline the erratic and unfortunate princess who became the wife of George the Fourth. The younger daughter of Frederick was married to Christian the Seventh, King of Denmark.

George the Third was the first sovereign of the Hanoverian dynasty born in England, and from his earliest years he appears to have gloried in being English. He was only a boy of thirteen when his father died, and he had been kept in such retirement, not to say seclusion, by his mother and her friend and counsellor the Earl of Bute, that little was known of him in the court or society till he became of age. It is recorded that "till he was twenty-one years old he had never been introduced to the privy-council, nor matriculated at either of the universities, nor had he ever been allowed to display the powers of his mind, his judgment, or his taste in the selection of his associates: that he had been held in a state of liberal seclusion as absolute and unbroken as if his capacity to fulfil the varied and weighty functions of a king had depended upon his remaining a stranger to those future functions, utterly ignorant of the character of his subjects."

This is taken from the point of view of a political opponent of Lord Bute; but it was unquestionable that when, at the age of twenty-three, George the Third came to the throne his attainments were not conspicuous, though it was pretty generally declared that the instructors who had the charge of forming his ideas had impressed upon him the power which he should exercise when he became King, and the personal authority which belonged to the royal prerogative, even if they had stopped short of preaching the doctrine of arbitrary rule. At the same time he was kept under the strict control of his mother and the Earl of Bute, with the object, it was believed, of their being able to retain power in their own hands by acting through his instrumentality. He was for some years even made to continue to dress in a more juvenile fashion than his age warranted, that his mother might subject him to those domestic restraints, which he never appeared to resent with any violence, though they were carried so far as to make him frequently listless and even sullen. Of course the influence of Bute was made the subject of gross and venomous scandals and caricatures against the dowager princess—for John Stuart, Earl of Bute, was considerably detested, and though, when he became the head of the ministry on the accession of the prince, he appeared to encourage literature and the arts, he was himself more conspicuous for his pride and overweening ambition than for his talents, and it soon became plain enough that the literature of which he became the patron was that of the men, amongst whom was Smollett, who were on what was called the Jacobite or high Tory side, and would write to support the royal authority and arbitrary power.

Frederick Prince of Wales had first made the acquaintance of the young Scotch nobleman at some private theatricals at the house of the Duchess of Queensberry, where he performed the part of Lothario in "The Fair Penitent." He was invited to Leicester House and became a companion of the prince, after whose death he remained the confidant of the dowager princess, who gave him the office of groom of the stole, a position from which, by participating in the political intrigues that were carried on at Leicester House, he contrived to obtain an influence which, after the resignation of the elder Pitt, who was created Earl of Chatham, led to his succeeding Newcastle as first lord of the treasury.

There can be no doubt that the education of George the
Third was seriously neglected, but it is at the same time doubtful whether his intellectual power was such as to have enabled
him to attain any distinction in the higher branches of study.
He never could be induced to apply himself to Greek and Latin,
and though he was said to have gained some proficiency in
music, of which he was a good judge, and also to have a knowledge of mathematics and mechanics, and more than a mere
taste for the study of astronomy, it is probable that the sub-
jection in which he was held, the strife and suspicion which
were too prominent in the household, and his own natural inclination for a quiet rural life, united to increase a natural
depression which was habitual with him. All accounts agree
in representing him to have been, even as a youth, singularly
temperate in his habits, precise and careful in his demeanour,
and with a simple kindliness and affection in his relations to
his family. It would appear that, to use a common expression,
the dowager princess was of a "nagging" temper in her relations
to her eldest son. Perhaps she could not admire or appreciate
a youth who displayed neither scholarly accomplishments nor
what were then regarded as elegant manners. But George
maintained a dignity of his own, though he dressed plainly and
his manner was quiet even in his amusements. He was never
lacking in courage, was fond of riding spirited horses, was tall
and well-proportioned enough to look well in the saddle, and was
distinguished for a certain determination of demeanour, and a
directness and honesty of purpose which are often associated with
the kind of firmness that may degenerate to obstinacy under
opposition. It was unfortunate that the lessons which he received
on the subject of royal authority served to warp an intellect somewhat narrow, and to lead to violent assertions of determined

self-will on occasions when his opinions were opposed to those
of his advisers who could best estimate the attitude of the
nation. His really strong religious principles and his genuine
desire to rule wisely and for the benefit of the country did not
always enable him soon to overcome the smouldering anger
with which he regarded any representation which he fancied
was an attempted infringement of his prerogative, and for which
he expressed his resentment by secluding himself from his
ministers and nursing his wrath in moody contemplation of the
affront offered to his royal authority by any strong expression of
an opinion contrary to his own. There can be little question that
these fits of obstinate self-assertion and the accompanying irrita-
bility at any contradiction or remonstrance were attributable to
a defective training acting on a tendency which in later years
became so pronounced as more than once temporarily to impair
the mental balance when subjected to strong provocation, and
this may be sufficient to account for the malady which rendered
it necessary on two or three occasions for him to go into retirement, leaving his son, the Prince of Wales, to act as Regent.

This, however, belongs to a later date, and forms no part of
the narrative with which these pages are concerned. Nor need
we enter for more than a moment upon the records of the
comparatively pure and blameless life of the youth who, at
twenty-three years old, succeeded to the throne of George the
Second. By the real goodness of his intentions and the
practical virtues which distinguished his personal character
George the Third may be said to have commenced a new era
in the history of court life; and one or two stories of early
attractions are by contrast so innocent, that even if they were
proved to be true they would have no weight against the
untarnished chronicle of a domestic fidelity which afforded no

opportunity even to the unscrupulous libellers and scandal-mongers who were ever on the watch to assail the private, no less than the political, relations of the throne. It was generally known and accepted at the time that Prince George of Wales had formed a youthful but still a deep and ardent attachment to the young and charming Lady Sarah Lennox, daughter of the Duke of Richmond. The prince, who was much engaged in out-door recreations, was said to have seen the young lady on some occasion when she was at a haymaking, in which she and some aristocratic companions were taking a playful part, but, at anyrate, they had many opportunities of meeting, and the prince earnestly urged his suit, to be met with a refusal, which had the effect of making him so unhappy that he gave up his field-sports and neglected dogs and horses. Then, it is said, the young lady relented, and there was really an engagement between them, which, though it was not cancelled by the dowager princess and her adviser, neither of whom, perhaps, dared to carry matters with such a high hand, came to an end on the sudden accession of the prince to the throne, when the view of public duty which was adopted by the young King, and had probably been constantly presented to him, led him to relinquish his intention to marry Lady Sarah and to make her his consort. The conviction that such a marriage was not permissible seems to have grown in intensity afterwards, and to have led him not only to endeavour to control his brothers in their choice, and to prevent them from forming any other legal ties than those that would mate them with royal families, but also at a still later date to his promotion of the Royal Marriage Act—a measure which secured little and inflicted much, as it probably caused more evils than it was designed to prevent.

The intelligence of the death of his grandfather was conveyed to the young prince on The Hundred Acres of Banstead Downs, whither he had ridden to follow a stag that was to have been turned out. The prince was preparing for the chase when the messenger arrived, and he at once got off his horse to question the man. Accounts that were afterwards published professing to be from the statements of attendants remind one of the declarations of Mr. Perch, the messenger to the firm of "Dombey and Son," who used to confide to his acquaintances the remarks made to him by eminent clients of the house during the crisis of its history. One report represents the prince as saying, when he heard the tidings of the King's death, "Poor old gentleman! I little expected these tidings this morning, for the King was remarkably well last night;" and represents him to have been much affected by the thought of the grief of his aunt Amelia. Another equally authentic addition to the story is that he said, "God rest his soul and enable her to bear this heavy blow! All the pleasures of this life are now for ever past with me;" a sufficiently remarkable observation unless it had reference to his dread of responsibilities which he afterwards undertook with no little resolution, or to the conviction that he would now be compelled to relinquish the object of his affections. Similar accounts, including that of Sir Levett Hanson, imply that the means taken by the dowager princess and Lord Bute to separate the lovers and to impress the prince with the dire effects of his persisting in the determination to marry Lady Sarah, had the effect of convincing him that it was necessary for the sake of his mother's happiness and the good of the nation to sacrifice his deepest feelings: and it is even represented that he expressed some fear that his mind would not bear up against the shock of disappointment, but that he finally wrote a letter full of bitter regret and tender sorrow to the lady, explaining that he was called upon to make this sacrifice to duty.

These representations, however, have to be regarded with caution; for, at all events, Lady Sarah Lennox having been, of course, prohibited from all further correspondence with the prince, recovered from her disappointment sufficiently to be present at the marriage of her former lover to the princess whom he had chosen for his consort.

It says something also for his firmness and determination that in an extraordinary council in the year following his accession he announced that he had made his choice; that ever since his accession he had turned his thoughts towards a princess for his consort, and that, after mature deliberation, he had come to a resolution to demand in marriage the Princess Charlotte of Mecklenburg-Strelitz. In the following year the marriage took place, and the joint coronation followed in September, so that no time was lost in vain regrets, if any such existed.

With the court of George the Third there is no need to occupy these pages. Enough to say that the simple decorum and the orderly domestic character of the king was shared by his consort, a precise, somewhat formal, but not arrogant and not unkindly little woman, with no pretensions to beauty, but with a very decided opinion of what was due to the somewhat exacting etiquette and assiduous attention which she demanded of maids of honour and attendants, and with a keen eye to economy. It should be recorded, however, that her alleged avarice, and even the supposed parsimony and stinginess with which both she and the King were charged in endless libellous pictures and coarse lampoons, had little foundation except in comparison to the extravagance of their sons, and the examples set by those who could be profuse at the expense of creditors.

or in the expectation of obtaining aid from parliament to pay their debts.

The court was no longer held at Kensington Palace, nor did the King and Queen ever reside there. Perhaps not without reason George the Third seems to have had a dislike for the place or its associations, and preferred Buckingham House, where the levées of the King were held from the year 1806 to 1810, in fact till he became unable to attend even though they were private receptions. Buckingham House, or "the Queen's House" as it was then commonly called, was not a palace, but was a large and finely arranged mansion, very beautifully situated in St. James's Park on the site occupied by the present palace, to make room for which the original house was pulled down in 1825 by order of George the Fourth. Buckingham House was built by a Captain Wynde, a native of Bergen-op-Zoom, for John Sheffield, Duke of Buckingham, the poet and patron of Dryden. At his death in 1721 the Prince and Princess of Wales (afterwards George the Second and Queen Caroline) endeavoured to purchase it of the widow, but did not succeed; but in 1761 George the Third bought it of Sir Charles Sheffield for £21,000, and settled it on Queen Charlotte as a substitute for Somerset House, the former palace or house of the Protector Somerset, which then occupied the site of the present pile of public buildings, and had always been recognized as part of the jointure of the Queen consort.

When George the Third and Queen Charlotte left their favourite Windsor to come to London, Buckingham House was their home, and there all their children were born, excepting their eldest son, George, Prince of Wales.

The royal family was a large one, and was not in all respects distinguished for the docility which might have been better developed under a less precise and rigid domestic government than that which appears to have been employed by the royal parents. George the Third was not only deeply influenced and very injuriously affected by the seclusion and suppression to which he had in early life been subjected, but he made the mistake of displaying, in the domestic sphere, the arbitrary power which he had afterwards been taught that he possessed. In the domestic sphere, however, it is most desirable that such power, if it be exercised at all, should never be allowed to show itself in sullen, unreasoning obstinacy, but should be tempered with parental wisdom. This wisdom it may be feared the head of the nation did not possess, though he had a kindly heart and a fund of sound common sense which supplied the place of judgment when it was not obscured by gusts and fits of a temper, doubtless partly attributable to the effects of a mental malady, which recurred in a marked form only at long intervals until near the end of a protracted life, when he remained altogether in retirement.

If the discipline of the royal family was somewhat rigid and monotonous, the court etiquette was also precise and even severe, while it was simple and unostentatious. The royal household was unpretentious, there were no magnificent hospitalities, few splendid festivities—too few, perhaps, since some of those which had in earlier times been regarded as essential to the royal state and of which a revival was expected, were not observed. Queen Charlotte was a shrewd, sensible, gentle-speaking, decorous, very plain-looking little woman, with a certain pride which exacted not only the deference of state courtesy, but the drilled manner of conventional respectability and morality. This was perhaps all that could be enforced in a society which had to be reconstituted among the persons chosen by the sovereign as personal attendants. That the court was dull, and the duties of the ladies and maids of honour arduous and even exhausting, may be learned perhaps from the pages of the diary of Madame d'Arblay—the Miss Burney whose name is so intimately associated with the Johnsonian recollections;—but probably nobody who had the means of knowing anything of the royal family really doubted the goodness and underlying her narrow precision and parsimony the kindly nature of Queen Charlotte. Most certainly she did not accumulate money for the purpose of indulging in personal extravagance or selfish gratification. At her death, when her will was proved, it was found that she had no hoard of wealth—that her possessions were in fact so few that except by the sale or distribution of her valuable jewels she was unable to leave any considerable legacies to her daughters. Possibly such money as she could command had been spent in trying to avert the effects of the extravagance of some of her sons, who had as vast a faculty for public display, for enormous extravagance, and getting into debt and endeavouring to shift the responsibility of it, as their mother had for avoiding such liabilities. It is only fair to believe she may have contrived to secure much privacy and seclusion not only because of her own disposition, but for the purpose of preserving the quiet mode of living which she thought was essential to the health of the King, whose condition no less than his tastes made it desirable that he should have frequent intervals of retirement from public excitement.

The more domestic life of the royal family during the boyhood of the sons of George the Third was frequently passed at Kew, where the royal dukes received their early education under preceptors who prepared them for school or college. Kew House had belonged to Samuel Molineux, who was secretary to George

the Second while he was Prince of Wales. He was known as
"an ingenious astronomer." The Prince took a lease of the
house, and often resided there, and it afterwards came into the
possession of his son Frederick, who commenced the formation
of Kew Gardens, and his widow continued to reside there, and
in 1760 established the Botanic Garden. After her death George
the Third renewed the lease; and the associations of the place,
unlike those of Kensington, were so agreeable to him that he
commenced building a new palace on a spot nearly opposite the
familiar house, but the building was unattractive in appearance
and inconvenient in its arrangements, was never completed, and
remained unfinished until it was taken down. Close to the spot
where this building was erected, however, was an old house
which, in 1781, had been bought in trust for the Queen, who
had taken over a long lease of it, and this ancient mansion was
in reality the residence of various members of the royal family.
It was here that George the Fourth was educated, and here
Queen Charlotte died in 1818.

The history of political and national events of the period
over which we have been passing forms no part of the intro-
ductory references necessary to the narrative which is to occupy
the following pages. The tremendous episodes of the establishment of American independence; the French Revolution, the
excesses of which had the result of consolidating and maintaining British loyalty and patriotism; and the long and
determined opposition by which England became instrumental
in breaking down the usurpation of Napoleon Bonaparte on the
Continent of Europe were all included in the long and, speaking
after the manner of loyal histories, "the glorious" reign of George
the Third. Our retrospect, however, has been for the purpose
of tracing the succession by which a reign truly noble, and

attended with beneficent influences, inaugurated a new era of the
social and domestic life of the nation. It is, of course, to be
remembered that the accession of George the Third was also
an event which exercised a vast influence, because of the
character of a sovereign who from early youth had manifested
a simple and sincere regard for religion and morality. At the
moment that he ascended the throne he emphatically declared
his intention to uphold the claims of both, and by his domestic
example, and his determination to discountenance the vices which
had too long prevailed in society, he gave powerful aid to those
who were earnestly engaged in promoting the moral and religious
improvement of the people. Excesses that had been regarded
without abhorrence, even if not with complacency, while they
seemed to be countenanced by the manners of a dissolute circle
associated with the court, were no longer openly tolerated by
those who sought the favour of a King and Queen who during a
long married life maintained mutual confidence and faithful affection. The royal approval and assistance were never sought in
vain for efforts to raise the standard of public virtue above the
brutal debauchery and gross sensual indulgence which had too
strongly marked the manners of a vast section of the population.
At the same time, various institutions for increasing education
and promoting art and science, which had already been established or proposed, were rapidly developed. Numbers of
energetic and enthusiastic men found that the time had come
when their efforts would be successful in organizing and directing
well-devised means for the rescue of society from much of the
vice and ignorance by which it was debased.

Though the court of George the Third was unlike that of
his predecessors, there appeared to be much quarrelling and
disorder among the members of the royal family. The royal

dukes were perpetually opposing each other in politics, and frequently disregarding the opinions of the King, but there seems to have been a good deal of genuine affection, especially between the elder brothers, in times of trouble and domestic sorrow.

Perhaps the exception was Ernest, who became Duke of Cumberland on the death of his uncle, the brother of George the Third. There has scarcely been a man in the history of the country for the last seventy years who contrived to make himself less popular, or indeed more generally detested, than " the dreary, galloping duke," as he used sometimes to be called; but we shall have to say a few words about him presently.

It can scarcely be said that George the Third was ever on very good terms with all his sons at the same time, even if he was heartily in sympathy with any of them after they had passed the days of childhood. In fact, from boyhood they were a troublesome family, and as they grew older some of them had to be sent away to Germany or elsewhere to school or college. Neither of their royal parents possessed the qualities necessary to control or to direct a number of lads who inherited a considerable amount of self-will, and were by their position able to disregard many of the restraints to which youths in ordinary stations are more easily subjected.

There were very remarkable differences of character in the princes, and neither father nor mother appears to have been able wisely to discriminate, so that the more really amiable, sincere, and obedient member of the family—Edward Augustus, afterwards Duke of Kent—appears to have received the fewest marks of regard, his very frankness, and a certain fearless truthfulness and independence of character, placing him at a peculiar disadvantage, which led to his being left out of the

family circle, so far as a cordial recognition of his real merits
was concerned. He spent most of his time in military service
abroad, and was so strict and assiduous in the performance of
his duties that on more than one occasion those under his
command were inclined to resent, as exactions, the details of
discipline which he conceived to be necessary for restoring and
maintaining efficiency. While his elder brother, the Duke of
York, was, as commander-in-chief of the army, occupying a high
position in England, and (apart from the episode which led to his
being accused, and put on his trial, for conniving at the reception
of bribes for promotion) effecting reforms which not only compelled officers in the army to study their profession, but vastly
increased the comfort and efficiency of the men, the Duke of
Kent was left almost entirely without the kind of personal support
which should have been extended to one whose courage and
ability commanded public distinction. He always felt that he was
neglected, and that he had little to hope either from his father
or his two elder brothers—the Prince Regent and the Commander-in-Chief. It is not easy to determine whether this sense
of being neglected and excluded was partly owing to a kind of
sensitiveness which was too ready to take a gloomy view of the
apparent indifference which comes of separation and the worldly
maxim of "everyone looking after his own interests." It is
true that the debts which the Duke of Kent incurred—and
explained as being inevitable, because of the position in which
he was placed and the orders he received—were paid, after some
delays, and that he received promotions, but the latter came
at times when they had the effect of increasing his financial
difficulties. It would appear, also, that he was conscious of
being left unnoticed, unless he made repeated applications, which,
as they might be resented as extortions, he patiently deferred

until his condition seriously affected his spirits. This led him to believe that he was, from some unexplained cause, out of the pale of family sympathy, and compelled to occupy a position such as that endured by the "whipping boy" in ancient school-days, when an unfortunate lad was nominated to receive the punishment deserved by but not inflicted upon royal or aristocratic scholars.

It might have been suspected that his impressions were the result of a morbid fancy, but singularly enough there were evidences that the complaints which he afterwards made had considerable foundation. It would appear from the testimony of those best able to judge that the very frankness and uncompromising truthfulness of his nature caused him to be oppressed. "He could not dissemble;" and if he had committed a fault, would not deny it, but if questions were asked would at once take the consequences of acknowledging it with outspoken courage, even in the face of impending severe punishment.

It seems highly probable that to a temper like that of George the Third this would come like defiance and obstinacy, which required to be broken by any means that could be made effectual; while the boy himself may have been unconscious that he had done anything which had not been demanded by a regard for honour. However this may have been, he was sent when he was eighteen years old to the dreary town of Luneburg to study military science under the direction of a Baron Wagenheim, whose chief aim, whether under orders from the king or not, seems to have been to keep his charge under the strictest and most oppressive discipline, and on his own account to pocket the allowance of £1000 a year granted to the prince, to whom he doled out a guinea and a half a week, which, after it had been reduced by the infliction of certain fines, was to provide for all personal expenses.

This short allowance does not seem to have been an exception, however, for the Duke of Sussex declared late in life to a friend that till he was one-and-twenty his pocket-money never exceeded a guinea a week; that when he was one-and-thirty an income of £2000 a year was allotted to him, and that at that time he was always in arrears and poor. The younger dukes at all events seem to have been but meanly provided for in their early years; and yet they saw with what reckless profusion their eldest brother the Prince Regent spent money, and either witnessed or heard of the showy splendour and costly hospitalities of Carlton House. They knew of the vast sums of debt incurred for excesses and indulgences, which were paid for, even though they were continually resented and denounced, by the nation, and when their turn came it can scarcely be wondered at that, with a common tendency to extravagance which seemed to be a glaring and almost an alarming reaction against the personal economy of the king and queen, they should launch into expenses without any very serious apprehension of the consequences. The Duke of Sussex, however, was in England, and led for the most part a quiet life; while the Duke of Kent was abroad, and engaged in military duties in various parts of the world. After a year at Luneburg he was transferred to Hanover to continue his studies, where he was under the same restrictions, and subjected to a surveillance which he declared included intercepting his letters to his father, who, not hearing from him, attributed his silence to an undutiful temper, and at the same time received false reports of his conduct and complaints of his extravagance, though he was still limited to his guinea and a half a week, and was not allowed either horse or carriage.

From Hanover he was sent to Geneva, but without any increase of pocket-money, though his governor received £6000 a year for maintaining an establishment. He had now passed his twenty-second year, and being unable any longer to endure the position in which he was detained, and receiving no satisfactory reply to his requests, he started for London without asking permission of anybody, and after five years' absence found himself at an hotel in King Street, writing for permission to see his father, who angrily refused to receive him, though his two elder brothers—the Prince of Wales and the Duke of York—interceded for him. After a fortnight of suspense he received orders to go at once to Gibraltar, with an intimation that the King would grant him a short interview on the night before his departure.

Whatever may have taken place during this hurried visit, the position of the young prince was altered, for it would appear that he went out to Gibraltar to take command of the 7th Fusiliers, of which he was made colonel, and that he was allowed £5000 a year. He still, however, required a sum of money to pay for an establishment and outfit, as he had nothing provided for him, and no sufficient sum being forthcoming, he went into debt, with the not unusual result of so far exceeding his immediate expectations that he had to make prospective arrangements with his creditors, to whom he gave bonds which were to be redeemed in seven years. His debts amounted to £20,000, so that when he was ordered with his regiment to Canada he was obliged to sell off everything belonging to him at Gibraltar, and to pay his most pressing creditors; and as he was again without any allowance for outfit and equipment, he had no resource but to incur fresh liabilities. Like a good many other young men who have extravagant tastes and have not learnt how to begin to practise economy, he complained that he never had a fair start, and in his case the complaint was not groundless. He was compelled to go into debt for the personal and household equipments which were immediately necessary; and, perhaps for the very reason that he could not pay for them at once, ordered many more than he really required, only to find that the position and appearance which he desired or was expected to maintain absorbed his entire income. His pecuniary misfortunes were enormously aggravated by the actual loss of consecutive outfits on which he had expended money or credit. In 1793 he had to leave Quebec (in little more than two years) to join the expedition against the French West India Islands, and his effects were again sold, as an entirely different equipment had to be obtained. This was lost in crossing Lake Champlain, which was frozen over, and a supply of necessary articles was procured at Boston.

The prince had already taken rank as an organizer, and had in fact promoted one section of army reform at an earlier date than that at which his brother, the Duke of York, commenced his efforts to achieve complete reconstruction of the service, and those endeavours to increase the well-being of the men in the ranks, which had gained for him the name of "the soldier's friend." In the West Indies, where he joined Sir Charles Grey, Edward Augustus entered upon the serious business of a campaign in which he took a prominent part, heading the flank division at the storming of several strong and important forts in Martinique and Guadaloupe, where the commander-in-chief remonstrated with him for his reckless bravery. He was in command of a battalion of grenadiers who disembarked at Marigot des Roseaux, under Vice-Admiral Sir John Jervis (afterwards Earl St. Vincent), for the attack of Morne Fortunée, and who conducted themselves so admirably in that affair, under the immediate command of his royal highness, as to entitle them to particular notice in the commander-in-chief's despatch. Their leader himself hoisted the British colours on the post, the name of which was changed to "Fort Charlotte" in honour of his mother the Queen. The conquest of the whole island was soon after accomplished without the loss of a single man, though the troops were exposed to a heavy fire from the batteries and works of the enemy. In the following month, at the capture of Guadaloupe, the prince led on the first division, consisting of the first and second battalions of grenadiers and a hundred of the naval battalion, to the attack of the post on Morne Mascot, and he and his companions received the thanks of the English and Irish Parliaments for their distinguished services. In fact the father of our Queen had his full share of the courage for which the line of Hanover-Brunswick has mostly been famous. George the Third is reported to have declared, "All my sons are courageous except one, and him I will not name as he is to succeed me." This is a remarkable example of Georgian reticence, and seems to accord somewhat with the declaration of George the Fourth that he had been at the battle of Waterloo—an assertion so often repeated that, perhaps, the prince had come to believe it, and actually on one occasion appealed to the Duke of Wellington to confirm it. "I was there, wasn't I, Arthur?" "I have often heard your royal highness say so," was the cautious but truthful reply. After the West Indies expedition, Prince Edward was raised to the rank of lieutenant-general and made commander of the forces at Halifax; but his former ill-luck attended him with regard to an expensive outfit, which was the fifth that he lost. The vessel in which it was sent out was, like its predecessor, captured by the French, and the same fate befell two succeeding ones, so that he had lost altogether about the value of £10,000

at the time that he was further promoted to the rank of general
and commander-in-chief of the forces in North America. Another
vessel had disappeared with his library, maps, plans, and a stock
of wine.

In 1798 he returned to England and took up his temporary
abode in Kensington Palace, and in the following year, when
he was thirty-two years of age, was made Duke of Kent and
Strathern and Earl of Dublin. At last he seems to have gained
the position which he had deserved, and for which he had so
long waited in vain. The king had previously written to him
expressing approbation of the whole of his conduct, and after
his reception had appointed him to the command of the army
of the interior. When he became Duke of Kent he was made
commander-in-chief of the English forces in North America and
Lieutenant-governor of Nova Scotia.

After this he was closely engaged in official work, and had
some expectation of having command of the troops in Ireland,
the union having been then nearly completed. He was again
called to England, partly because he was in ill-health and partly
by desire of the King, with whom he stayed for some time at
Weymouth. In 1802 he went out as governor to Gibraltar,
where the garrison had become so disorganized that his efforts to
restore discipline resulted in an attempted mutiny, and it was
said that a plot for seizing him when he was on parade, and
flinging him from the Rock, was frustrated by a whispered
warning given to the duke, while he was visiting the hospital,
by a soldier who lay there dying from the effects of a long course
of intemperance. Whether this was the chief cause of the recall
of the duke or not need not be discussed,—but no sooner had
he succeeded in restoring order than he was ordered to leave the
command in the hands of the officer next in authority and to

return to England. The order was of course obeyed, but he felt that some explanation should be given of such an unusual proceeding, and on arriving in London he asked for a court-martial to be appointed to inquire into the circumstances. This was refused on the ground that it would not be expedient in the case of an officer of his rank; and consequently he was once more left to feel that he had been subjected to some adverse influence, which in this case was attributed by the public—and it would also seem by the duke himself—to his brother the Duke of York, who was omnipotent at the Horse Guards.

Though the duke had enough troubles of his own, he was always ready to listen to the troubles of others, and to help his friends as far as his duty and his limited influence and limited means would permit. Strict, and even severely punctilious and minutely methodical as he was reputed to be in his military capacity and in the ordering of his establishment, he had a loyal and tender heart and an affectionate nature. That his influence was comparatively small, so far as any military or government patronage was concerned, may be well imagined from the manner in which his own requests were received or rather rejected, and his own money difficulties prevented him from exercising to the full his generous disposition.

It cannot be denied that the duke shared to some extent the expansive views of his brothers as to the purchasing power of a sum of money either in hand or in prospect, but it is also certain that he did not share in the money itself. When the King, with a munificence for which he has seldom been fully credited, made very large presents to his sons from the balance which came to him from prize-money, the Duke of Kent had the smallest portion; and yet when he applied to Pitt to bring before Parliament his claims for losses incurred through no fault of his own, but in the public service and in consequence of delay in the settlement of his "parliamentary establishment," he took the opportunity of representing that the allowances of his younger brothers were insufficient for the position those princes were expected to maintain.

The death of Mr. Pitt soon afterwards, though it did not prevent an increase in the allowances of the younger brothers, left the promises of the minister to the Duke of Kent unfulfilled. The consequence was that the engagements which he had made with creditors, on the assurance that his claims would be considered, and in the conviction that their justice would be acknowledged, could not be fulfilled, and he had to arrange with trustees to devote half his income for the extinction of his debts. It will be enough to say that neither then, nor at a later date, when, as a husband and a father, he might "reasonably" (that is, without an appeal to sentiment) have expected some consideration, did he receive any aid either from the government or from his brother the Regent, whose demands, added to the less alarming but still excessive expectations of the Duke of York, exhausted the supplies to be obtained from Parliament. As we are referring for a moment to this later period (1819), when the duke was driven to offer his house at Castlebar (valued at £51,000) for sale, it may be interesting to note that Mr. Hume, the sworn foe to extravagance, but at the same time the sworn foe to injustice, stood up for him to the extent of showing that if, in respect of parliamentary allowance, he was placed on the same footing as the Duke of Clarence he would have to receive £96,000, and if on a footing with the Duke of Sussex £20,000.

Though we may not linger upon these preliminary pages, they are of some importance in what purports to be a really intelligible narrative of the life of our gracious and beloved Queen, for they show what were the conditions against which her noble and excellent father had to contend, and they will explain the unobtrusive but truly dignified conduct of the widowed duchess, who, in the quiet seclusion of her home, devoted herself to the loving care which should make the best attributes of childhood and of womanhood the foundation for the character of Princess and of Sovereign.

Without projecting the faintest shadow of politics upon the page it may be permissible to say that the fact of the Duke of Kent having decidedly taken the "Liberal" side, so far as he entered upon political questions, was not likely to have advanced his interests, the very pronounced Liberalism of the Duke of Sussex having perhaps emphasized the profession of any such opinions in other members of the family. Thus we find the Duke of Kent speaking at a banquet in response for the toast of the royal family, and saying, "I am a friend of civil and religious liberty all the world over. I am an enemy to all religious tests. I am a supporter of a general system of education. All men are my brethren; and I hold that power is delegated only for the benefit of the people. These are the principles of myself and my beloved brother the Duke of Sussex. They are not popular principles just now. That is, they do not conduct to place or office. *All* the members of the royal family do not hold the same principles. For this I do not blame them; but we claim for ourselves the right of thinking, and acting as we think best." These were broad sentiments, and by no means likely to be palatable either to the King, the Duke of York, or the Duke of Cumberland, who were dead against such sentiments and against the removal of political disabilities from the Roman Catholics. Doubtless the Duke of Kent had the courage of his convictions. At the same time it should be remembered that the *practical* political "Liberalism" of the Duke of Kent so far as he entered upon political matters at all, might now probably be regarded as resembling what has been called democratic Toryism. As a matter of fact, however, he would not have anything to do with pronounced politics. The royal dukes were rather given to "orating" in or out of the House of Lords, and the Duke of Sussex was always good for presiding somewhere or other, especially at charity and other dinners, or meetings for promoting philanthropic objects, while his position as grand-master of freemasonry possibly gave to his addresses the peculiar effect which is supposed to belong to the utterances that distinguish the occupants of "the chair of King Solomon." The Duke of Kent, however, though he was amiably willing to preside at anniversary festivals and assemblies for promoting benevolent objects, and though his good-nature, easy eloquence, and imposing appearance, in addition to his royal rank, made him a model chairman, and led to his having to work harder than he would have done "in his place" in the Upper House, chiefly confined his speaking in public to such kindly efforts. He had enough of family opposition without exasperating it by party debate, for which he had no inclination. He wrote to Lord Eldon respecting attendance in Parliament, reminding him of a conversation on the day of the opening of the session, in which he had said he would always be ready to attend the House of Peers whenever he had the slightest direct intimation that his presence was wished for. "In doing this," he added, "I am anxious your lordship should understand that I am actuated by that principle I have ever professed of supporting the King's government, and never taking any part in political disputes, for which I have the utmost abhorrence, and, indeed, am less fit than any other member of our house, having never given my attention to any other pursuit but that of my own profession."

The necessity for his acting with constant precaution in relation to public affairs soon became apparent, for he was now raised to the rank of field-marshal, and yet his position in the royal family made it very difficult for him to avoid being personally implicated in the scandals which were then exciting public attention. Charges of receiving bribes had been brought against the Duke of York, and these accusations, as well as the conduct of the Prince Regent in insisting on a separation from his wife the Princess Caroline, affected all the members of the royal family in different ways, so that it was exceedingly difficult to maintain a neutral position. To add to these embarrassments, just before the inquiry into the allegations made against the Duke of York, pamphlets were published professing to defend the Duke of Kent against the persecution and neglect to which it was stated he had been subjected by his brother. He had nothing whatever to do with these publications, and he went to the House of Lords to assure their lordships that there was no animosity between him and his brother, that all reports to the contrary were unfounded and untrue, and that he was fully persuaded that all the charges made against his brother were false, and would be proved to be without foundation.

From the allegations made against the Princess Caroline and the so-called "investigations" instituted by her husband the Prince Regent, he was less able to hold aloof, and such part as he took in that miserable business ended in his incurring the resentment both of the Prince and of the unfortunate but most indiscreet and incorrigibly flighty Princess, who had intrusted to the Rev. Dr. Randolph to take with him to Germany a packet of letters, which he protested he had sent back to her, declining to be responsible for conveying them. They were either intentionally intercepted or by some means fell into the hands of some one who took them to Queen Charlotte, and as they were full of strong expressions and some injurious representations with regard to almost every member of the royal family who was then at court, they contributed not a little to increase the aversion felt by many relatives of the Prince to the misguided woman who had written them. The whole transaction was discreditable to both sides, and of course the letters should not have been conveyed to the court, and should not have been read by those who complained of their aspersions. The Duke of Kent had not seen and would not receive them. He afterwards wrote a precise memorandum in which he said, "These letters (most unhappily for the writer) fell into hands for which most certainly they were never intended. I have not seen them myself. I never would see them, nor allow them to come into my possession (though they have been more than once offered for my inspection) for various reasons, among them a conviction that their being in existence at all, and certainly in the hands of the parties who held them, was a breach of that honourable confidence which ought to actuate all persons in matters where private correspondence is concerned." It is evident that the duke was not at all the kind of man for exercising the "diplomacy" necessary for promoting the ambitions of the Prince Regent, who had already been offended with him for having used his influence to prevent a scandal being made of a former "anonymous letter and a drawing" which had been attributed to the Princess, and had also got into mischievous hands.

The conduct of the duke, however, appeared to be that of an honourable and an amiable man, and it is not surprising that the

Regent afterwards asked him to take some trouble in reference to the disputes which had already arisen with the Princess Charlotte.

Finding that nothing would be done to bring his claims before the House of Commons, and that he had little to hope from the Prince Regent, whose lavish expenditure had set so ill an example to his brothers, and who, now that he was in royal authority, because of the condition of the aged King, was little likely to abate his demands on the public purse, the duke retired to Brussels. There he took up his residence, occasionally travelling on visits to Germany, where he had several friends, doubtless included among the numerous correspondents who kept him so extensively employed that he had to engage a secretary and a couple of sergeants of his regiment who acted as clerks. This business of letter-writing had grown upon the duke in consequence of his readiness to interest himself in the affairs of everybody who sought his counsel or patronage. He was accessible to almost anyone who needed his aid and had any reasonable plea for his assistance, and it may therefore be easily imagined that he was always communicating with one or other of the public departments, forwarding petitions, and seeking favourable consideration for people who sought redress or asked for appointments.

At that time (1816) the King had been for six years in permanent seclusion, and there was no hope of his recovery. In 1789 he had been obliged to retire from all public life for three months, but the cloud which then obscured his mental faculties passed away, and he had, with his family, attended at Saint Paul's Cathedral to give thanks for his restoration to health. In 1809, twenty years afterwards, commenced the fiftieth year of his Majesty's reign, and the event had been observed as a public festival, with many appropriate celebrations. In the following year, however, there was a return of the malady from which he had previously suffered.

The death of his favourite and youngest daughter the Princess Amelia had greatly affected him, and it became evident that his condition at such an advanced age was too serious to allow any sanguine hopes of his recovery. To the Duke of York was intrusted the personal care of the sovereign, and the Prince of Wales, who was appointed Regent, practically succeeded to the throne, and assumed the rights of royalty, with the consent, though it can scarcely be said with the hearty concurrence, of the people, a large proportion of whom regarded him with a dislike not far removed from contempt. This was partly caused by the self-indulgent and dissolute life that he had led, and by his enormous extravagances, which had resulted in frequent appeals to the public purse, - but all the ill-will which was manifested towards him had been accentuated by his unhappy relations with his wife, from whom he had separated in 1796, almost immediately after the birth of a daughter, who became next in succession to the throne. George the Third, who constantly protected the unhappy Caroline, took charge of the young princess, and the mother retired to a private residence at Blackheath, and when in London occupied a house in Connaught Place, facing Hyde Park. When the King's condition became hopeless the child was placed under the care of the Queen, who, it is to be feared, was not over-kind to her, and only allowed her mother to see her once a week.

With the miserable and unedifying story of the Regent and his unhappy Princess—especially with its later episodes when he became King and her alleged wrongs led to popular tumults - we need not here be concerned. It is necessary, however, to refer as briefly as may be to her daughter, the Princess Charlotte, for whom, as she grew older, there was manifested by the nation a deep and almost passionate regard, which owed much of its strength to the very opposite feeling with which her father was greeted, especially as there was a general conviction that he was treating her with indifference and neglect, if not with actual cruelty and oppression. These suspicions were not without foundation. The Prince Regent cared chiefly for his own selfish ease and amusements. His child knew nothing of parental affection, and had never had any of the care and happiness that belongs to true home life, nor the moral developments that come of close and generous friendships in early youth. Before she had reached womanhood she had learned to pity and to excuse, if not to defend, much that was blameworthy in her mother's conduct. Her very deep sense of justice added to a genuinely affectionate disposition and a yearning for affection in return caused her to side with her mother, and may have had much to do with the strong opposition to her father's imperious orders which she sometimes manifested. One sentence—a remark which she made at a rather later date to Baron Stockmar (of whom we shall see more presently)—is vastly significant of the decided impression which she had formed and of the injurious circumstances amidst which she must have been placed. "My mother was bad, but she would not have become as bad as she was if my father had not been infinitely worse:"--a terrible sentence, look at it how we may.

The Princess Charlotte possessed admirable and some noble qualities, such as were well calculated to make the people idolize her, and abundantly to justify the enthusiasm with which her name was mentioned, although she was allowed few opportunities of appearing in public in such a way as to call forth regular expressions of loyalty. She grew to be a handsome woman, above the ordinary height, with a fine figure, an expansive and genial beauty, manners frank, vivacious, and sometimes unconventional enough to give a kind of charm to her conversation with those whom she liked. There was an occasional caprice almost approaching to flightiness, which, however, was corrected by her frank good-humour and her modest dress and decorous though rather careless demeanour. Her great characteristic seems to have been a deeply-loving nature and a very amiable and charitable temper, amidst much that was wilful and wayward in her conduct. She needed the guidance of true, strong, and one might add sedate affection, and this she found but for one happy year—the last year of her earthly life.

When she was sixteen a separate town residence was provided for her at Warwick House, near her father's palace of Carlton House, and there or at Windsor she lived among comparative strangers with her governess, and for companion Miss Cornelia Knight, who afterwards wrote an account of the life that was led there. She was only allowed to see her mother once a fortnight, and for the next three years her experiences may be inferred from the fact that at seventeen she had not been confirmed—which was then considered to be a very serious negligence for a girl of that age. Neither had she appeared at court, which, considering what the court was, perhaps places some small grain of credit to the account of her father, if his motive was a higher one than to save himself trouble and responsibility. His conduct towards her was summed up in the directions he gave to Miss Knight: "Remember that Charlotte must lay aside the idle nonsense of thinking that she has a will of her own: while I live she must be subjected to me, as she is at present, if she were thirty, or forty, or forty-five." This may seem to show that he had already been made to feel that she had a will of her own and might unexpectedly exercise it, and she did exercise it when, at eighteen, an offer of marriage was made by the Prince of Orange, who afterwards became King William the Second of the Netherlands.

The Prince Regent saw that here was an opportunity of getting rid of a great responsibility, and therefore he consented with alacrity to the proposed alliance, and so hurried on the engagement that the princess was betrothed almost before she was aware of it, although on her first meeting with the Prince of Orange she was not very favourably impressed either with his manners or appearance. It would seem that she immediately began to insist on conditions, the discussion of which would delay the marriage, and she was supported in her demands by the "opposition" in Parliament and by her mother, to whom the Prince of Orange had already shown himself to be inimical.

So strongly did the Regent endeavour to overcome her objections to leave England and take up her residence in Holland for a considerable part of each year, that he was suspected of indifference to her succession to the throne; and it may well be imagined that the influence of the Duke of Cumberland was in this direction, since—as after events proved—he was alive to the possibility of his own claims being put forward if the salique law observed in Hanover could be established in England.

The princess soon showed that she could be as determined as her father or as either of the royal dukes, and so persisted in her objections to a foreign residence that the marriage was delayed.

On the 7th of June, 1814, the allied sovereigns and their victorious generals visited London, and were sumptuously entertained by the Prince Regent, who at the same time refused to allow his wife to be present at the court festivities, from which his daughter was also excluded. This prohibition increased the indignation of the Princess Charlotte, who saw in it a deliberate design to injure the reputation of her mother in the opinion of the royal and imperial guests, and her resentment was excited by the conduct of her affianced husband, who, with an utter disregard of her sentiments, attended the assemblies from which she had been peremptorily banished.

She now demanded not only that she should remain in England immediately after the marriage, but that her future home should be open to the visits of her mother, and as the intended bridegroom refused his consent to such an arrangement she distinctly told him that the marriage was impossible, and he accepted the decision with so little emotion that it was evident not much love had been lost on either side. The Prince Regent was in a fury, and characteristically went to Warwick House, suddenly dismissed the household of the princess on the ground that they had connived at her disobedience, and commanded her at once to prepare to go to Cranbourne Lodge at Windsor, where, as she well knew, she would be kept in seclusion, and under the espionage of strangers. When it was supposed she was preparing for the journey, she stole out of the house and entered a hackney-coach, in which she drove to her mother's house in Connaught Place.

There was a great commotion when her flight was discovered. The Regent was baffled, and had to send to the Duke of York and others to assist him in bringing back the princess. The Duke of Sussex was out at a dinner-party when a hastily-scribbled note from his niece was put into his hand. She implored him to protect her, and said she had sought refuge with her mother. Without waiting to find his carriage he had a hackney-coach called, and drove off to Connaught Place. Hackney-coaches were in remarkable request that evening for the conveyance of distinguished passengers to the same destination. When the duke arrived he found Mr. Henry Brougham there. This rising advocate was already employed as the legal adviser of the Princess of Wales. When the duke heard who he was, he turned to him and asked, "Pray, sir, supposing that the Prince Regent, acting in the name and on behalf of his Majesty, were to send a sufficient force to break open the doors of the house and carry away the princess, would resistance in such a case be lawful?" Brougham replied that it would not. "Then, my dear," said the duke to his niece, "you hear what the law is, and I can only advise you to return with as much speed and as little noise as possible." The princess was now inclined to yield. Her mother joined in urging her to show obedience to her father. When the Duke of Sussex left the house he found the lord chancellor and two chief-justices in a coach together, waiting to be admitted. In another coach came the Duke of York, and eventually he persuaded the princess to return with him to Warwick House.

The end of it was that she stayed for a few days at Carlton House with her father, who seems to have shown a less arbitrary temper now that he saw what she might dare if driven to extremities, and she was afterwards taken to Windsor, all her attendants having been changed. But the marriage was irretrievably broken off—and what was more, she had already seen somebody whom she believed she would love much better than she ever could have loved the Prince of Orange, who two years afterwards married a Russian grand-duchess.

By that time the Princess Charlotte had married that somebody else. No other, indeed, than Prince Leopold of Coburg, a man whose bereavement by her death after a year of happy conjugal affection was deeply felt by the whole nation, and whose noble qualities, solid acquirements, and sincere character gave him a distinguished place in the councils of Europe for many years afterwards, when he had by general consent been elected to the throne of Belgium.

Prince Leopold was directly descended from the old and noble house of the great Elector of Saxony, Frederic the Wise. This elder, or as it was called the Ernestine, branch of the great Saxon family was represented by the owners of various duchies, which were acquired after the electorate had passed to the younger or Albertine branch of the family in consequence of devotion of the elder family to the Protestant religion. Frederic the Wise, Elector of Saxony, the friend and protector of Martin Luther, was powerful enough to hold his own, but the defeat of John Frederic by the Emperor Charles the Fifth, in 1547, changed the succession to the younger branch, the treacherous Maurice having deserted the Reformed faith, and thus secured elevation to the electorate. At the death of the great grandson of Frederic the Wise, Ernest the Pious, Duke of Saxe-Coburg-Gotha-Coburg,—the several duchies acquired by the family and now possessed by his descendants were divided. They included the dukedoms of Saxe-Gotha-Altenburg, of Saxe-Meiningen (the family of the Princess Adelaide, consort of William the Fourth), of Saxe-Hildburghausen, and Saxe-Coburg-Saalfeld. Of these, Saxe-Gotha-Altenburg went to the eldest son, Frederic; and Saxe-Coburg-Saalfeld[1] to the youngest,

---

[1] By subsequent family arrangements as to succession he took the Duchy of Gotha and surrendered that of Saalfeld to the Duke of Meiningen.

John Ernest, the ancestor of Ernest the First, eldest brother of Leopold and, as we shall see hereafter, father of Prince Albert.

This Duke Ernest was eldest son of Duke Francis and of a very clever and sensible woman, Augusta, daughter of Prince Henry the Twenty-fourth of Reuss-Ebersdorff. He had succeeded to the dukedom in 1806 when it was in the occupation of the French, from which it was not set free till 1813. The second son was Ferdinand George, who married the Princess Kohary of Hungary, and whose son married Donna Maria the Second, Queen of Portugal. Prince Leopold was the third son, and with him we are more concerned. There were four daughters: Sophia married Count Mensdorff Pouilly, who left France at the Revolution and obtained a high position in the Austrian service, his son, Count Alexander Mensdorff, having been well known at a much later date as Austrian minister of foreign affairs; Antoinette, the second daughter, married Duke Alexander of Wurtemburg; Julie, the third daughter, the Grand-duke Constantine of Russia, from whom she separated in 1802, taking up her residence in Switzerland; Victoria Marie Louise, the youngest daughter, had been married to Emich Charles, Prince of Leiningen, and had (in 1813) been left a widow with two children, a son and a daughter, to whom, though she was still a young, handsome, and accomplished woman, she devoted herself with maternal care and affection.

Prince Leopold was distinguished even in a distinguished family for a remarkable personal charm—keen intellect, much tact, and courtesy of manner, the sagacity which includes a knowledge of men and enables its possessor to estimate character, and a fine sense of humour. His "record" was clear as to character and conduct, and he was just one of those men who are not only generally attractive, but who command esteem and regard. To the temperate blood, sound brain, and habitual self-possession of the Coburg family he added a wisdom and consistency of conduct which is usually only the result of age and experience. In England he was popular almost immediately that he became known. His characteristics were those that the English appreciate, and rightly or wrongly claim for themselves. The highest praise they could give him was "What a complete English gentleman!" He had, however, had some experience, for at fifteen he had entered the Russian army, just before the battle of Austerlitz; and though there were some family disagreements with the Grand-duke Constantine—he did not sever his connection with the imperial court, but in 1813 was the first German prince who joined the Russian army for the liberation of Germany, and was on Constantine's staff. He had visited Napoleon at Paris in 1807, and was at the Congress of Erfurt in 1808. He was a successful negotiator at the Congress of Vienna, and in 1815, at Paris, obtained an increase of territory for his brother the Duke of Coburg. In the previous year (1814), he also was one of the honoured guests who came to England, and were magnificently received at Carlton House. Though the Princess Charlotte was excluded from these superb gatherings, she had met Leopold, and was anxious to become better acquainted with him. She confided her wishes to her aunt, the Duchess of York (the Princess Frederica of Prussia, daughter of Frederick William the Third), who, knowing that there would otherwise be great difficulty in bringing these young people together, promised to give a ball for her, and to invite the prince. This was done, and it need scarcely be said that the meeting, at which there was soon a mutual understanding, sealed the fate of the proposed Orange marriage. It was a critical position for Prince Leopold, and the Prince Regent was

at first inclined to oppose him, especially as it had been represented that he had taken means to supersede the Prince of
Orange; but his invincible amiability and patient good sense,
no less than his admirable manners, actually won over the
Regent. The Duke of York as well as the Duke of Kent were
generally favourable to the suit, and the marriage was afterwards
arranged, though for some time after Leopold had left England,
in 1814, the whole matter seemed to be doubtful, and but for
the kindly Duke of Kent, who enabled the lovers to correspond,
the difficulties might have become insuperable. In January,
1816, however, Leopold received an invitation to return to
England, and the marriage took place amidst the congratulations
and rejoicings of the nation, who regarded the wedded pair with
the utmost delight and complacency.

When Prince Leopold arrived in England he stayed first at
Brighton and there awaited the arrival of Christian Frederick
Stockmar, whom he had appointed to be his physician, but who
afterwards became his confidential secretary and most faithful and
trusted companion. Stockmar, who subsequently received the
title of baron and whose name has been associated with many of
the events relating to the early life of our Queen, was a very
remarkable man,—remarkable not only because of his undoubted
ability and accomplishments, but for a sincerity and integrity
which was never known to fail. His self-devotion led him to
give up family ties, many personal ambitions, and much prospect
of ease and comfort, in the service of the prince, for whom he
had the greatest esteem and affection.

There is a peculiar self-effacement by which some men of
keen perceptions, an intense sense of humour, and yet with an
undercurrent of melancholy, apparently keep themselves in the
background, at the same time experiencing deep self-satisfaction

in the notion that they are exercising a powerful influence on those about them by their advice and the results of their observations. Stockmar had something of this quality, and undoubtedly possessed a remarkable talent for what is called "reckoning people up." As a politician or as a theoretical statesman, and as one who had more than usual opportunities of observing and associating with ministers and leaders of opinion, he set himself to diagnose character as unhesitatingly as he would, in his capacity of physician, have diagnosed disease. He had been educated at the Coburg Gymnasium and at Wurzburg, Erlangen, and Jena. In the period of the war dating from 1812 he became "town and country physician" at Coburg, where he had been practising medicine, and there he organized a military hospital. In January, 1814, and again in 1815 he had as physician accompanied the Saxon ducal contingent to the Rhine, and in the latter year into Alsace. In that campaign Prince Leopold had become acquainted with him, and such was their mutual regard that when the marriage of the prince with Princess Charlotte was settled, Stockmar received and accepted the offer of the appointment of physician in ordinary to the prince, whom he followed to England on the 29th of March, 1816.

As an example of the manner in which he would by a few vivid touches of description indicate his impressions of important people whom he met we may quote from his diary (not at the time of course intended for any eye but his own) his remarks on some members of the royal family. Of the Regent he wrote: "Very stout, though of a fine figure; distinguished manners; does not talk half as much as his brothers; speaks tolerably good French. He ate and drank a good deal at dinner. His brown scratch-wig not particularly becoming." The Duke of

York was "tall, with immense *embonpoint*, and not proportionately strong legs; he holds himself in such a way that one is always afraid he will tumble over backwards; very bald, and not a very intelligent face. . . . Spoke a good deal of French with a bad accent." The Duchess of York, daughter of Frederick William the Second of Prussia, is described as "a little, animated woman; talks immensely and laughs still more. No beauty; mouth and teeth bad. She disfigures herself still more by distorting her mouth and blinking her eyes. In spite of the duke's various infidelities their matrimonial relations are good. She is quite aware of her husband's embarrassed circumstances, and is his prime minister and truest friend, so that nothing is done without her help. As soon as she entered the room she looked round for the banker, Greenwood, who immediately came up to her with the confidentially familiar manner which the wealthy go-between assumes towards grand people in embarrassed circumstances." The Duke of York had married the Princess Frederica Charlotte Ulrica, Princess Royal of Prussia, in September, 1791, when he was twenty-eight and she was twenty-four years old, and the portion of £30,000 which she was said to have received from her father was probably a considerable attraction; whether the promise which the Prussian monarch was said to have made, also to pay the duke's debts to the amount of £20,000, was an expression of satisfaction at his daughter's marriage need not be discussed, but it is declared that on the marriage being settled he said to her, "Ma fille vous avez attendu longtemps, mais vous avez tirée le gros lot."

Of the Duke of Clarence, afterwards King William the Fourth, Stockmar wrote: "The smallest and least good-looking of the brothers (he must have meant the elder brothers), decidedly like his mother, as talkative as the rest." But the observation on the Duke of Kent is in accordance with the known character of that prince: "The quietest of all the dukes I have seen, talks slowly and deliberately, is kind and courteous." A very different estimate to that given of Ernest, Duke of Cumberland: "A tall, powerful man, with a hideous face; can't see two inches before him; one eye turned quite out of its place." This duke had in 1814 married his cousin, Frederica Caroline Sophia of Mecklenburg-Strelitz, who had been twice previously married; first to Prince Frederick of Prussia, and secondly to the Prince of Salms-Braunsch, from whom she had been divorced.

The Duke of Sussex did not at this time come within the diagnosis of physician Stockmar. He was living quietly, rather as an English nobleman than as a prince of the royal family. As we have seen he was an avowed Liberal; and he was probably the most really cultivated of all the royal dukes, his extensive library at Kensington Palace containing many rare books, and especially a fine collection of Bibles and ancient manuscripts, for he was a student of Biblical literature. He, like some of his brothers, was a great smoker, and possessed a remarkable collection of meerschaum and other pipes, some of them of considerable value. Another characteristic was a liking for rather handsome attire, especially gorgeous dressing-gowns. One can scarcely think of the Duke of Sussex in this regard without associating some of his peculiarities with his experiences in freemasonry. There may have been much in masonic ceremonies and decorations to account for a few of his ways.

The Duke of Sussex, while in Italy, when he was only a youth of nineteen, had fallen distractedly in love with Lady Augusta Murray, daughter of the Earl of Dunmore, a governor of one of the American provinces. The lady was staying in

Rome with her mother, and so vehemently did the prince urge his suit that, unknown to the mother, the young people were married by an English clergyman there. In the winter the whole party returned to England, and the ceremony was repeated, the duke figuring as Mr. Frederick. It was a love-match, and the lady was of high lineage, descended in fact from the same royal lines as the duke himself; but the union was pronounced to be void, and was set aside by the King, under the terms of the Royal Marriage Act of 1773, which made the marriage of any descendant of George the Second under twenty-five and without the King's consent absolutely null and void.

Of the youngest of the royal princes—Adolphus Frederick, Duke of Cambridge—Stockmar wrote: "A good-looking man with a blonde wig. Speaks French and German very well, but, like English, with such rapidity that he carries off the palm in the family art." He was a popular prince in many respects, and deservedly so, for he was a pleasant and good-natured man, unpretentious, quiet, and reputable in his conduct, had served in Flanders not without distinction, was a ready patron of movements intended to ameliorate the condition of the poor, and was not only a promoter of the art of music and of musical education, but was a very good singer. At the time of the wedding of the Princess Charlotte he was unmarried, but in May, 1818, was united to Wilhelmina Louisa, youngest daughter of the Land-grave of Hesse-Cassell. In 1814 he had been appointed governor of Hanover, and held that position till 1839, when, on the death of William the Fourth, the Duke of Cumberland succeeded to the Hanoverian throne.

Of the surviving daughters of George the Third (one, as we have seen, had died in 1810) two were married—the elder to the King of Wurtemburg; the Princess Elizabeth (third daughter) to the Landgrave of Hesse; the Princess Augusta (the second daughter) remained unmarried. The fourth daughter, Princess Mary, was then unmarried, but in 1816 married her cousin the Duke of Gloucester, son of the brother of the King, and a prince who was usually regarded as deficient in intelligence, and decidedly was somewhat of a cipher, but quiet and inoffensive, and capable of very genuine friendship. The Princess Sophia, the younger daughter of George the Third, was unmarried.

There had been no children of the marriages, and therefore intense interest was manifested in the Princess Charlotte, and in her approaching alliance with Prince Leopold. The union seemed in most respects to promise great happiness, for the young couple thoroughly understood each other, and were mutually devoted.

On the 2d of May, 1816, they were married, and immediately afterwards went to the Duke of York's residence at Oatlands, returning in a few days for the London season, during which they remained at Camelford House, Park Lane, afterwards going to reside permanently at the prince's own beautiful house at Claremont, near Esher, which had been purchased for them by the government for £69,000.

Stockmar, though he was only one of the chief officers of the simple household (which, besides himself, consisted of Mrs. Campbell, lady-in-waiting to the princess, and three gentlemen equerries or aides-de-camp), was in so confidential a position that he could well estimate the happy relations of the prince and princess. "In this house reign harmony, peace, and love," he wrote in October, 1816; "in short, everything that can promote domestic happiness. My master is the best of all husbands in all the five quarters of the globe, and his wife bears him an amount of love, the greatness of which can only be compared with the English national debt." Ten months afterwards: "The married life of this couple affords a rare picture of love and fidelity, and never fails to impress all spectators who have managed to preserve a particle of feeling."

Alas! a shadow was gathering over that abode of mutual affection—the curtain of death was to be drawn across the picture. The princess was about to become a mother, and the event was looked forward to with anxiety, not only by all England but by foreign nations. There appeared to be no reason for apprehension: all was apparently going well. Stockmar had firmly and wisely enough refused to undertake any responsibility, or to attend the princess even as resident physician, and the result showed that it was prudent for him as a foreigner to abstain from interference. The physician in ordinary was the famous Dr. Baillie; Sir Richard Croft was accoucheur. In those days a good deal of medical treatment consisted of depletion,—bleeding, cupping, and means for lowering the system were considered necessary in cases where quite a different course would now be pursued. The strength of the princess had, it was said, been greatly diminished. The period of suffering before the birth of her child was unusually protracted: the ministers, the Archbishop of Canterbury, and other important personages had assembled at the house awaiting the result. A male child was born, but born dead. It was a terrible disappointment, but the prince bore it with resignation, and, worn out with long watching by his wife, retired to rest, the princess appearing to be well and free from pain. At midnight Stockmar was awakened by Sir Richard Croft coming to his bedside, and begging him to inform the prince that the patient was in a dangerous condition. Two hours afterwards, at two o'clock in the morning of the 6th of November, 1817, the dead mother lay beside the dead child; and the husband, broken down with grief, felt as though his life had been wrecked and there would be no more joy for him in the world.

The terrible event caused profound grief throughout the nation. The country was in mourning, and was pervaded by a sense of gloom, amidst which sinister accusations against the Regent and Queen Charlotte found extravagant expression. The unfeeling conduct of the father, and the dislike and harshness manifested towards the princess by the Queen, were bitterly remembered, and suspicions of neglect, and worse than neglect, were first whispered, and afterwards more openly disseminated.

They were entirely without foundation, for the princess had been under the unceasing care of a devoted husband; and apart from the question of the erroneous medical practice of the time, no immediate responsibility could be placed upon anyone in attendance upon her. But the calamity was so awfully sudden and unexpected that people sought for some further explanation than was to be found in mistaken treatment. This state of public feeling was painfully increased by the suicide of Sir Richard Croft, whose mind had been so affected that he was in a state bordering on insanity. He could not endure the grief and anxiety which, added to the conviction that he was the object of public denunciation, overthrew his reason, and while attending the wife of a clergyman, whose condition seemed somewhat to resemble that which preceded the death of the princess, he shot himself with a pistol which he found in the room that he occupied in the house.

The Duke of Kent was still in Brussels, where he had been completing the stables and gardens of a mansion which he had obtained for his residence. He was now fifty years of age; but his manner of living had been different to that of his elder brothers, and as compared with them he was still in his prime. In one of his visits to Germany he had met the youngest sister of Prince Leopold—the Princess Victoire (Victoria) Maria Louisa—widow of the Prince of Leiningen, who with her two children lived at Amorbach in Bavaria, in a residence assigned to her as princess-dowager. The princess was but thirty years old, her husband having been much her senior. She had now been for four years a widow, with a son, Charles Emich, Prince of Leiningen, about twelve, and a daughter, Anna Feodora, about nine years of age.

The duke, a man of handsome presence, courteous and most kind and attractive manners, and with accomplishments which give distinction even to princes, had probably soon won the regard of this lady, as her singularly engaging appearance, amiable and unselfish disposition, and admirable character, had certainly secured his affection. Stockmar in his journal recorded that she was of middle height, with a good figure, fine brown eyes and hair, fresh and youthful; naturally cheerful and friendly, most charming and attractive; naturally truthful, affectionate, unselfish, full of sympathy and generous. This is a description which might seem to derive some eulogy from the language of a courtier; but Stockmar was no courtier, and wrote in his diary only what he had reason to believe of the sister of his beloved Prince Leopold. His estimate of the mother of our Queen was verified by the long and consistent life of that gracious lady, who, by the characteristics here attributed to her, and by her gentleness and patience, overcame the prejudices and innumerable difficulties which awaited her on her arrival in England.

The Princess Charlotte, heiress to the throne, was dead. The Prince Regent was separated from his wife, from whom he desired to be divorced. The Duke of York had no children.

There was none to succeed the princess in relation to the future accession to the throne. The regular life of the Duke of Kent had made it probable that he would survive his elder brothers. It was not surprising therefore, that after receiving the sad intelligence of the death of his niece, which greatly affected him, he should consider what would be its political result, and make definite arrangements for his marriage, which took place on the 29th of May in the following year (1818) at Coburg, where it was solemnized according to the rites of the Lutheran Church. It was necessary, however, that, in accordance with the Royal Marriage Act, the ceremony should be performed in England, and on the 11th of July two royal weddings took place at Kew, for William, Duke of Clarence (afterwards William the Fourth), at same time took to himself a wife—the Princess Adelaide of Saxe-Meiningen. Queen Charlotte, full of years and full of cares for the husband with whom she had spent a long life was already dead to the world, almost dead to sense, and to mental as well as physical light—exerted herself to be present. It was the last time that she was able to appear at any ceremonial observance, and she died shortly afterwards. The Prince Regent had so far relented as to give away both brides, and after the ceremony had been performed by the Archbishop of Canterbury and the Bishop of London, and the Queen had retired, he presided at a grand banquet in honour of the occasion. The comfort of the happy re-married pair had been cared for by the bereaved Prince Leopold, and in his carriage they drove to Claremont House, where they were to stay for a time before returning to Germany to take up their residence at the house of the duchess at Amorbach.

The duke was an "amiable, courteous, and even chivalrous husband" to quote Stockmar again), and the marriage was an

eminently happy one; but his financial embarrassments continued, and he could neither obtain a settlement of them, nor any adequate assistance from the government or from his brothers, the Regent acting as though the superficial reconciliation implied by his having given away the bride should be regarded as sufficient concession to compensate for any lack of further interest.

The Castle of Amorbach was part of the inheritance of the young prince, the son of the duchess; and she had, upon her marriage, relinquished an annuity which had been paid her as dowager, and amounted to about £5000 a-year. The want of money was pressing, and as time went on became serious, for it was the earnest desire of the duke that the child which he had reason to expect, should be born in England, the country over which he had a strong conviction either he or his offspring would one day be called to reign. The duchess, however, was prevented from making the journey, because of the want of means to pay the expenses, until some private friends of the duke in England proffered their aid. It may be interesting to know that these friends were Alderman Wood and Lord Darnley, the trustees who received the revenues of the Duke of Kent in trust for his creditors when he retired to Brussels, and received only a small amount of his income. His liberal politics had prevented him from enjoying the advantages of office conferred on other members of the royal family, and yet his debts were not to be compared with those of the Duke of York. When Alderman Sir Matthew Wood heard of the situation of the duchess, he wrote to the duke at Brussels to suggest his removing to England. The duke replied that a considerable sum would be necessary to defray the expenses; and as no funds were in hand, the alderman suggested to Lord

Darnley that they two should execute a personal bond to Messrs. Coutts, the bankers, for an advance to the duke, they taking their chance of his living long enough for them to be repaid out of income. By these means the duke and duchess were enabled to reach England, and it may be added that the advance was only just repaid at the time of the duke's premature death.[1] Knowing how anxious our gracious Sovereign was at the commencement of her reign not only to meet all the obligations contracted by her father, but also to acknowledge the aid which he had received, it is not surprising that the well-known alderman (a Liberal in more than one aspect) received a baronetcy offered him by Lord Melbourne, in accordance with her Majesty's commands. This is a digression, but it is not out of place.

Having obtained this friendly aid, at a time when further delay would have made the journey impossible (it already involved some risk), the duke promptly prepared for the journey to England. It is recorded, and it was eminently characteristic of the man, that feeling reluctant to intrust anybody with the responsibility, he himself drove the carriage in which the duchess travelled for the whole of the journey by land from Amorbach to London, where they arrived early in the month of April, 1819, taking up their residence in Kensington Palace, in which a suite of apartments had been prepared for them.

The rooms occupied by the Duchess of Kent were spacious, and all the more convenient and home-like for not being of too great a height. A room on the first floor at the north-east corner of the palace, and with three windows on one side looking out on the private grounds, was the bed-room, and there the

---

[1] *Memoir of the Right Hon. William Page Wood, Baron Hatherley.* Edited by his nephew, W. R. W. Stephens, M.A. 1883.

baby who was to be our Queen was born. The adjoining "north drawing-room" was converted into a nursery.

The state apartments of the palace at Kensington during the residence there of the Duchess of Kent and the Princess Victoria consisted of a suite of twelve rooms, approached by the grand staircase, the balconies of which, as already noticed, were painted with groups of figures, including the portraits of the "Turks" who were attendants of George the Second, a figure of "Peter the Wild Boy," and some other celebrities of the time when the work was executed. The state apartments were now used only on extraordinary occasions. The Cubic Room, or grand saloon, where the christening was held, was a showy room, 37 feet square, gaudily decorated and containing gilt mythological statues in marble niches, surmounted by gilt busts; a bust of Cleopatra over the mantel-piece, and a very fine marble sculpture by Rysbrach representing a Roman marriage. The paintings in the galleries and state rooms were numerous, and included a number of historical pictures and family portraits, and several of them had been collected by Queen Caroline, who took particular pleasure in regaining as many as possible of those that had belonged to Charles the First; but many changes had been made, and several of the most remarkable works had been removed to Windsor and Buckingham Palace.

It may be mentioned that the duchess had walked daily in the gardens, and that no ill effects had ensued from the long journey taken at a critical period. In her case, following the Coburg custom, the services of a famous accoucheuse named Charlotte Siebold were secured, the regular medical attendants being in waiting only in case of their advice being required; but all went well, and the ministers and noblemen who had assembled at the palace soon received the announcement of the birth of a princess. Amongst those present were the Duke of Sussex, the Duke of Wellington, the Archbishop of Canterbury, Lord Lansdowne, the Bishop of London, Mr. George Canning, and Mr. Nicholas Vansittart, afterwards Lord Bexley.

It is no flattery to say that the "new princess" was a beautiful baby. That was the universal conclusion. Even Stockmar said so, and he was not likely to be "carried away" amidst the general delight and congratulation which extended beyond this country, and was equally felt in the old home at Coburg: at the Rosenau, the palace of Duke Ernest (the elder brother of the Duchess of Kent), about four miles from the old town: and at Ketschendorf, the dwelling of their mother, the dear affectionate old dowager-duchess, the grandmother of the little baby-princess at Kensington, who, many years afterwards, could write of her: "The Queen remembers her dear grandmother perfectly well. She was a most remarkable woman, with a most powerful, energetic, almost masculine mind, accompanied with great tenderness of heart and extreme love for nature."

The mother's heart was in the letter that the dowager sent to her daughter, the Duchess of Kent. "I cannot express how happy I am to know you, dearest Vickel, safe in your bed with a little one, and that all went off so happily. May God's blessing rest on the little stranger and the beloved mother! Again a Charlotte, destined, perhaps, to play a great part one day, if a brother is not born to take it out of her hands. The English like queens, and the niece of the ever-lamented, beloved Charlotte will be most dear to them. I need not tell you how delighted everybody is here on hearing of your safe confinement. You know that you are much beloved in this your little home."

A charmingly simple and loving letter, with a truly home-like tone, just such as might have been expected, for the faithful Siebold having concluded her duties in London had returned to Coburg, and there had described the new-comer in terms that at once suggested to the nature-loving grandmother the sweet and appropriate name of "May-flower" for the princess born in May.

Madame Siebold was wanted at Coburg, for the Duchess Louise was about to present her husband the duke with a second child; and on the 26th of August (1819) at a little before seven in the morning a groom from the Rosenau rode into the court-yard of Ketschendorf to summon the dowager-duchess, bringing the news of the birth of a prince—a prince destined to sustain the closest and dearest relations to his cousin the infant princess then sleeping beside her mother in the room at Kensington. The good news was sent off to the Duchess of Kent by the dear old dowager on the following day. "Rosenau, August 27, 1819. The date will of itself make you suspect that I am sitting by Louischen's bed. . . . Siebold, the accoucheuse, had only been called at three, and at six the little one gave his first cry in this world and looked about like a little squirrel. . . . At a quarter to seven I heard the tramp of a horse. It was a groom who brought the joyful news. I was off directly, as you may imagine, and found the little mother slightly exhausted but *gaie et dispos*. She sends you and Edward (the Duke of Kent) a thousand kind messages. . . . The little boy is to be christened to-morrow,[1] and to have the name of Albert. The Emperor of Austria, the old Duke Albert of Saxe-Teschen, the Duke of Gotha, Mensdorff, and I are to be sponsors. Our boys will have the same names as the sons of the Elector Frederic

---

[1] The event was deferred till the 19th of September, when the baby prince was christened in the marble hall at the Rosenau.

the Mild, who were stolen by Kunz of Kauffengen—namely, Ernest and Albert. . . How pretty the *May Flower* will be when I see it in a year's time! Siebold cannot sufficiently describe what a dear little love it is. Une bonne fois, adieu! Kiss your husband and children. AUGUSTA."

Prince Leopold, watchfully kind in the midst of his own sorrow, had come to the aid of his sister and her husband when they needed it, but though he was heartily at one with them he could at present take little or no personal part in the rejoicings. The sorrow that had stricken his life had gone deep, the wounded heart was still bleeding, and he had to find in retirement that resignation and restoration which a man of his character would not seek in vain. "The Prince of Coburg," wrote Bollmann in one of the letters to be found in Varnhagen's reminiscences, "stands out in noble outline before the nation. If he does nothing in the opinion of the public to break the association with their loved princess and remains conspicuously the noble man of blameless life, I believe that further events may make his career a very remarkable one." This forecast was verified indeed, but for several years before it was fulfilled in any manner such as the writer contemplated, the good, sagacious, and accomplished prince had accepted the charge that he believed had devolved on him—that of giving his invaluable aid and counsel in protecting, instructing, and directing the education of the princess who would, he believed, occupy the position which once had been expected for his beloved Charlotte. The child loved him dearly, and spent the happiest days of her somewhat lonesome child-hood at the beautiful house at Claremont. On a visit to Coburg, where he went to arrange for a visit of the dowager-duchess to Italy, when the infant Prince Albert was but two years old, the same affection was manifested for him by the little boy, whose mother wrote: "Albert adores his uncle Leopold, and will not leave him for a moment; he looks sweetly (makes soft eyes) at him, kisses him every moment; and is only happy when he is by him." Assuredly the uncle was to become a foremost beloved figure in the story of those young lives. He could not take any leading part in the celebrations, but he was present at the christening of the infant princess, which took place at Kensington Palace on the 24th of June, a month after the date of her birth.

Although the Prince Regent took care to make it understood that in case of his obtaining a divorce from the Princess Caroline he might marry again, and though there was some probability of the Duchess of Clarence giving an heir to the throne, the Duke of Kent was firm in the conviction that the crown would come to the princess, and when showing the infant to his friends, who of course were much interested in her, would say with a kind of subdued delight, "Look at her well, for she will be Queen of England." It is not surprising therefore that the christening was an event which occasioned a little excitement and was made of some importance. The gold font was brought from the Tower of London, where it had long remained undisturbed, the draperies from the Chapel Royal, Saint James's, were hung in the grand saloon of the palace, where the solemn rite was performed by the Archbishop of Canterbury and the Bishop of London. The chief sponsors were the Prince Regent and the Emperor Alexander of Russia, represented by the Duke of York, and in whose honour the infant princess was to receive the name of Alexandrina. The godmothers were the Princess-dowager of Wurtemburg (the princess-royal and eldest aunt of the infant princess), represented by Princess Augusta; and the Dowager-duchess of Coburg (the grandmother of the infant princess), represented by the Duchess of Gloucester, the Princess Mary.

At first it was the wish of the Prince Regent, as a mark perhaps of great conciliation, to bestow on the child his own name and that of the former regnant members of the family, and to have her christened *Georgiana* Alexandrina. We may be thankful that the nation was spared *that*. The English may-flower, by any other name than Victoria, would have been as sweet, but it would have taken some time to get over "*Georgiana*." The Duke of Kent had wished the child to be named Elizabeth, as it was a favourite name in England; but the Regent seems to have only dropped "Georgiana" in favour of paying a compliment to the Russian emperor, and so the name was given as Alexandrina, and on the Duke of Kent saying that he should like a second name, the prince replied: "Then let it be her mother's, but Alexandrina must precede it." The future Queen was, therefore, named Alexandrina Victoria; but the first name was almost from the first abandoned for that of Victoria, a name that soon stole into the hearts of the English people, and for fifty years has represented to them the dominant grace and goodness of their sovereign Lady.

We have already[1] seen what is the lineage of her Majesty on her mother's side, and that it was also the lineage of the prince who was in years to come to be her royal consort, but it will be convenient here to show in a tabulated form the descent of her Majesty the Queen from Egbert, the first actual King of England; the line of Brunswick-Hanover joining the succession by the marriage of the Duke of Brunswick-Luneburg, afterwards Elector of Hanover, to Sophia, who was the youngest child of the Elector-palatine and Elizabeth eldest daughter of James the First. George the First was the son of the said Duke of Brunswick Elector of Hanover, and Sophia.

[1] Page 64.   The elder branch of the Saxon family—the Saxe-Coburgs.

DESCENT OF QUEEN VICTORIA FROM EGBERT. *(a 4 8 27)*

1. EGBERT.   2. ETHELWOLF.   3. ALFRED THE GREAT.   4. EDWARD THE ELDER.
5. EDMUND. 6. EDGAR. 7. ETHELRED. 8. EDMUND IRONSIDE.   9. Edward (not a king).
10. Margaret, wife of Malcolm, King of Scotland.   11. Matilda, wife of HENRY I.
12. Matilda or Maud, Empress of Germany, and wife of Geoffrey of Anjou.   13. HENRY II.
14. JOHN. 15. HENRY III. 16. EDWARD I. 17. EDWARD II. 18. EDWARD III.

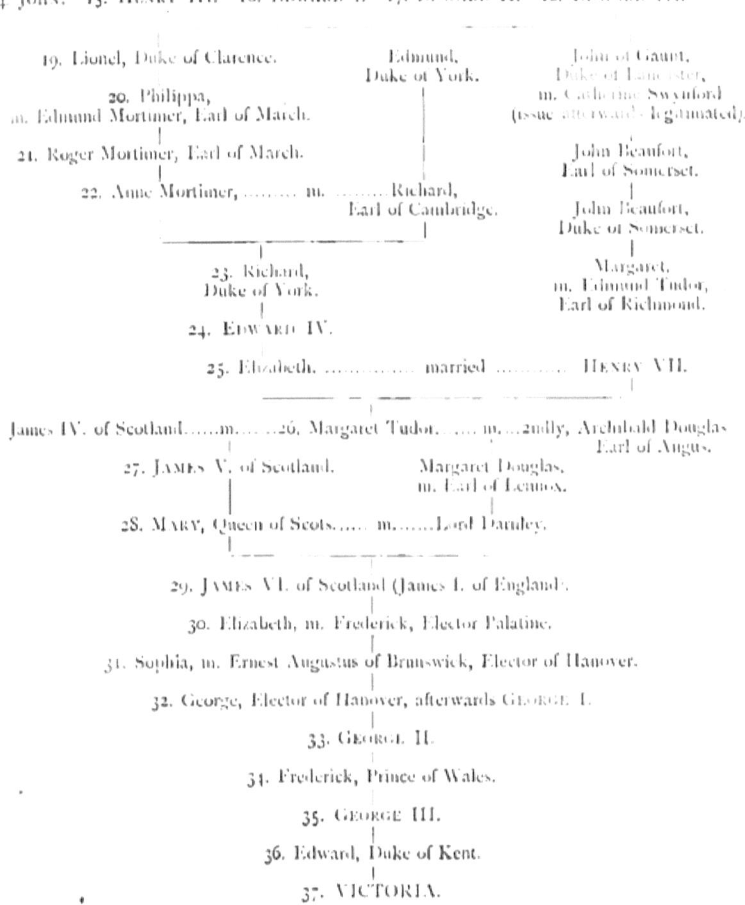

In the domestic suite of rooms at Kensington Palace the first months of the princess's infancy were passed, but even at that early age she was occasionally seen outside the world of the nursery. In the month of August the princess was vaccinated, and to use a common expression the vaccination "took well," a fact worth mentioning, because it was only just before that date that the discovery of the use of vaccine by Dr. Jenner had begun to supersede the old plan of "inoculation," and the baby Victoria was the first member of the royal family who was submitted to the new treatment.

The child throve famously, for her mother performed all those maternal duties which are, or were, too often neglected by ladies of high rank, and not only "nursed" her baby, but then and long afterwards personally attended to the daily bathing and the tiny toilette. These may appear to be small matters to record, but they have a very definite relation to the sound health which her Majesty has enjoyed, and for the strength which has enabled her cheerfully to fulfil her duties to the state even under very trying conditions.

The responsibility accepted by the Duchess of Kent was at all events sufficient to cause admiration if not surprise, for we find the duke writing in reply to Dr. Collyer: —" I appreciate most gratefully your obliging remarks upon the duchess's conduct as a mother, upon which I shall only observe, that parental feeling and a just sense of duty, and not the applause of the public, were the motives which actuated her in the line which she adopted. She is, however, most happy that the performance of an office most interesting in its nature has met with the wishes and feelings of society."

When the cold weather set in with some severity the duke made arrangements for spending part of the winter in the milder climate of Devonshire, and secured a pleasant abode at Woolbrook Cottage at Sidmouth. The journey was a long one, and the roads were so bad that it took nearly two days to go from Salisbury, so that it was necessary to stay for a night at an inn at Ilminster; but the destination was safely reached, and the good folk at Sidmouth were loyally delighted to receive the distinguished visitors, who, by the simplicity and kindliness of their manners, immediately became popular.

The first serious danger which threatened the infant princess was at this quiet abode. A careless boy who had contrived to get hold of a gun, and went out to shoot any small birds that he could find, carried his sport so close to the duke's cottage that he fired through the nursery window. The glass was shattered, and some of the shot passed close to the head of the child in the nurse's arms. The delinquent was captured and brought before the duke, who with the duchess had been seriously alarmed; but perhaps not much more alarmed than the culprit himself, who, however, escaped with a solemn warning and reprimand on promising to be more careful in future.

Alas! this was but a small trouble—a flutter of anxiety soon to be followed by a terrible calamity. The child for whom such tender care was manifested became fatherless,—the mother for the second time a widow,—the nation was again mourning—mourning the loss of a prince who had been distinguished for his kindly charities and personal virtues, no less than for a liberal patriotism. His constant delight was in the child for whom he presaged so great a future: but this was to be made a reason for simple and unpretentious training—the training of the heart and mind.

Amidst numerous current stories and anecdotes of the early life of the Queen, some of which are, of course, not authentic, but most of which have been recently repeated, is one which may be accepted as illustrative, not only of the earnest and anxious affection that the duke bore to his child, but of his deep religious feeling. It was originally related by a clergyman who was on most friendly terms with the duke, and who had called at Kensington Palace to take leave of him previous to the journey to Sidmouth. The duke asked him to see the infant princess in her crib, and said, "As it may be some time before we meet again, I should like you to see the child and give her your blessing." They went into the little princess's room, and on the visitor closing a short prayer that as she grew in years she might grow in grace and favour both with God and man, the duke responded with a fervent "Amen," and said with much emotion, "Don't pray simply that hers may be a brilliant career, and exempt from those trials and struggles which have pursued her father; but pray that God's blessing may rest on her, that it may overshadow her, and that in all her coming years she may be guided and guarded by God."

The pleasant cottage at Sidmouth had been occupied only a few weeks when the duke took an illness which proved fatal. He had been out for a long walk with his trusted friend and equerry Captain Conroy, and had returned probably somewhat heated and certainly with wet boots, which (neglecting the advice of his companion), he delayed changing, attracted to linger for a little while, it was said, to play with his baby daughter, whom he saw holding out her hands to him. Whatever may have been the cause, he appears to have taken a chill, and in the evening showed some of the symptoms of a bad cold, which increased to inflammation of the lungs and fever. It was, however, not of this that he died, but of the same kind of mistaken medical treatment which had killed the Princess Charlotte. The duke was a strong man, and the plan adopted for curing his disorder was to make him a weak one, by "cupping" and bleeding.

On the afternoon of the 22d of January (1820) it was known that he could not recover. He appeared to be losing consciousness, but he at once knew the voice of his old and attached friend General Wetherall, who had been brought to his bedside. He was able to talk coherently, and by a strong effort to listen to the reading of his will, which he signed slowly, taking pains to make each letter of the word "Edward" clearly legible. His "beloved wife Victoire, Duchess of Kent," was made sole guardian to the infant princess, and the estate was for their benefit, Captain Conroy and General Wetherall being left trustees. The duke died on the following day (Sunday the 23d) very early in the morning, and the duchess, who for days and nights had been by his bedside, was left desolate. The Princess Feodora, then a little more than nine years of age, deeply felt the death of her stepfather. Years afterwards, when she had long been married to the Prince Hohenlohe and separated from her little sister, who had become Queen of England, and whom she had tenderly loved, she wrote: "Indeed, I well remember that dreadful time at Sidmouth. I recollect praying on my knees that God would not let your dear father die. I loved him dearly; he always was so kind to me." There is something very charming in this; it is a testimony to the worth of the man, more valuable than a hundred studied eulogies.

The kind and faithful brother Prince Leopold was in Scotland, but hastened to the bereaved wife; not only to sympathize with her, but to console her by immediate support and generous assistance. Her position was a painful one; for she was almost a stranger to the English royal family, from whom she probably had few expectations, knowing what had been the experience of her husband and having heard something of the continued quarrels and divisions. She was also in comparative poverty. There had been no settlement of the duke's pecuniary difficulties, and she did not even possess the means to return with her establishment to Kensington until her brother's ready aid enabled her to make adequate arrangements.

Loving sympathy was not altogether wanting in the hearts of her husband's kinsfolk, however. The royal dukes were touched and grieved at the sad news of their brother's illness; and the Princess Augusta, to whom the Duchess of Kent had written (in French, for she could not write English), was, as she said, nearly heart-broken, for she sincerely loved her brother, and seemed to be the amiable pacificator, willing but not able to heal the animosities of the family. Speaking of the duchess, in a letter to Lord Harcourt, she said: "She has conducted herself like an angel; and I am thankful dearest Leopold was with her. I long to hear of her; but I fear we shall not for these ten days; it will be a sad meeting to us both. But she will be doubly dear to me now, and indeed I loved her dearly before."

Some days later, when the duchess and her children with their household had made the journey from Sidmouth and were at Kensington, the princess again wrote—"She is the most pious, good, resigned little creature it is possible to describe. She has written to me once; and I received the letter from her and one from Adelaide, *written together* from Kensington. Dearest William is so good-hearted that he has desired Adelaide to go to Kensington every day, so she is a comfort to the poor widow; and her sweet, gentle mind is of great use to the Duchess of Kent. It is a great delight to me to think that they can read the same prayers and talk the same mother-tongue together; it makes them such real friends and comforts to each other."

This reference to the Princess Adelaide, the wife of the Duke of Clarence (afterwards William the Fourth), is very touching, and suggests the amiable disposition and tenderness of that really good woman.

Hers was a gentle, unselfish spirit, apparently incapable of mean jealousy, and her affectionate heart was touched by the affliction of the mother and the apparent isolation which must be the lot of the fatherless girl, unless the duty of lovingkindness appealed to those who were themselves near the throne. Her own infant, a daughter born two months before the birth of the Princess Victoria, had lived only a few hours, but this loss of the child who would have stood near to the succession left no bitter feeling; and even two years later (on the 11th of March, 1821), when a second daughter died only a few weeks old, the sorrow and disappointment brought nothing but tender thoughts of the child at Kensington. "My children are dead, but yours lives, and she is mine too," wrote this dear lady to her sister-in-law. Such a message sent in the midst of grief needs no comment.

On the 29th of January, 1820, six days after the death of the Duke of Kent at Sidmouth, his father, King George the Third, expired at Windsor. "It has pleased the Almighty to release the King from all further suffering," was the announcement which told of his death, and the words were appropriate, for he had been long dead to most of those things that belong to the duties and the pleasures of life. The accession of the Prince Regent as George the Fourth was little more than a formal proclamation, for he had been practically on the throne for ten years, and was himself seriously ill with a cold which ended in a similar disorder to that of which his brother the Duke of Kent had died.

The funeral of the duke took place on the 12th of February at Windsor, whither his body had been brought from Sidmouth, the journey occupying nearly a week, the procession having to halt on successive nights at Bridport, Blandford, Salisbury, and Basingstoke, the coffin being deposited in the church of each town with a military guard. From Cumberland Lodge, where the body lay in state for a day, there went a long and stately funeral procession, consisting of the Dukes of York, Clarence, Sussex, and Gloucester, and Prince Leopold, in long black cloaks borne by attendants, and of field-marshals and generals bearing the pall and canopy—"poor knights," pursuivants, pages, and heralds. The funeral took place at night, and those who took part in it walked by torch-light amidst a large assembly of persons who, in that wintry weather, had arrived from London and other parts of the country to witness the solemn spectacle "viewed from the distance of three miles through the spacious long walk, amidst a double row of lofty trees, whilst at intervals the glittering of the flambeaux and the sound of martial music were distinctly seen and heard." A few days afterwards the body of the King was also laid in its last resting-place.

But happily even amidst sorrow and mourning the realities of life fail neither in their compensations nor their demands, and the Duchess of Kent, in obedience to her husband's last injunctions and with an unfailing sense of the obligations which she alone could adequately fulfil, prepared to face a situation of great difficulty and of what to one in her position was actual poverty. It would appear that by some flaw in the act of Parliament or the settlement she could not claim the amount which was to have come to her as jointure, and as she had already forfeited her previous settlement she was compelled to accept the aid of her brother Prince Leopold, and of other friends, until the error was rectified by the payment of the jointure, which amounted to £6000 a year. As she had consented to give up the property bequeathed by the duke, for the discharge of his debts, she had still for some time to rely upon the generosity of her brother, who, it was understood, made her a considerable annual allowance.

She, however, possessed much calm courage, supported by the consciousness of integrity, and stimulated by the responsibilities which devolved upon her. Her own brief and simple statement explains her situation as seen in the first months of her widowhood: "A few months after the birth of my child, my infant and myself were awfully deprived of father and husband. We stood alone, almost friendless and unknown in this country. I could not even speak its language. I did not hesitate how to act. I gave up my home, my kindred, and other duties to devote myself to a duty which was to be the sole object of my future life."

That duty was commenced with a reverent and hopeful belief that it would be a blessed one; and the belief was well founded. Her life at Kensington with her children was an example of pure and simple domestic peace, and she had the deep and abiding satisfaction of seeing under its influence the formation of elements which were to give a new character to royalty, and silently to work in unison with the highest and best form of that social reformation which was approaching though not yet distinctly perceived. She gained the esteem, the affection, not only of her children, but of the pure in heart who recognized the value of her labour of love. Withdrawn, almost secluded, from the court and from the conventional gaieties and pleasures of fashionable life, she was within the borders of a better and nobler kingdom. She had secured the regard and respect of the people and the true leaders of the nation even before she had thoroughly acquired the language, which she was not slow to learn.

Viscount Morpeth and Viscount Clive waited on the Duchess of Kent with an address of condolence from the House of Commons, and she met them with her child in her arms—a simple unceremonious reception, but affecting and significant. Many friends of her late husband, and several representatives of charitable and benevolent institutions in which he had been personally interested, also went to pay their respects, and the baby princess was, so to speak, introduced to a considerable number of loyal and loving persons, who kept a place in their hearts and memories for the fair, rosy, smiling face, above which some of them fancied they saw the reflected light of a not-far-distant crown. The Duke of York, who, with all his great faults, had a kindly heart, called to encourage and to sympathize, and, if we are to accept a story which has often been repeated, baby Victoria unconsciously won that heart at once. The duke had scarcely entered the room when the child, recognizing in him a likeness to her father, held out her arms with a smile accompanied by infantile exclamations which quite overcame him. Warmly embracing her he declared with emotion that he would indeed be a father to her, and he appears to have shown real kindness to her and to her mother until his death in 1827. One of his early presents was a beautiful donkey on which the child afterwards learned to ride, much to the benefit of her health, and this donkey, which was a docile and excellent animal, became popular, if not historical, so frequently did it appear gaily caparisoned in Kensington Gardens, or at a later date at Tunbridge Wells and elsewhere, sedately bearing its little mistress. It is said that when, soon after her fourth birthday, her uncle, George the Fourth, had sent an invitation for her to visit Carlton House, she gleefully asked, "Oh! mamma, shall I go upon my donkey?" for she could not doubt that his Majesty would be pleased to see an animal of which she held such a good opinion.

Among the earlier visitors to the duchess after her bereavement was Mr. Wilberforce, who was invited to Kensington as an old and esteemed friend of the duke, who agreed with him in his philanthropic opinions and in his efforts to abolish negro slavery. He lived at Gore House, Kensington, afterwards famous as the dwelling of Lady Blessington and Count d'Orsay, and much later, during the Great Exhibition of 1851, as the "symposium," or refreshment-house, where the culinary art of various nations was exemplified under the direction of the celebrated Alexis Soyer. Mr. Wilberforce, who is described by Leigh Hunt as a "worthy ultra serio-comic person,—a little, plain-faced man, radiant by nature with glee and good humour, very 'serious' at a moment's notice, an earnest devotee, a genial host, a good speaker, and member of parliament," wrote to his friend Hannah More on the 21st of July, 1820: "In consequence of a very civil message from the Duchess of Kent I waited on her this morning. She received me with her fine animated child on the floor by her side with its playthings, of which I soon became one. She was very civil, but as she did not sit down I did not think it right to stay above a quarter of an hour, and there being but a female attendant and a footman present I could not well get up any topic so as to carry on a continued discourse. She apologized for not speaking English well enough to talk it; but intimated that she might talk it better and longer with me at some future time. She spoke of her situation, and her manner was quite delightful."

The princess was early trained to simple and regular living, and was carried frequently in the open air. As she grew older she took plenty of exercise, either riding on her pet donkey or running at a remarkable pace about the lawns and gardens of Kensington Palace, so that she was often observed by passers-by, who could see her from the other side of the railings, and to whom she often used very gracefully to proffer pretty infantile greetings. Of course she had not been made to learn many lessons before she was four years old. "Do not tease your little puss with learning. She is so young still," wrote the dowager-duchess to her daughter; but she had learned to read almost before she could speak plainly, and though she was afterwards sometimes as wayward with regard to her lessons as many other children are, and even when being taught her alphabet is said to have asked, "What good this? what good this?" she was no sooner convinced of the advantage of learning than she studied with much regularity, and even with avidity. But then it must be remembered that her mother was her early instructress, constantly watched over her, and wisely arranged that in work or play, physical, as well as mental and moral health and development should receive due attention. In childhood and in girlhood the princess slept in her mother's room. An account which has been received as authentic says: "At eight, in summer, the family party met at breakfast; Princess Victoria had her bread and fruit and milk on a little table by her mother's side. After breakfast the Princess Feodora studied with her governess Miss Louise Lehzen, or the two princesses would walk or drive for an hour. From ten to twelve Princess Victoria received instruction from her mother, and would then run about or amuse herself with her toys in the suite of rooms that formed two sides of the palace. Mrs. Brock was the name of the nurse, who, however, was generally saluted as 'dear, dear Boppy!' At two o'clock the duchess had luncheon, and the princess partook of her plain dinner by her mother's side. Then till four o'clock lessons again occupied the time, after which there was a visit or a drive, and then perhaps a ride or walk in the gardens. Occasionally on fine summer evenings the whole party would sit out under the trees on the lawn. When the time came for her mother to dine, a simple supper was laid beside her for Princess Victoria. After a little time to play with her nurse, the princess joined the party at dessert, and at nine retired to her bed, which was placed beside her mother's."

It was a well-ordered child life, and though we can fancy a sense of loneliness when the rosy plump child, or, later, the little girl with much capacity for fun and social pleasures, broke the rather subdued echoes of the old galleries and rooms with the sound of her flying feet, or loitered sometimes to gaze at the pictures and scan the portraits, some of them of rather puffy-faced juveniles representing members of the previous royal families, there was some compensation in the hours spent out of doors.

A very tender affection existed between the little princesses, the half-sister Feodora evidently loving "the baby" dearly, and being well satisfied to accompany the miniature phaeton drawn by an attendant, or the almost equally diminutive pony carriage. It was in Kensington Gardens, while "taking the air" in this carriage, that the infant Victoria met with an accident which, but for the quickness and presence of mind of a private soldier who was passing, might have had a very serious result. The pony was being led by a page, a lady— presumably the duchess —walked on one side, and a young woman beside the chaise. A large water-dog gambolling on the road got between the legs of the pony and caused it to plunge, bringing the wheels of the carriage on to the pathway. The child was falling out, and the carriage appeared to be toppling over upon her, when, before she reached the ground, head foremost, the soldier, whose name was Maloney, caught her by the dress and swung her upward into his arms. After restoring her to the lady, amidst the congratulations of the few people assembled, he was told to follow the carriage to the palace, where he received a guinea and the very fervent thanks of the duchess, and it is said that he was afterwards not lost sight of.

In her very early days, when riding on her pet donkey, the princess was often attended by a pensioner, presumably Hillman, a soldier who had been with the Duke of Kent's regiment at Gibraltar, and remained faithful to him at the time of the attempted mutiny. This man continued in the duke's service, and he and his family had a cottage provided for them near the palace at Kensington, and were not forgotten in later years. The princess was sometimes reluctant to dismount from her donkey that she might walk or run on the grass as she was encouraged to do by her mother or the attendants, and it was occasionally necessary for the old soldier to use his persuasive powers, or for a representation to be made that the donkey needed to be fed or to have a rest; and these arguments were usually effectual, for the princess had a remarkable regard for animals, and was very careful of their well-being. It may be readily understood that the tiny Victoria, though usually good-tempered and docile, had a strong will of her own, and we have yet to learn that this is any other than a good attribute when that will is conformable to right convictions. It had the effect, however, combined with a love of fun, to make it difficult always to control the exuberant spirits of the child; and when

she had begun to run—and she ran at an extraordinary rate—
along the length of the broad gravel walk, or up and down the
green slopes, it was difficult to induce her to leave off, even
when a considerable number of ladies, gentlemen, and children
had assembled and stood in a semicircle watching her. In
fact, on these occasions it is said the infant princess would
occasionally speak to the lookers-on as though they were taking
some part in her amusement. It may be imagined how many
"little dears," and "sweet little loves," were elicited from the
women who watched her; for the baby princess loved to be
noticed, and to notice everybody in return by dainty little
curtseys and kisses of her chubby hand. This frank and unaffected demeanour towards everybody whom she met, either in
London or at the various places which she visited, remained
even after the unconscious freedom and merry familiarity of first
childhood had passed; and it is potent to-day, because it proceeds,
not from any studied method of conduct for the purpose of
courting popularity, but from simple and healthy training of a
heart naturally trustful of loyalty, and believing in mutual good-
will.

The general regard, or we might say the respectful familiarity
with which the frequent presence of the little princess was
noticed, was repeated at Ramsgate, whither the Duchess of Kent
went for the summer, when the child was five years old, and
where she afterwards stayed on several occasions. There one
hears of Princess Victoria on the sands in her simple dress, a plain
straw-bonnet with a white ribbon round the crown, a coloured
muslin frock looking gay and cheerful, and as pretty a pair of shoes
on as pretty a pair of feet as anyone could wish to see. There,
too, we hear of William Wilberforce again conversing with the
duchess and laughing as a wave unexpectedly rippled over these

little shoes and feet. Here, too, we hear of the visit of the child to the bazaar, or shops where shell-boxes, coral ornaments, and knick-knacks were and are still sold, or of her bestowing her weekly allowance of pocket-money on some poor old creature whom she notices as she passes along the High Street.

The name of Miss Jane Porter is still remembered by people who in their youth were acquainted with her stories, *The Scottish Chiefs* and *Thaddeus of Warsaw*. This lady was living with her sister, Anna Maria (who wrote *The Hungarian Brothers* and *The Recluse of Norway*), with their aged mother at a cottage not far from Claremont, and when the duchess and her daughter were staying there these three ladies were never tired of waiting or walking when they would be likely "to meet the young hope of England taking her morning exercise," either "walking by the side of her governess, or running forward in the eagerness of childhood's happy impulses with a bounding elasticity of active enjoyment, which full health only, or the spring of earliest youth can know." Miss Porter in a letter describes the infant princess as "a beautiful child, with a cherubic form of features, clustered round by glossy fair ringlets; her complexion was remarkably transparent, with a soft but often heightening tinge of the sweet blush rose upon her cheeks that imparted a peculiar brilliancy to her clear blue eyes."

But the early domestic life at Kensington was probably of the most interest, at all events to Londoners, and many brief but always loyal and pleasant references were made to it and to the appearance of the princess, who had already begun to dwell in the affection of people holding very different views and opinions on political and other matters, but in excellent accord on the subject of the healthy training of the child, her bright and attractive ways and appearance, and her unaffected simple manner.

It will be seen that even in these very early days the little princess attracted a good deal of public notice. On more than one occasion references were made in magazines and newspapers to the appearance of the child as, holding the hand of her sister the Princess Feodora, and drawing a toy cart by a string, she returned the salutations and compliments of the persons who were passing. It is said that even then, but more particularly when she was a little older, she took the greatest interest in other children, and was always particularly pleased to be allowed to speak to any infant that was being carried in the gardens. She would also take great pleasure in meeting a school of young ladies out for a walk, and would stop and talk to the younger ones of the party. When the princess was only three years old a correspondent of a daily paper wrote: " Passing accidentally through Kensington Gardens a few days since, I observed at some distance a party, consisting of several ladies, a young child, and two men-servants, having in charge a donkey, gaily caparisoned with blue ribbons, and accoutred for the use of the infant. The appearance of the party, and the general attention they attracted, led me to suspect they might be the royal inhabitants of the palace. I soon learnt that my conjectures were well founded. . On approaching the royal party, the infant princess, observing my respectful recognition, nodded, and wished me a ' good morning ' with much liveliness, as she skipped along between her mother and her sister the Princess Feodora, holding a hand of each. Having passed on some paces, I stood a moment to observe the actions of the child, and was pleased to see that the notice with which she honoured me was extended, in a greater or less degree, to almost every person she met. Her royal highness is remarkably beautiful, and her gay and animated countenance bespeaks perfect health and good temper."

On her fourth birthday the princess received a superb and characteristic present from the King her uncle, who had not seen her since she was a year old. He sent her a miniature portrait of himself set in diamonds. Soon afterwards, by his Majesty's special request, she was taken to visit him at Carlton House, where she was introduced with her mother to special guests invited to a state dinner party. It has been recorded that the princess was dressed in a plain white frock, of which the left sleeve was looped up and fastened with the costly miniature.

The King like other people was delighted with the bright and frank good humour of the child, and from that time showed more kindness to the Duchess of Kent, while his interest in his niece was shown by his causing an application to be made to Parliament for a grant for her maintenance and education. The princess, as we have seen, received her early instruction from her mother, who was also competent to superintend her later studies, but she had also the inestimable advantage of being under the care of the lady who had come to England as the governess of the Princess Feodora, and who remained to carry on the education of the little Princess Victoria, to whom she was devotedly attached. This lady was Louise Lehzen, daughter of a Hanoverian clergyman, and in 1827, three years after she had been officially recognized as governess to the princess, she received the rank of a Hanoverian baroness, conferred on her by George IV. at the request of the Princess Sophia. The household at Kensington was characterized by mutual regard and esteem—and it appears to have been a harmonious one, although it was quiet, and was, so to speak, pitched to a subdued tone. As governess and lady-in-attendance the Baroness Lehzen remained till the princess was to become queen, and long afterwards, amidst the cares of state and domestic duties, the former pupil continued regularly to write to the governess, who had retired to Hanover, where she died in 1870 at the age of eighty-seven. "My dearest, kindest friend old Lehzen expired on the 9th," wrote the Queen in her journal on that occasion. "She knew me from six months old, and from my fifth to my eighteenth year devoted all her care and energies to me with the most wonderful abnegation of self, never taking one day's holiday. I adored, though I was greatly in awe of her. She really seemed to have no thought but for me."

According to precedent the princess was also instructed by a "preceptor," who, in due time, taught her Latin, mathematics, and some Greek. The tutor or preceptor chosen by the duchess was the Rev. George Davys, who appears to have thoroughly deserved the confidence that was reposed in him, and to have been an excellent and judicious instructor. Afterwards, when the princess became direct heir to the throne, and it was suggested to the duchess that a bishop should be appointed instructor, she acutely replied that she had such reason to approve of Dr. Davys that she objected to any change being made; but that if it were thought necessary that the tutor to the princess should be a dignitary of the church, there could be no objection to Dr. Davys receiving the preferment which he so well merited. The result of this reply was that Dr. Davys was afterwards made Dean of Chester. At the close of his duties as tutor he became Bishop of Peterborough.

The infant princess had already been educated to obedience, to affectionate regard for the claims and feelings of others, and to a certain observance of orderliness; but it may be supposed there could have been little actual suppression of her naturally buoyant spirits, little "lecturing" as to the proprieties or the dig- nities, or she never would have acquired that simple but dignified self-possession, which is the reverse of what is usually called self-consciousness, and is her Majesty's truly royal characteristic. Eminent truthfulness, she may be said to have inherited from her parents. "The Queen always had, from my first knowing her, a most striking regard for truth." Dr. Davys told Bishop Wilberforce. "I remember when I had been teaching her one day she was very impatient for the lesson to be over once or twice rather refractory. The Duchess of Kent came in and asked how she had behaved. Lehzen said, 'Oh, once she was rather troublesome!' The princess touched her, and said, 'No, Lehzen, twice, don't you remember?' The Duchess of Kent, too, was a woman of great truth."

It will be easily understood that sound judgment and much discretion was necessary to enable the Duchess of Kent to maintain a certain independence in the management of her household and the education of the princess, and to avoid being implicated in party or family quarrels. Her child, as was well known, might at no very distant date become the sovereign of a great empire; but for some years such an event remained only remotely probable, as there might yet have been a nearer successor to the throne, and at her tender age the Princess Victoria could only be truly prepared for the great responsibility by being kept from any expectation of it. To have made the possible accession to a throne an incentive to obedience, docility, and childlike purity of intention would have been a mistake, and was a danger to be avoided.

This, with the need for refraining from any appearance of seeking to form a coterie, may have so limited the circle of visitors as to make the childhood of the little princess sometimes lonely for the lack of playfellows and companions. Her sister the Princess Feodora was so much older than herself, that though

they loved each other they could scarely be constant associates,
and it should be remembered that the elder sister was married
and had left England before the younger was ten years old.
There is little doubt that many of the early days of the young
Victoria were not altogether happy, and needed the cheering
influence of play-fellowship to relax the sense of precision
and watchfulness, which may be oppressive, where the child life
does not find some sphere of its very own, and into which only
rarely endowed adults who have never lost the childlikeness
can expect frequently to enter. There is an anecdote of an
occurrence, which, if it be true, sweetly and almost pathetically
illustrates this need on the part of the princess. The duchess,
always wishing to find suitable amusement to interest her
little daughter, and knowing how delighted she was to listen to
music, for which she had a remarkable talent, sent for a precocious juvenile performer on the harp, a child who, under
the name of Lyra, had caused considerable sensation in the
musical world. Lyra arrived at the palace, where she played to
the princess, who sat listening with that intent and absorbing
interest which was habitual to her when her attention was secured.
In the midst of the performance the duchess was called to receive
a message from an attendant, and was absent for some time. On
her return the sound of the harp had ceased, and on re-entering
the room she found the two children seated on the hearth-rug
in happy consultation over the toys with which the princess
had enticed the young musician, and some of which had been
generously offered for her acceptance. If this story be true, and
it has often been repeated without contradiction, it would make
a charming subject for a picture; the direct assertion of the
instinct for companionship in the two children who missed so
much—one because of family claims and the exactions of royal

rank, the other probably because of family needs and the exactions of her art.

But we cannot regard the Princess Victoria as having had even a tinge of what is called a "moping" temper, and knowing how assiduously she followed the instructions of her teachers, it is something of a relief to learn that her usual good spirits and sense of fun sometimes led to a smart reminder of the fact that she recognized the possibility of asserting a will of her own if she chose to do so. The princess could sing with a very sweet and clear voice when she was yet little more than an infant, and could play the pianoforte very creditably at an age when few young ladies could accomplish more than the simplest scales. She must therefore have been young indeed when on being exhorted to make herself "mistress of the pianoforte," and that there was no royal road to learning music, she gaily retorted by locking the instrument, putting the key in her pocket, and saying, "There! that is being mistress of the piano! and the royal road to learning is never to take a lesson till you are in the humour to do it." We must imagine this to have been said with a smile of mock defiance, for the story ends with the intimation that having made her amusing demonstration she went and finished her lesson.

The little wilfulnesses of the princess appear to have given greater emphasis to the frank and charming submission or acknowledgments which appear to have followed, and were sometimes unexpectedly candid.

When walking in the grounds of Earl Fitzwilliam, whom she had visited with the duchess during a journey in the north of England, one of the under-gardeners called to her not to go along one of the paths as it was "slape," meaning that it was very slippery after a heavy rain.

"Slape, slape! and pray what is slape?" inquired the princess.

The meaning of the word was explained, but she was such an accustomed pedestrian, or rather runner, that this was not likely to cause her to hesitate, and she therefore went on without heeding the warning, and in a few seconds came rather heavily to the ground.

"Now your royal highness has an explanation of the term 'slape,' both theoretically and practically," cried Earl Fitzwilliam, who was standing at some distance.

"Yes, my lord, I think I have," replied the little lady with humorous meekness as she was assisted to pick herself up. "I shall never forget the word 'slape.'"

On another occasion—the story belongs to Ramsgate—the fearless child, always fond of animals, was playing with a dog, and was told that the creature was uncertain of temper, but she was not to be deterred, and presently there came a snap at her hand, and her cautioner ran up, expressing great fear that she had been bitten.

"Oh, thank you!" was the artless acknowledgment. "You are right and I am wrong; but he didn't bite me, he only *warned* me. I shall be careful in future."

There was a truly healthy tone of mind and body, and consequently there was no affectation, and there has always been in the character of our Queen that characteristic which is potent in maintaining consistency and tact—a genuine sense of humour. Not much verbal wit is expected of children, but more than one very amusing utterance of this kind has been repeated, as having been among the early utterances of the child, who began early to learn three or four European languages, and asked little favours in German as easily as in English, though she always persisted in protesting that she was a little English girl, and spoke her native language in preference.

These are but small chronicles of a young life, but they may be interesting, even if they are less authentic than the announcements of the court newsman. In truth the little princess was not much concerned with the court newsman, for though her education was superior to that of most children, and she became more really "accomplished" than most young ladies even amongst the nobility, she was in the "fashionable" sense far less conspicuous than many girls who were members of wealthy middle-class families.

The princess had made no state appearance at court, although of course she had visited her uncles and aunts, especially the Duke and Duchess of Clarence, and we hear something of her being taken to Windsor, where she was pleasantly received. The king was living there in comparative seclusion, his health seriously broken, his popularity not increased.

The records of some of those who at that time saw the child who was so soon to become next heir to the throne were to be permanently associated with a new era of English literature.

Lord Albemarle, when he wrote his Autobiography, described the interest that he, like many other people, took in observing the outdoor recreations of the little princess when she was about seven years old.

"One of my occupations of a morning, while waiting for the duke, was to watch from the windows the movements of a bright, pretty little girl seven years of age. She was in the habit of watering the plants immediately under the window. It was amusing to see how impartially she divided the contents of the watering-pot between the flowers and her own little feet. Her simple but becoming dress contrasted favourably with the gorgeous apparel now worn by the little damsels of the rising generation —a large straw hat and a suit of white cotton, a coloured *fichu* round the neck was the only ornament she wore. The young lady I am describing was the Princess Victoria, now our gracious Sovereign, whom may God long preserve."

But there is a still more striking reference by the hand of a man, to whose memory this country owes a tribute which it is more ready to pay for any other service than for that of the author or of him who, by toiling, often with very restricted means and little opportunity for rest or leisure, to provide pure and elevating literature, promotes the best education of the people. This is not the place to speak of the remarkable development of what came to be called popular literature which took place at about the time that the little princess was playing in Kensington Gardens. Then, and for a good while afterwards, "albums," "keepsakes," "books of beauty," generally called "annuals," were among the principal lighter periodical literature for family reading, and there were the heavy quarterlies; but the age of truly popular periodicals may almost be said to have commenced with the *Penny Magazine*. Charles Knight, who succeeded his father as a bookseller at Windsor, was the projector and publisher of that, the *Penny Cyclopædia*, and a host of other admirable and entertaining books issued in weekly or monthly parts, to which he himself contributed (for he was a bright and instructive writer), assisted at various times by men of the advanced school of literature. Among these were Macaulay (then a young man), Brougham, and others, of whom Charles Lamb and Leigh Hunt already occupied a foremost place as contributors of light scholarly essays, stories, poems, and criticisms, which were highly entertaining and delightful in style and moral purpose.

We have from the hand of Charles Knight himself, in his *Passages of a Working Life*, a very charming reference: "In the early morning, when the sun was scarcely high enough to have dried up the dews of Kensington's green alleys, as I passed along the broad central walk, I saw a group on the lawn before the palace, which, to my mind, was a vision of exquisite loveliness.

"The Duchess of Kent, and her daughter, whose years then numbered nine, are breakfasting in the open air— a single page attending upon them at a respectful distance—the matron looking on with eyes of love, whilst the 'fair, soft English face' is bright with smiles. The world of fashion is not yet astir. Clerks and mechanics, passing onward to their occupation, are few; and they exhibit nothing of that vulgar curiosity which I think is more commonly found in the class of the merely rich than in the ranks below them in the world's estimation.

"What a beautiful characteristic it seemed to me of the training of this royal girl, that she should not have been taught to shrink from the public eye— that she should not have been burdened with a premature conception of her probable high destiny—that she should enjoy the freedom and simplicity of a child's nature—that she should not be restrained when she starts up from the breakfast-table and runs to gather a flower in the adjoining parterre that her merry laugh should be as fearless as the notes of the thrush in the groves around her.

"I passed on and blessed her; and I thank God that I have lived to see the golden fruits of such training."

These and similar expressions, which appear enshrined in the published sentiments of famous people, ring with a true note; and it may be remarked that they are not the words of courtesy or of flattery, by men and women who had any personal end to gain. On the contrary, they are remarkable for being frequently the spontaneous utterances of persons who were neither politically nor by temperament of the courtier class. Charles Knight was broadly liberal in his views, and was responsible for many a shrewd satirical hit and genial but remarkably telling touch of satire directed against certain persons in high places. Leigh Hunt, as everybody knows, was what was then regarded as a violent Radical, if the term violent could be applied to so gentle and cultured a publicist. At any rate, the plain, bold strictures upon the government published in the *Examiner*, had subjected him and his brother John to official prosecutions. The first, which was for an attack on the Regency, was abandoned; another for an article on military floggings, was defeated by the able defence of Lord Brougham; but a third was too dreadful. Leigh Hunt, in his light satirical vein, had referred to the Regent as "a fat Adonis of fifty," and the brothers were sent to the Marshalsea prison for two years and fined £500 a-piece,—a sentence which, of course, caused them to become popular, and to receive the support of many leading wits, poets, and reformers; while the time in prison was not ill spent, for there Leigh Hunt wrote some admirable poems.

But let us see what he wrote, late in his long life, of a recollection which stirred his kindly heart and made his after loyalty as true as it was consistent.

"We remember well the peculiar kind of personal pleasure which it gave us to see the future Queen, the first time we ever did see her, coming up a cross path from the Bayswater gate, with a girl of her own age by her side, whose hand she was holding as if she loved her. It brought to our mind the warmth of our own juvenile friendships; and made us fancy that she loved everything else that we had loved in like measure,—books, trees, verses, Arabian tales, and the good mother who had helped to make her so affectionate.

"A magnificent footman, in scarlet, came behind her, with the splendidest pair of calves in white stockings that we ever beheld. He looked somehow like a gigantic fairy, personating, for his little lady's sake, the grandest kind of footman he could think of; and his calves he seemed to have made out of a couple of the biggest chaise-lamps in the possession of the godmother of Cinderella. As the princess grew up, the world seemed never to hear of her, except as it wished to hear,—that is to say, in connection with her mother; and now it never hears of her, but in connection with children of her own, and with her husband, and her mother still, and all good household pleasures and hospitalities, and public virtues of a piece with them. May life ever continue to appear to her what, indeed, it really is to all who have eyes for seeing beyond the surface; namely, a wondrous fairy scene, strange, beautiful, mournful too, yet hopeful of being 'happy ever after,' when its story is over; and wise, meantime, in seeing much where others see nothing, in shedding its tears patiently, and in doing its best to diminish the tears around it."

Claremont, the fine mansion which had been bought for Prince Leopold, was now seldom visited by him, but it was left much at the disposal of his sister and her daughter, who were very dear to him. The house, being large and with lofty commodious rooms, and commanding fine views from the front, was a most agreeable residence, especially in summer, for the home demesne extended to about 420 acres, and the park and farms were about 1600 acres. It was not without sad memories. On an eminence in the garden a small Gothic building, erected for the Princess Charlotte, had, after her death, been converted into a mausoleum, dedicated to her memory, and containing a very fine bust.

The situation of the place, near Esher in Surrey, and only seventeen miles from Hyde Park Corner, made it easily accessible from Kensington; and the walks and drives were so delightful that the princess always rejoiced when the time arrived to spend a season there. But there was a stronger reason even than her keen appreciation of the pleasant park and homestead, the beautiful gardens, and the long rambles in summer days. Her uncle Leopold, though he had ceased to reside at Claremont, came as a visitor while his little niece and her mother occupied it, and in his loved society the child was always happy, for he devoted much attention to her, walked with her, talked to her, and, with a rare faculty for teaching without books, gave her pleasant lessons on botany, in which he was fairly proficient, and contrived to make his companionship the means of changing the monotony of ordinary lessons, and giving each day the aspect of a holiday. It must have been some keen remembrance of this which caused the Queen - when writing to her uncle years afterwards (in January, 1843)—to say of Claremont, where she was staying after Prince Leopold had visited England: "This place has a peculiar charm for us both, and to me it brings back recollections of the happiest days of my otherwise dull childhood, when I experienced such kindness from you, dearest uncle, kindness which has ever since continued. . . . Victoria (the princess royal, her own little daughter) plays with my old bricks, and I see her running and jumping in the flower-garden as *old*, though I feel still *little* Victoria of former days used to do." Even when this letter was written the Queen was only twenty-four, and doubtless often inclined to join in the frolics of Victoria the second.

We hear of a visit of the kind, sensible grandmother, the Dowager-duchess of Coburg, to Claremont, where there was quite a pleasant family reunion, and she could see the little May-flower whose portrait she had cherished, and to whom her heart went forth with genuine affection. We hear, too, of the celebration of the seventh birthday of the little princess in that pleasant home, and of a grand procession of her fifteen dolls, each representing a member of the royal family, and dressed by herself, aided by her nurse Mrs. Brock; and, moreover, there is a record of presents, among which stand forth a pair of the smallest mouse-coloured Highland ponies ever seen, brought especially from Scotland by Lady Huntly, who afterwards became Duchess of Gordon.

But we have already touched upon a later date, when the princess was approaching her eleventh year, and the time was coming at which she would have to occupy a more clearly defined position in relation to the throne, of which neither the glory nor the shadow had yet fallen upon her.

On the 26th of June, 1830, George the Fourth died at Windsor. As we have noted, the Duke of York had died in 1827, and therefore William Henry, Duke of Clarence, succeeded to the throne, and the Princess Victoria, who was just entering on the twelfth year of her age, stood next in succession.

The world had been moving since, in 1822, Mr. Canning became foreign secretary and devoted his splendid abilities to opposing the " Holy Alliance" formed after the Peace of Paris between France, Russia, Austria, and Prussia, to maintain what were, in most cases, despotic governments in Europe.

In 1824 Louis XVIII. had made way for his brother Charles X.; and in the same year Alexander I. of Russia had been succeeded by Nicholas I., who, as grand-duke, had paid a visit to Prince Leopold and Princess Charlotte at Claremont in 1816. He was then just twenty years old, singularly handsome, tall and erect in figure. Mrs. Campbell, the lady-in-waiting to the Princess Charlotte, had said of him: "What an amiable creature! he is devilish handsome: he will be the handsomest man in Europe." According to his usual custom the grand-duke slept on a leathern sack filled with hay from the stable. Almost immediately after his accession Russia began to push its claims in the east of Europe at the expense of Turkey; while the attempts of Turkey and Egypt against Greek independence led to the alliance of the English, French, and Russian fleets, and to the battle of Navarino, which ended the war and made Greece into a kingdom, the throne of which Prince Leopold would have occupied, but for his refusal to accept certain conditions.

In 1825 Brazil had become an independent empire under Dom Pedro, son of John VI. of Portugal, and on John's death in 1826 Pedro renounced the Portuguese throne in favour of his daughter Donna Maria, a child of about the age of the Princess Victoria. Dom Pedro gave the Portuguese a national constitution when he resigned the throne, but his brother, Dom Miguel, was as averse to the liberties thus secured as he was to seeing his niece wearing the crown, and promoted a civil war which lasted till 1834, when the youthful sovereign was established on the throne. She soon after (in 1835) married the Duke of Leuchtenberg, who died three months afterwards. She then married (in 1836) the Roman Catholic Prince Ferdinand of Coburg, who was son of Prince Ferdinand, the younger brother of Duke Ernest of Coburg by Antoinette, the daughter of the Prince of Kohary.[1]

But to the young Princess Victoria the most important event on the continent of Europe occurred in this very year (1830), in which she was to take a more prominent place in the eye of the world. The revolution in Brussels, which had the effect of severing the Belgian provinces from the rule of Holland, took place

---

[1] See page 65.

early in the year, and though it did not secure that result till September, it led to negotiations which in 1831 ended in the establishment of Belgian independence, with Leopold as an elected constitutional sovereign, in whom the people and indeed other European states were already displaying the confidence which comes of genuine esteem. It may easily be believed that the prospect of parting with her beloved uncle was a great grief to the princess, to whom he had been father, friend, and counsellor; but, as we shall see, he maintained these relations with unabated regard, and amidst the arduous duties of government paid frequent visits to this country, and maintained the same loving care which he had always manifested.

Events in England during the years just preceding 1830 had also shown that vast changes were imminent, that a new era was soon to open. In Parliament the questions of Roman Catholic emancipation and parliamentary reform had loomed large, illuminated by the eloquence of Canning and of Brougham. O'Connell in 1824 had organized a Catholic Association, and in 1825 a Roman Catholic Relief Bill, brought in by Sir Francis Burdett, had passed the House of Commons, to be thrown out in the Lords, where the Duke of York had solemnly sworn that if he came to the throne he would never consent to the repeal of the Catholic disabilities, but it was felt that the rigorous exclusion of Catholics from office and from Parliament could not be long maintained.

The death of the Duke of York in 1827 was followed by the paralysis which ended the official life and the administration of Lord Liverpool; and little as George the Fourth liked Canning, because he had refused to countenance the persecution of Queen Caroline, and had supported the Catholic claims, Canning was made premier. But he was in ill-health, and his attendance at the funeral of the Duke of York hastened his death, which took place in a few months, and shortly afterwards the Duke of Wellington formed an administration, of which Mr. Peel was home secretary. The friends of Canning, Mr. Huskisson, Mr. Grey, Lord Palmerston, and Mr. Lamb (who almost immediately afterwards, by the death of his father, became Viscount Melbourne) abandoned the ministry. Lord John Russell moved for the repeal of the Test and Corporation Acts, and Mr. Peel, left in a minority, withdrew his opposition. In the Lords the motion was supported by Lord Holland (the nephew of Charles James Fox), and the Duke of Sussex, whose ardent support of civil and religious liberty had not diminished, and had been resented by the King. The measure passed, and this, with the election of Daniel O'Connell to represent the county of Clare in Parliament, gave new and irresistible stimulus to the demand for the relief of the Catholics, who could not consistently be longer excluded. Both the Duke of Wellington and Peel saw that the claims of a large body of their fellow-countrymen must be acknowledged; and neither Wellington nor Peel was such a bigot as to refuse concession to demands which were obviously supported by the nation. The duke declared with deep emotion that there must either be concession or civil war, and Peel brought in the bill which, after strong opposition in the Lords, and warning tears from Lord Eldon (who had a weakness for crying on special occasions), opened Parliament and offices of state to the Catholics, for whom a new form of oath was prepared in place of the oath of supremacy. They were still excluded from the offices of Regent, of Viceroy of Ireland, and of Lord Chancellor. It is to be noted, however, that the words in the new oath, "on the true faith of a Christian," had the effect of excluding Jews from Parliament till 1858, when they also had a special oath. Eight years afterwards (in 1866) the separate form of oath for Catholics was abolished.

The King gave his royal assent to the bill with an ill grace, and showed no little resentment; but the ball of reform and improvement was set rolling. Many mitigatory changes in the criminal law, and a commission on the state of the law proposed by Brougham, which led to great improvements, were followed (in 1830) by the measure establishing the new police force. There was everywhere apparent an accession of earnest political activity, which, to experienced eyes, showed that a great measure of reform could not be far distant.

Before the end of the year (1830) another revolution had changed the aspect of affairs in France. Charles X. and his minister Polignac, reverting to the high-handed Bourbon policy, attempted to stifle political discussion in the press by prosecuting editors, and issuing "ordinances" forbidding publication of pamphlets or newspapers without official permission. There had been a bad harvest and a severe winter in the previous year, and there were not wanting signs of discontent ready to break out into open disaffection on any adequate provocation. The provocation soon came. When the elections came on in May a royal proclamation was issued attempting to influence the popular votes, and when this failed, the elections were declared to be annulled on the ground that the people had been misled, and directions were given altering the number and qualifications of the deputies and the manner of electing them. These "ordinances" were issued at midnight on the 26th of July. The next day there was a panic on the Bourse, and ominous gatherings of groups of citizens were to be observed in various parts of Paris. The editors, acting on counsel's opinion, declared that the ordinances were illegal. Polignac sent out police to stop the publication of the newspapers, but the offices were closed against them, while the journals were being thrown out of the windows to the crowds of people who assembled in the streets. The Tribunal of Commerce and the legal authorities were opposed to the demands of the king, but the police broke open the doors of the printing-offices and destroyed the types and presses. About thirty of the elected deputies met and were waited on by a party of citizens, who told them that Marshal Marmont, who only had in Paris about 4000 troops whom he could trust, was posting soldiers all round the city. Next day the streets were blocked with barricades; the Hôtel de Ville was seized by the insurgents, who rang the alarm-bells and sent the tricolor flying from the steeples. The marshal sent to assure the king that he must make concessions or there would be an insurrection; but history was to repeat itself. The king was at cards; the court was amused; and the marshal was told to put down the insurrection. He withdrew to the Tuileries with as many of the soldiers as had not gone over to the insurgents. Two of the peers waited on Polignac and urged the immediate withdrawal of the ordinances; and as he refused, they ordered Marmont to arrest him. He escaped to St. Cloud, and the king, now really alarmed, agreed after some parleying to revoke the ordinances and appoint a new ministry. But it was then too late, for the revolution had become an accomplished fact. Charles was left with only a few soldiers. Marmont could do nothing with his doubtful troops, for whom he could not provide rations. Late on the 1st of August the king and his companions were informed that a strong provisional government had nominated Louis Philippe, the Duke of Orleans, Lieutenant-general of France. Charles then offered to abdicate in favour of the Grand Duc de Berri, but his proposals were received with indifference.

He was strongly advised to hand over the regalia without further parley, and to depart from France by way of Cherbourg. He may be said to have left the kingdom without a hand being raised in his favour. He and his escort could not arouse the least demonstration of loyalty. It was like the departure of James the Second from England, and though nobody offered him violence, he did not feel safe until he embarked in an English vessel for Spithead.

It was not a "bloodless revolution," for there had been a good deal of fighting in the streets, and 800 citizens of Paris had been killed and 4500 wounded, while a large number of the opposing soldiers had been slain. Decorations and pensions were given to the wounded citizens, the dead received honourable burial; the ministers were tried and sentenced to imprisonment and forfeiture of property. Lafayette, who was ready to take advantage of any turn of the tide, espoused the new cause by proposing Louis Philippe as "the best of republics" for France, and the result was that under the title of King of the French, that astute and experienced personage swore fidelity to the charter, and France had an elected instead of an hereditary sovereign.

This reference is not out of place here, for we shall soon have to meet Louis Philippe again in these pages, and moreover, the excitement in favour of parliamentary reform in this country at the time of the accession of William the Fourth in 1830 was raised to extreme activity by events in France.

One cannot now read the current political comments of that time without a smile when we come to William being called the "reforming king" and the "patriot king," in the sense that he initiated or even effectually promoted the "Reform Bill." That he yielded to political necessity or expediency goes without saying, but he scarcely did so with a good grace, and not until he perceived that the country and the Whig ministry of Earl Grey would take no denial.

Not to speak of less respectful appellations, he was more truly and popularly called "the Sailor King," for he had been a sailor, and had much of the bluff hearty kind of bonhomie and good-nature which was usually associated with sailors. There can be little doubt that he had much of the bluntness and some of the coarseness that were also attributed to manners on board ship; and it is said on the authority of Greville that though at the meeting of ministers on the death of George IV. he behaved very well, he forgot himself when he was about to sign the constitutional declaration,—and blurted out, "This is a d—— bad pen you have given me." The Archbishop of Canterbury was present, and this was supposed conventionally to have made the expression less excusable.

One of the first provisions which Parliament thought it necessary to make on the accession of William was that of the appointment of a regency in case of his death, for the King was sixty-six years old, and there were no children of his marriage. His relations with the famous Mrs. Jordan (Dorothy Bland) the actress, long previous to his marriage, had been known and recognized; and it has been recorded that his amiable consort, finding that he had given orders for the removal of certain portraits of Mrs. Jordan and her children (who had been named Fitz-clarence), ordered them to be restored to their former position in the King's apartments.

It is to be regretted that this and other more striking traits of her kindly nature—notably her unselfish affection for the Duchess of Kent and the Princess Victoria, who now stood next the throne—were not publicly known at that date, for such knowledge would have gone far to mitigate the unfounded dislike which was manifested to her by those who regarded her as an enemy to popular freedom, and resented her quiet ways her German nationality her want of popular accomplishments. Brougham was partly responsible for the political animosity, and much mischief was done by coarse caricatures, which were designed to bring this gentle lady into contempt, but she survived both.

There is not the least probability that Queen Adelaide desired to be appointed Regent, or that she tried to prevent the provisional appointment of the Duchess of Kent to that position, but the King seems to have regarded the possible regency of the duchess with no little antipathy. Under the circumstances it was inevitable that she should be appointed, or that the office should be conferred on the Duke of Cumberland, and such a proposal would have raised a popular tumult, which would have been very serious indeed. In his first message to Parliament, however, the King said nothing about the appointment of a regency in case of his death, and though the Houses of Lords and Commons both made reticent allusions to the matter, they were assured that the King was very well, and that they need not trouble themselves. The Tory ministry of the Duke of Wellington, Peel, Goulbourn, and Aberdeen, remained in office, though Parliament was dissolved as usual on the accession; but the government of Earl Grey succeeded it, and the consideration of the appointment of a provisional regency had to be resumed. Towards the end of the year a bill was introduced into Parliament providing that Queen Adelaide, in the event of her giving birth to a child after the death of the King, should be guardian of such child and regent of the kingdom. If that event should not occur, the Duchess of Kent was to be regent during the minority of her daughter the Princess

Victoria, who was not to marry while a minor without the consent of the King, or, if he died, without the consent of both Houses of Parliament. The duchess was to be assisted by a Council of Regency, consisting of members of the royal family and ministers of state; and she was to forfeit the regency should she marry a foreigner during the lifetime of the King, and without his consent.

The Princess Victoria herself was unacquainted with the fact that she was next in succession to the throne. The utmost care had been taken to keep her from the knowledge of her position while there was any considerable doubt of her being the next heir, or until she was of an age to understand what were her expectations without being injured by the knowledge.

Her own shrewd observation had led her to note some difference between the salutations offered to her and to her elder sister, and it is said that at a very early date she inquired why all the gentlemen took off their hats to her instead of to the Princess Feodora. This, of course, could be explained by the reminder that she was a princess of the English royal family while her sister belonged to a foreign house; but it was difficult sometimes to avoid her questioning glances and quick observation. The elder sister had now (in 1830) been two years married to Prince Ernest Hohenlohe, one of the most upright and blameless of men. The wedding had taken place at Kensington Palace in February, 1828, according to the simple rites of the Lutheran Church, the ceremony being performed by Pastor Dr. Kuper, the chaplain of the Royal Lutheran Chapel. The King (George IV.) was too ill to be present, but the Duke and Duchess of Clarence, the Duke of Sussex, the Duke and Duchess of Gloucester, the Princess Sophia, the Princess Sophia of Gloucester, and Prince Leopold had been present, and the Duke of

Clarence gave away the bride, who almost immediately afterwards accompanied her husband to Germany. It was probably in view of the increased dulness of the household to the princess, then not quite ten years old, that the Duchess of Kent afterwards spent a considerable part of the year either at the seaside or at some other agreeable resort.

At Broadstairs or at Ramsgate—where they occupied Towneley House, overlooking the harbour,—at the Marina of St. Leonard's, and at Tunbridge Wells, the Duchess of Kent and the Princess Victoria were already well known and loyally welcomed; but they visited these places in simple and unpretentious fashion. The princess—plainly, but always becomingly attired—rode, or walked, or ran, without much regard to the weather, for she had been trained to healthy exercise; and her own ingenuous manner and ready appreciation of the courtesy of everybody around her, enabled her to appear without restraint in places where visitors congregated, or to visit shops and bazaars and spend her pocket-money as other children did.

The mention of pocket-money may remind us that it was very well understood by everybody concerned that habits of economy were observed and inculcated. The Duchess of Kent had reason to know that extravagance has to be paid for by somebody, probably at the cost of much inconvenience if not of suffering; and she also recognized that the duty had fallen to her to pay debts which had not been incurred by herself, and carefully to avoid giving occasion for reproach by increasing her liabilities.

There can be no doubt that the little princess was taught quite early that pocket-money was not illimitable, and that she learned to be contented with a very moderate allowance, and to be satisfied with such recreations as were inexpensive, that is to say, visits to some of the galleries and show places in London, and the "parade," the morning assembly, or the esplanade and the band at the summer resorts. An incident said to have occurred at Tunbridge Wells has often been repeated. The princess was buying a few presents to give to her friends, and had spent all her money, when she remembered that there was another person to whom she would like to give a little souvenir, and at the same time her attention was attracted by a very pretty box, the price of which was half-a-crown. The woman who kept the shop would have sent the box with the rest of the purchases, though it had not been paid for, but the princess's governess could not permit it. "As the princess has not got the money she cannot buy the box," she remonstrated. "But I will put it aside then, and keep it for her royal highness," said the shop-keeper. "Oh, if you will be good enough to do that, the princess can come for it when she has the money." This was done, for punctually on pocket-money morning the princess appeared at the shop on her donkey and completed her purchase. There is not much in the story; but it was told on the authority of Harriet Martineau, and it was one of many which were current at the time, and then and afterwards people in London, as well as at Ramsgate, Brighton, St. Leonard's, Tunbridge Wells, and elsewhere showed unmistakable pleasure in hearing and repeating such anecdotes.

When George the Fourth died the Duchess of Kent and her little daughter were at Malvern, where the same good-will and admiration for the princess attended them. The simple life of the princess, who appeared almost daily on her donkey as any other young lady of her age might do, the kindly manners of the duchess, the unostentatious gifts to the poor and the distressed in the neighbourhood, were spoken of here as they had been elsewhere, and doubtless a pleasant holiday was passed amidst the beautiful scenery of Herefordshire and Worcestershire; but it was necessary to return to London, and the time soon arrived when it was thought desirable that the princess should learn in what relation she now stood to the throne, for, as we have seen, the Regency Bill was already before Parliament.

It was not easy to suppose that the knowledge had really been concealed from her; but assiduous care had been exercised to direct the bright intelligence and the young ambition to a disinterested attainment of those qualities and distinctions that fit their possessor for exercising eminent personal influence in any station. Sir Walter Scott, who was one of the honoured visitors at Kensington Palace, had written in his diary on May 19th, 1828: "Dined with the Duchess of Kent. I was very kindly received by Prince Leopold, and presented to the little Princess Victoria, the heir-apparent to the crown, as things now stand. . . This little lady is educating with much care, and watched so closely that no busy maid has a moment to whisper, 'You are heir of England.' I suspect if we could dissect the little heart, we should find some pigeon or other bird of the air had carried the matter."

This was a reasonable conclusion, but Sir Walter was mistaken. It was not till after the accession of William the Fourth that the secret was told, and for a good many years the manner of its being imparted was the subject of stories more or less conjectural, and mostly representing the Duchess of Kent delivering a stilted didactic discourse to her daughter, somewhat after the manner of examples in *Enfield's Speaker*.

What really took place was made known by the Baroness Lehzen, the old governess, in a letter to the Queen in December, 1867, in which she said: "I ask your Majesty's leave to cite some remarkable words of your Majesty's when only twelve years old, while the Regency Bill was in progress. I then said to the Duchess of Kent that now, for the first time, your Majesty ought to know your place in the succession. Her royal highness agreed with me, and I put the genealogical table into the historical book. When Mr. Davys [the Queen's instructor, afterwards Bishop of Peterborough] was gone, the Princess Victoria opened as usual the book again, and seeing the additional paper, said, 'I never saw that before.' 'It was not thought necessary you should, princess,' I answered. 'I see I am nearer the throne than I thought.' 'So it is, madam,' I said. After some moments the princess resumed, 'Now, many a child would boast, but they don't know the difficulty. There is much splendour, but there is more responsibility.' The princess having lifted up the forefinger of her right hand while she spoke, gave me that little hand, saying, 'I will be good. I understand now why you urged me so much to learn, even Latin. My aunts Augusta and Mary never did; but you told me Latin is the foundation of English grammar, and of all the elegant expressions, and I learned it as you wished it; but I understand all better now,' and the princess gave me her hand, repeating, 'I will be good!' I then said, 'But your aunt Adelaide is still young and may have children, and of course they would ascend the throne after their father William IV., and not you, princess.' The princess answered, 'And if it was so, I should never feel disappointed, for I know by the love aunt Adelaide bears me, how fond she is of children.'"

This frank and tender reply of the princess is to be associated with her knowledge that her aunt had lost her children, and had written to the Duchess of Kent the few affecting words already noticed in a previous page. In reference to this, the Queen makes a note upon the letter of the Baroness Lehzen—"I cried much on learning it, and ever deplored this contingency."

With the recognition of the position occupied by the princess came a grant from Parliament of £10,000 a year for her maintenance and education, and the Duchess of Northumberland was appointed governess, which, of course, meant general directress of the princess's studies, and not that the invaluable Baroness Lehzen should be superseded. Her other teachers were mostly English. Mr. Amos instructed her in the elements of constitutional government, Dr. Davys continued his tuition, and music lessons were still given by Mr. Sale, singing was taught by the famous Signor Lablache, dancing by Madame Bourdin, and writing and arithmetic by Mr. Steward, writing-master of Westminster School. In music the princess excelled, as she was not only an excellent singer, but an admirable pianist, and the lessons in drawing which she received from Mr. Westall, R.A., the well-known painter, developed a talent which she has ever since exercised, much to her own pleasure and occasionally to the gratification of those of her subjects who have seen some of the Queen's sketches. In languages the princess had already been well instructed, and those who know what an excellent horsewoman the Queen has always been will not be surprised that she received riding lessons from Mr. Fozard, the most famous teacher of his day.

These studies demanded much time and attention, and the old quiet life was not very materially changed. Though we have referred to a certain loneliness, or a need for youthful companionship in these early days of the young princess, there were, of course, uncles, aunts, and cousins enough to claim recognition, and to increase the number of visitors who were occasionally received at Kensington; and it need scarcely be

said that now there was no longer as much occasion for reticence and seclusion. The princess was already in correspondence with some of her relatives at Coburg, but neither of the cousins there had yet visited London, and the dear old grandmother, the Dowager-duchess of Coburg, was no more to look upon the face of the little May-flower whom she loved so well.

She had written to the Duchess of Kent on the princess's eleventh birthday: "My blessings and good wishes for the day which gave you the sweet blossom of May! May God preserve and protect the valuable life of that lovely flower from all danger that will beset her mind and heart! The rays of the sun are scorching at the height to which she may one day attain. It is only by the blessing of God that all the fine qualities He has put into that young soul can be kept pure and untarnished. How well I can sympathize with the feelings of anxiety that must possess you when that time comes. God, who has helped you through so many bitter hours of grief, will be your help still. Put your trust in Him."

She wrote again in the following June, after the death of George the Fourth: "God bless old England, where my beloved children live, and where the sweet blossom of May may one day reign! May God yet for many years keep the weight of a crown from her young head! and let the intelligent, clever child grow up to girlhood before the dangerous grandeur devolves upon her."

Again, after the provision of the Regency Bill on the 30th of December, 1830: "I should have been very sorry if the regency had been given into other hands than yours. It would not have been a just return for your constant devotion and care to your child if this had not been done. May God give you wisdom and strength to do your duty if called upon to undertake it! May

God bless and protect our little darling! If I could but see her once again! The print you sent me of her is not like the dear picture I have. The quantity of curls hide the well-shaped head, and make it look too large for the lovely little figure."

In the following November (1831) the family at Coburg, the daughter and grand-daughter at South Kensington, and the son at Brussels, had to mourn the loss of this steadfast friend—this loving heart. There were two boy princes at Coburg, Ernest and Albert,—the latter of whom was, as we have seen, born in the same year as the Princess Victoria,—who felt that loss bitterly. Their father, Duke Ernest, was near his mother when she died. Her next son Ferdinand was present also,— but Leopold, the younger and favourite son, last saw her when she visited him at Brussels in the summer, on his election as King of the Belgians. He could not leave the affairs of his new kingdom to attend her in her last hours, nor would his new responsibilities permit him to be so constantly near his little niece in England, to direct and regulate her studies, of which he used previously to receive a weekly report.

CHAPTER II.

The princess had now to appear at court and at the various places to which she paid holiday visits, in a new capacity. Little change was made in the simplicity of the domestic life at Kensington, and studies and recreations went on much as usual: nor had the frank, winning manners of the child been lost in the more sedate girlhood: but when she was present on public occasions, or even when she appeared walking or driving, there was just the difference that she was now the acknowledged heir to the throne, and that people regarded her more directly as the future Queen. As we have noted, there was also more "company" at Kensington Palace. Sir John Hobhouse, after dining at the Palace, where the princess was seated at her mother's right hand as in the old days, says, "The young princess was treated in every respect like a grown-up woman, although apparently quite a child. Her manners were very pleasing and natural, and she seemed much amused by some conversation with Lord Durham, a manifest favourite at Kensington. When she left the room, she curtsied round very prettily to all the guests who were present, and then ran out of the room." This would seem to point to the early hours which the princess observed, and there are other references of the same kind at a still later date—one by the poet Moore, who was present at a party when the princess delighted the company by her singing, and would have continued for some time longer but for premature intimation of bed-time. There is also a record of a ball at which the princess was permitted to be present while on one of the visits to the provinces, but she only graced the occasion for a short time, and after one dance retired at quite an early hour.

The first appearance of the princess at court "in state," was at the "drawing-room" held by Queen Adelaide in February, 1831. It was the Queen's birthday, and therefore there was an additional reason for the presence of the youthful princess, who was already sufficiently self-possessed to stand on the throne on the left of her Majesty, and to note all that took place with evident interest. She was herself probably the chief object of attraction to that brilliant assembly, amidst which her bright, ingenuous face, her beaming blue eyes, and the modest dignity of her bearing consorted well with the simple frock of English blonde over white satin of Spitalfields manufacture, the pearl necklace, and the diamond ornament which fastened the braids of fair hair.

It was the most magnificent drawing-room that had been seen since that which had taken place on the presentation of Princess Charlotte of Wales upon the occasion of her marriage, for it was intended to do honour to the new Queen, and to introduce to her proper place in the royal circle the young maiden who, in simple becoming guise, attended with her mother the Duchess of Kent, her suite consisting of the Duchess of Northumberland, Lady Charlotte St. Maur, Lady Catherine Parkinson, the Hon. Mrs. Cust, the Baroness Lehzen, General Wetherall, and Captain (then Sir John) Conroy, with Lady Conroy.

Before this appearance at the drawing-room, the absence of the princess from the coronation of the King and Queen on the previous September had excited a good deal of remark, and was the cause of innumerable comments in the newspapers. Of course the world of politics no less than the world of fashion was interested in speculating on the cause of what was set down as the premeditated absence of the princess, and as usual, any interpretation but the simple and obvious one was likely to be adopted. When it was discovered that no place had been assigned to the princess in the ceremony at Westminster Abbey a hundred rumours found tongue. It was the fault of Earl Grey; it was the fault of the Duchess of Northumberland, who was seeking to assert political influence with her pupil; it was the fault of the Duchess of Kent, who refused to allow her daughter to be present because she had herself not been treated with proper respect by the King; it was the fault of Lord Adolphus Fitzclarence, who, in arranging the plan for the procession, had placed the princess last of the royal family, instead of giving her the proper place immediately after their Majesties.

These were the reports which were circulated, until a simple explanation was given by the announcement that the sanction of the King had been obtained for the absence of his niece from a ceremony, the fatigue and excitement of which it was believed would be injurious to her health. Here was another topic of discussion; all kinds of forebodings were indulged in, and a temporary indisposition or, at worst, a slight declension of strength, which made it necessary to avoid the excitement and exhaustion caused by repeated state ceremonials, was magnified into a report of symptoms betokening some inherent weakness or constitutional defect

The Duchess of Kent was, for more than one reason, reluctant to see her daughter drawn into the court atmosphere, and she had repeatedly to run the risk of offending the King, and perhaps even of seeming to slight the kindness always displayed by the Queen, because of her determination that the child, who had been reared with so much care, should not sacrifice domestic peace and order, and the education which was to raise her above the ordinary court measure, by being at her early age committed to the intrigues, the slanders, and, it may be added, the contaminations of those who would have endeavoured to secure an influence over her. Such a result neither the King nor the Queen might have perceived till it was too late to prevent it, though the King would certainly have resented it as he afterwards resented the infrequency of his niece's visits. At anyrate the Princess Victoria, instead of taking part in the coronation and the subsequent festivities, was quietly pursuing her studies. In the following autumn (1831) the Duchess of Kent went with her household to the Isle of Wight, where they occupied Norris Castle, near East Cowes, which was from that time retained as a marine residence, and where they were removed from the rioting and disturbances which shook not London only, but the great provincial towns, during the excitement caused by the opposition to the Reform Bill.

The coronation ceremony had not been of a very splendid character, as compared with that of George the Fourth, which had become historical not only for its extravagant cost (£268,000), but because of the attempts of the unhappy Queen Caroline to assert her rights by seeking to force her way into Westminster Abbey, from which she had been excluded. Yet the quiet celebration of investing William the Fourth and Queen Adelaide with the insignia of royalty involved an expense of over £43,000, of which £22,234 was for the several departments of the household, and £12,000 for the office of works for fitting up Westminster Abbey, &c., while £3034 was spent in fireworks and for opening the theatres to the public on the night of the coronation.

The King and Queen spent a good deal of their time at Windsor, and brilliant court festivities were not very numerous; but the King was remarkably fond of giving dinner parties, at which it is not surprising that the Duchess of Kent and her daughter were seldom to be seen. We hear, however, of some important state assemblies where the Princess Victoria was present, and, indeed, more than one was given in her honour by Queen Adelaide. The principal of these was a grand ball given on the 24th of May, 1832, to celebrate the thirteenth birthday of the princess, who was much impressed by the brilliant scene which she now witnessed for the first time, but amidst which she moved with the frank grace that was habitual to her, and with a modest self-possession which even in those early days seems to have enabled her to sustain her part in all such ceremonial assemblies, and preserved her from any appearance of disadvantage, notwithstanding her youth and inexperience. Doubtless her attractive appearance and behaviour caused the dissatisfaction expressed by the King at the comparative seclusion in which she was educated. He grumbled that she was not more at court, and every time he saw her the grievance was emphasized by his perceiving that, to use a common phrase, she "would be a credit to him," though he appeared to lose sight of the credit due to the Duchess of Kent. To her judicious care, and her reluctance to subject the "May-flower" to the blighting influences of a court circle, were largely due the natural ingenuous address which delighted the Sailor King, and was probably far more keenly appreciated by his gentle Queen. When the King went to prorogue his first Parliament the Queen had invited her niece to see the state procession, and, standing in the balcony, was perceived by the crowd below, who raised a hearty cheer. The kind lady took the little girl by the hand and led her to the front of the balcony to share in the homage of the people, and this may be said to have been the first official introduction of the princess as immediate heir to the crown. In January, 1831, too, the princess had appeared, for the first time, at the theatre—Covent Garden —where she witnessed the entertainment with evident pleasure.

Not only the manner of her education, but the disposition and appearance of the Princess Victoria were pretty well known to the public, and the just reasons for her comparative seclusion at that early age were also understood. A correspondent of the *Mirror*, in the later months of 1831, says: "The heiress presumptive to the British crown is gradually becoming an object of great interest to all classes of her future subjects . . . and it is well known that no mother has more anxiously studied to inculcate on her daughter's mind a due sense of moral and religious duties, and the practice of kindliness, gentleness, and forbearance to all those about her, than has the Duchess of Kent towards her precious charge. Her studies have been pursued with as unremitting attention as her health would bear: she is quick in acquiring languages, and speaks fluently English, French, and German, is well read in history, and has attained such perfection in music as to be able to take part in the private concerts frequently given by the Duchess of Kent, who is herself extremely fond of music. Many contradictory reports of the state of her health have been spread, arising, possibly, from the physician of the household paying her regular visits for form's sake, and to satisfy the duchess's natural anxiety. We know, however, from good authority, that the princess's health is satisfactory, and the exuberance of her spirits is a sufficient proof of there being no cause for alarm on this head. . . . Her disposition is spoken very favourably of, and her good humour never fails her, though she is not much in the habit of associating with young ladies of her own age, but leads, on the whole, a secluded life. From everything that is known, therefore, of this interesting young personage during her yet short career, there is every reason to induce us to look with confidence to the day when she will be called on to wield the sceptre of the most powerful empire in the known world."

With the personal appearance of the princess a few of those who had not seen her had gained some knowledge from pictures and engravings. Mr. Fowler, an artist at Ramsgate, had painted two portraits of her, one of which, completed in her ninth year, was sent for exhibition to the Royal Academy, but was rejected. There was some correspondence on the subject between the president, Sir Thomas Lawrence, and the Duchess of Kent, who considered that, with one exception, the portrait was the best likeness of her daughter which had then been accomplished, the exception being a very fine bust by Behnes, which is now to be seen at Windsor Castle. An oil-painting of the duchess seated on a sofa, on which her little daughter stood beside her, had been made for the King of the Belgians by Sir William Beechey; and there was a bust of the infant princess by Turnerelli, the sculptor, the father of a gentleman who more recently became conspicuous in relation to some rather remarkable endeavours to raise a popular testimonial to Lord Beaconsfield. The most satisfactory likeness of a later date, however, was the full-length portrait painted by Mr. Westall, R.A., her instructor in drawing, when the princess was in her twelfth year.

On the 28th of May, 1832, four days after the birthday

ball, we hear of the princess at her second "drawing-room," and then of her retirement till the summer, when she accompanied the duchess on a tour, which continued during the autumn, through some of the most attractive historical and picturesque portions of England and Wales, a journey designed to serve the higher purpose of education as well as to delight the imagination—to maintain the health of the princess, at the same time that it removed her and the household from the disquieting influences of that political crisis, of which it is necessary to note some of the circumstances, since they will have associations with subsequent pages of the present narrative.

After the coronation of William the Fourth there had been no immediate change in the government, but the administration presided over by the Duke of Wellington was detested by the people, and had to sustain not only the powerful opposition of both Radicals and Whigs, who were pledged to support the urgent demand for reform, but also the demands of extreme Tories, who seemed determined to oppose to the uttermost a government which had granted Catholic emancipation. All over the country ministerialists were defeated, and a number of the successful candidates were ardent representatives of popular rights. The scenes at the elections were more violent than anybody has seen on similar occasions during the past fifty years; for the riot and confusion at the hustings and at polling places before the passage of the Reform Bill could not be imagined by the present generation; and when the country was eager to assert its dissatisfaction with the government the tumult was so exaggerated that it became alarming evidence of the probability of further demonstrations of a very dangerous kind. The result of the general election, however, was that the ministry lost about fifty votes in the House of Commons, and that the reformers were victorious in many places where the power and influence of the government were set against them.

On the 2d of November, 1830, the King had opened Parliament in person, and the address in reply passed, but not without some allusions to the subject of reform; in the House of Commons by Brougham, and in the Lords by Earl Grey. The Duke of Wellington took up the matter without hesitation, and concluded his remarks by saying, " I am not only not prepared to bring forward any measure of this nature, but I will at once declare that, as far as I am concerned, as long as I hold any station in the government of this country, I shall always feel it my duty to resist such a measure when proposed by others."

This was quite characteristic of " the Iron Duke," for he was a man of " unbending" opinions, one of which was that in this country, where property of various descriptions required to be protected, and where, to sum up what he conceived to be his political duty in his own phrase, the matter of the first importance was " to carry on the King's government," no better form of legislation could possibly be devised than that which already existed. This was in effect what he actually said, and when he concluded by avowing his determination to resist any suggestion of reform in the parliamentary representation of the country, his declaration meant war, and was taken as such. The ministry of which he was the head was not likely to last long after that, but he was not a man to yield at once.

It will show how strongly the unsympathetic feeling between the duke in his ministerial capacity and the representatives of those who desired political progress and out-and-out reform was accentuated, if we recall the fact that when Wellington was appointed prime-minister Henry Brougham, in a remarkable speech, said, among other things, that the appointment was unconstitutional. This was, of course, an extreme statement, but was explained, after he had expressed the greatest respect for the duke's illustrious character and abilities, by his saying that he could not feel gratified to see the regular and confidential adviser of the crown at the head of the civil and military establishments, dispensing all the patronage of the crown, the army, and the church. It was in this speech that there occurred the remarkable passage which introduced the phrase of "the schoolmaster abroad." "Let it not be supposed," said Brougham, "that I am inclined to exaggerate. I have no fear of slavery being introduced into this country by the power of the sword. . . . The noble duke might take the army, he might take the navy, he might take the mitre, he might take the seal—I would make the noble duke a present of them all. Let him come with his whole force, sword in hand, against the constitution, and the energies of the people will not only beat him, but laugh at his efforts. There have been periods when this country has heard with dismay that the soldier was abroad. This is not the case now. Let the soldier be ever so much abroad in the present age, he can do nothing. There is another person abroad—a less imposing person, and in the eyes of some an insignificant person—whose labours have tended to produce this state of things. The *schoolmaster is abroad*, and I trust more to the schoolmaster, armed with his primer, for upholding the liberties of the country, than I fear the soldier with his bayonet."

There is something enormously significant in this—as an indication not only of the "situation" at that date, but of the signs of the times. But Wellington never pushed his convictions to such an extreme as to carry compulsion against the evident will of the nation. He has been debited with saying that the people would be quiet, and that if they did not keep quiet

there was a way to make them; but if he said so he never meant
by it a forcible opposition to the unmistakable demands of the
country. He and Peel were ready to accept accomplished facts,
after having these facts hammered into them so that they were
beyond dispute, and the grand old soldier grew simply eloquent
when, in spite of his previous honest convictions and prejudices,
he had to yield intellectual and even moral consent to a course
which he saw was inevitable, and not only to retreat himself
but to take others with him, including the King. Probably
Wellington never quite realized that he was not a highly
capable minister, well acquainted with the theory of government,
but he modified a good deal as he grew older, when his autocratic
notions had sobered down before the conviction that the forces
of public opinion could not be beaten—that the armies he had to
encounter were not those of the enemies of the country abroad,
and that, in fact, the government would have to be carried on
without him, or in spite of his former theories.

Peel, as most middle-aged people know, was the son of a
cotton manufacturer, or rather of a calico-printer, in a very large
way of business, as many as 15,000 hands having been employed
in his father's factories at one time. The elder Peel was exceedingly wealthy, and was made a baronet (so Cobbett declared),
because he contributed £10,000 to the "Loyalty Loan," which
was the Royal Patriotic Fund of his day. He was in Parliament, where he distinguished himself as a thorough-going Tory,
and his elder son Robert, who was a steady and studious lad at
Harrow, and afterwards took a "double-first" at Oxford, was also
returned to the House while still little more than a youth, and
almost immediately took office with the near prospect of a place
in the cabinet. In 1830 he had succeeded to the title and a
large fortune and estate on the death of his father. Sir Robert

Peel would never accept any honorary distinctions on his own behalf, putting all such offers aside with a manner which appeared to be an almost haughty intimation that he considered they would add nothing to his dignity or social position. He was a man of scrupulous honour and integrity, much sensitiveness and humanity, and with great tenacity of opinion, which did not, however, prevent him from holding broad and generous views, or from being open to conviction. It may easily be understood that such a man would be cherished by the Duke of Wellington, who was much inferior to him in high culture and true breadth of perception.

Everybody was ready to give homage to the duke as the great general who had broken the power of France, but popular demonstrations against him as head of the government became so violent that it would have been almost impossible for him to have continued to hold office. Brougham had announced an intention to introduce a measure dealing with parliamentary reform, and approved by a large number of members, but the day before he was to bring it forward Sir Henry Parnell moved for the appointment of a select committee to consider the estimates on the civil list, and as this was carried against the government by a majority of twenty the ministry took the opportunity of sending in their resignation.

The King at once sent for Earl Grey, whose high character and consistent advocacy of moderate reform, no less than his ability and experience, made him the head of the Whig party, and the new ministry was soon completed, on the clear understanding that a measure for an extensive reform in Parliament should be at once introduced, and that in the prosecution of his plan for effecting it the prime-minister should receive the King's countenance and support. The Whigs had not been in office for five-and-twenty years, and now was the opportunity for carrying a measure the demand for which was shown by political demonstrations in various parts of the country. Henry Brougham was made lord-chancellor with the title of Lord Brougham and Vaux, but he hesitated at first to accept it, for he preferred to be free as a leader of the party of independence, and he had such a splendid practice at the bar that the emoluments of the office of lord-chancellor were not much temptation. He had to be persuaded to accept it by Lord Althorp (son of Earl Spencer), one of the most disinterested men living, who became chancellor of the exchequer. The Hon. E. G. Stanley, afterwards to become famous as the Earl of Derby—"the Rupert of debate"—was appointed chief secretary for Ireland, but failed to be elected for Preston because he refused to pledge himself to support vote by ballot. Lord Melbourne, a rather neutral friend of reform and by no means anxious for the promotion of an extensive measure in that direction, was home secretary; Viscount Palmerston, foreign secretary; the Marquis of Lansdowne, president of the council; Sir James Graham, first lord of the admiralty; and Lord John Russell paymaster of the forces, without a seat in the cabinet.

The work of framing the government measure of reform was assigned to a committee composed of Lord Durham, Lord Duncannon, Sir J. Graham, and Lord John Russell; but it was the scheme of Lord John Russell which was the foundation of the bill. This was as it should have been for more reasons than one. Lord John was the representative of the great historical Whig family, and was a consistent upholder of principles that were at that time in advance of those of many of his own political associates. His speech and manner displayed the quality of caution more than of temerity; for he seldom rose to a display of eloquence; often hesitated for the right word, though he seldom used a wrong one; was never brilliant, but never either tried or pretended to be so, and mostly spoke sensibly and much to the purpose. When, in addition to his negative qualities, it is remembered that he was rather plain-looking, so short as to be almost dwarfish in person, with a large head, hidden mostly by a large hat slouched down over his forehead, so that when he sat in the House of Commons little could be seen of his face but his mouth, which bore an expression of dry humour; it may be wondered at that he was for the greater part of his long career a popular man, and at the time we are now considering, when he was still comparatively young, the best liked of the leaders of the cause of reform. He had always been a consistent Liberal; he had carried the repeal of the hated Test and Corporation Acts in the teeth of the Wellington government. He was a man of honesty and integrity and with strong religious principles, and an advocate for religious freedom, and the traditions of the noble family to which he belonged, joined with a kindly recognition of his earnest political convictions, caused the people to like and to trust him. "Little Johnny," as he was too often irreverently designated—or Lord John, as he was quite familiarly called—was always true to his colours, and mostly had a good following; though he was as little as possible like Brougham, who, at the time of the Reform Bill of 1832, made speeches so vigorous, varied, and defiant of opposing powers, that they were read with boundless delight by "the masses."

On the 1st of March Lord John Russell was to bring forward the bill, and the House of Commons, its lobbies, passages, and approaches, were crowded to excess. As the clock struck six a little active figure—a calm, pale, determined face—appeared entering the house. There was a momentary hush, and then followed a tremendous cheer; then, amidst a profound silence, Lord John commenced an exposition of the bill, which he declared was founded on the ancient constitution of the country, which declared that no man should be taxed for the support of the state who had not consented, by himself or his representative, to the imposition of these taxes. That reform was a matter of right and of reason, as well as of policy and expediency, he unhesitatingly asserted. A stranger who was told that this country was unparalleled in wealth and industry, and more civilized and more enlightened than any country was before it,—that it was a country that prided itself on its freedom, and that once in every seven years it elected representatives from its population to act as the guardians and preservers of that freedom,—would be anxious and curious to see how that representation was formed, and how the people chose their representatives, to whose faith and guardianship they intrusted their free and liberal institutions. Such a person would be very astonished if he were taken to a ruined mound and told that that mound sent two representatives to Parliament; if he were taken to a stone wall, and told that three niches in it sent two representatives to Parliament; if he were taken to a park where no houses were to be seen, and told that that park sent two representatives to Parliament; but if he were told all this, and were astonished at hearing it, he would be still more astonished if he were to see large and opulent towns, full of enterprise, and industry, and intelligence, containing vast magazines of every species of manufacture, and were then told that these towns sent no representatives to Parliament. Such a person would be still more astonished if he were taken to Liverpool, where there was a large constituency, and told, "Here you will have a fine specimen of a popular election." He would see bribery employed to the greatest extent, and in the most unblushing manner; he would see every voter receiving a number of guineas in a box as the price of his corruption; and after such a spectacle he would, no doubt, be much astonished that a nation whose representatives were thus chosen could perform the functions of legislation at all, or enjoy respect in any degree.

This was the prefatory appeal, and it indicates tersely, but sufficiently, the conditions for which a reformation was being demanded. There is no need in these pages to give an exposition of the various parts of the measure which was then proposed. The number of persons who would be entitled to the suffrage under the bill not previously possessing that right was supposed to be, in the counties, 110,000; in the towns, 50,000; in London, 95,000; in Scotland, 50,000; in Ireland, about 40,000; and it was believed that the measure would add to the constituency of the Commons House of Parliament about half a million of persons, all connected with the property of the country, having a stake in it, and deeply interested in its institutions. The number of members of the house would be decreased by 62, the number of representative constituencies from 658 to 596, as 168 seats which were to be abolished by disfranchisement of boroughs would not be compensated by the additions effected by redistribution, or the accession of representation in other places.

The debate on the bill was long, and members of the opposition set themselves to impede the progress of the measure, which they succeeded in doing for fifteen months, during which not only the ministry but Parliament itself underwent repeated vicissitudes, while the country was kept continually disturbed by riots and deeds of violence. On the 14th of March the bill was read for the first time. The second reading was moved on the 21st of March, and was carried by one vote only. The excitement in and out of the House was tremendous; but no more could be done till after the Easter recess, when Parliament reassembled on the 12th of April. Then General Gascoyne moved an instruction that the number of members ought not to be diminished, which Lord Althorp said was the first of a series of obstructions, but after an acrimonious discussion it passed by a majority of eight.

The opposition thought that they had effectually "mated," if not checkmated, the ministry, for the countercheck was the dissolution of Parliament, and it was known that the King, who was by no means so "patriotic" as to desire as wide a measure of reform as that represented by the bill, had a great aversion to this alternative.

An address was being prepared in the House of Lords asking him not to dissolve Parliament. There was no time to lose, and Brougham was equal to the occasion. He went at once to his Majesty and urged him to go down to the House of Lords and exercise his royal authority by announcing a dissolution. The King was in a dilemma. He could not sacrifice the ministry after the promises that he had made to support them in the measure that they now sought to carry through Parliament by an appeal to the country, and yet he disliked the appearance of committing himself to the provisions of the bill. There was no compromise; and though he would have liked to "run with the hare and hunt with the hounds," it was in this instance impossible; or, as he afterwards said, incompatible with his character as a sovereign and a gentleman. He was next angry with the Lords, who were preparing to petition him against a dissolution; and hurrying on his robes he called out, "Bring me a hackney-coach," as though he had no time left even to wait for the royal carriage. But the royal carriage was soon ready, and off he went in semi-state, the Life Guards riding wide as an escort; the people in the streets huzzaing with a demonstrative energy that for the time reminded him he had done the right thing for maintaining his popularity.

The House of Lords was in a tumult when the King entered, and the disturbance was barely hushed to listen to his Majesty when he said that he had come to prorogue Parliament prior to a dissolution. Parliament was dissolved the next day, and the public rejoicings were sufficient to prove to the anti-reformers that there would be a fierce struggle at the elections. There were illuminations in the city and in many parts of the West End; which, however, was no decisive sign of political satisfaction, since it was pretty well known to householders that unless they exhibited lighted lamps or candles in their windows the mob outside would probably smash every pane of glass. This took place at the houses of known anti-reformers, who would not illuminate; and at Apsley House, the residence of the Duke of Wellington, not only was every pane of glass that looked upon the streets ruthlessly demolished by showers of stones, but a yelling mob remained for a long time uttering execrations, for which the duke probably cared little, though he afterwards had his mended windows provided with external shutters of iron.

When the elections came on there were truer and nobler signs that numbers of people were in earnest, though in the fourteen days during which the poll continued enormous sums of money were spent in bribing and treating, and the scenes of riot and disorder, in which crowds filled the streets and processions marched hither and thither with bands and banners, were made the more feverishly exciting by the unusual heat of the weather.

Parliament opened on the 14th of June, and on the 24th Lord John Russell again brought forward the bill, which, with some modifications of details, was read without opposition. The second reading was fixed for the 4th of July, and again a vast and expectant crowd filled the house and all its approaches. The debate lasted for three nights, and at five o'clock on the morning of the 7th the measure was carried by a majority of 136, and then went into committee. It was not till the morning of the 22d of September that the bill passed by 345 votes against 239, and then the question was, What will the Lords do? Solemnly Lord Althorp and Lord John Russell, followed by a hundred reformers, carried the bill to the bar of the Upper House. Solemnly it was received; but in spite of the serious and dignified appeals of Earl Grey and the impassioned eloquence of Lord Brougham, it was thrown out. Lord Eldon and Lord Lyndhurst and other anti-reforming peers had already made up their minds against " the revolutionary violence of the measure." Wellington was, of course, immovable; the bishops were against it, and by a considerable majority it was rejected.

The news went through the country like flame. In London and other large towns the shops were closed, the church bells were muffled, everywhere meetings were held, and violent speeches were made in all parts of the country. At one of these meetings 100,000 persons were present, and a resolution was passed to pay no more taxes till the bill became law, and this example was afterwards followed elsewhere. The common council of the city of London held a meeting at Guildhall in favour of the measure, and there was another assembly of leading merchants and bankers at the Mansion House. The corporation voted an address to the King, and it was carried up attended by 50,000 people, the lower sort among whom again vented their fury by attacking Apsley House, and committing other acts of violence.

On the 20th of October the King again went down and prorogued Parliament, delivering a conciliatory speech, which referred to the general manifestation of a desire for constitutional reform in the Commons' House of Parliament, to the certain direction of the attention of the next Parliament to the question, and to his unaltered desire to promote its settlement. The violence of public meetings somewhat abated, but the political organizations became more formidable, and their proceedings were declared to be illegal. There was indeed reason for alarm, for in various parts of the country the riots had approached to attempted revolution. At Nottingham the castle, which was the property of the Duke of Newcastle an extreme Tory was fired and destroyed.

The Bristol riots were still more serious in their results, for the whole town was terrorized by a furious and madly drunken mob, who sacked and burned numbers of houses, destroyed furniture and valuables which were thrown from the windows, and ruined a great many respectable people by the wanton destruction or seizure of their property, and the casual sale of their valuable effects in the public streets. A mob of the vilest miscreants, under the pretence of a political demonstration, set up an insurrection of brigandage, and would have destroyed the whole city, while the military officer in command of the troops sent to quell the riot would do nothing effectually to prevent these atrocities. The arrival of an officer of a different stamp put an end to the riot after a great slaughter, in which five hundred wretched creatures were killed, and hundreds wounded: nor could any other remedy have been applied, for the mob had by that time taken possession of a quarter of the town where they prepared a desperate resistance to the troops and the thousands of sturdy constables enrolled from the crews of merchant ships and the respectable inhabitants of the city

But there were meetings which, by their orderly organization and peaceable but intense earnestness, were immeasurably more effectual as demonstrations than any display of unreasoning violence. Such was the great Midland meeting at Birmingham, at which there were present 150,000 men, with 200 bands of music and 700 flags. Assembled at the foot or on the lower slope of Newhall Hill, this vast multitude was hushed to silence as they heard a trumpet blown— a signal that they were to unite in singing:

> Lo! we answer! see we come,
> Quick at freedom's holy call,
> We come! we come! we come! we come!
> To do the glorious work of all:
> And hark! we raise from sea to sea
> The sacred watchword. Liberty!
>
> God is our guide! from field, from wave,
> From plough, from anvil, and from loom.
> We come our country's rights to save,
> And speak a tyrant faction's doom.
> And hark! we raise from sea to sea
> The sacred watchword, Liberty!
>
> God is our guide! no swords we draw.
> We kindle not war's battle-fires;
> But union, justice, reason, law
> We claim, the birthright of our sires;
> We raise the watchword, Liberty!
> We will, we will, we will be free!

We have scarcely improved upon this kind of national song

or hymn in later times. Without committing ourselves to political opinions, we may acknowledge that it is more real, more earnest and impressive than most of the "patriotic" productions of the present day, whether they invoke Juggernaut or Jingo. But these men were seriously and reasonably in earnest; they knew what they wanted; they wanted nothing that was subversive of law and order.

That they thought the aspect of affairs was serious—serious for political and civil liberty—may be gathered from the fact that after singing the "national hymn" the multitude, with uncovered heads, followed a fugleman in reciting a vow or declaration:—"With unbroken faith, through every peril and privation, we here devote ourselves and our children to our country's cause." There could, perhaps, be no better proof of the sober reasonableness of their intentions than the fact that a fortnight afterwards, when there was a promise of the crisis being over and a belief that the ministry would carry the bill, these 150,000 men again met on Newhall Hill and united in solemn thanksgiving.

A very great deal had happened in that fortnight. The ministry saw that there was but one course for them beside resignation, and they were pledged to the country not to resign while there was any other course open. It was evident either that the King must create as many new peers as would suffice to make a majority for the bill, or the Lords must give way. During nine days when there was no ministry there was little business done. Crowds and knots of persons were everywhere discussing the situation; the King's head, wherever it appeared on a signboard, was covered with crape, and that of the poor Queen, who was suspected of high Tory principles, was smeared with lampblack. The National Union petitioned the

House of Commons to refuse supplies and to put the exchequer in commission. O'Connell, who was an ardent reformer, and went for manhood suffrage and vote by ballot as well as for the repeal of the Union, was addressing vast assemblies in London; so also were Sir De Lacy Evans and Mr. Hume. There was a general cry to "stop the duke," and to run on the bank for gold. Members taking up petitions for stopping supplies were charged to say that no more taxes would be paid until the bill had passed. It was reported that the Unionists were preparing to march on London. The country was turning against the King himself. He was hooted, and the newspapers contained insulting references to him; dirt was flung at his carriage, and the guards had to ride close for his protection. There was nothing for it but to recall the ministry.

The result of their return was the abandonment of the King's objections to increase the peerage, but there was no need to put the prerogative in force. The peers gave way, many of the opponents of the bill remaining absent from the house, and after some amendments, which were agreed to by the Commons, the great measure was adopted. The King would not give his assent to the bill in person, but on the 7th of June (1832) it received the royal assent by commission, and a new political era had begun.

Events moved apace, and in 1834, after a period of enthusiastic public meetings and great debating in Parliament, slavery was abolished in all the British dominions, and the enormous sum of £20,000,000 was paid to the West India planters as compensation. Great advances had already been made in other directions, and the years 1830-1834 were a period of great ecclesiastical and religious as well as philanthropic activity. In 1831 the "Congregational Union of

England and Wales" was founded, Dissenters were actively and vigorously forming various societies for missionary and educational effort, and "Exeter Hall" became a power. In 1834 the Wesleyan Methodist association was founded, and in 1833, while the Whigs had abolished ten bishoprics of the Established Church, what was known as the Tractarian movement began to show signs of organization at Oxford. The repeal of the Test and Corporation Acts had not removed all disabilities from Nonconformists, and the grotesque but not absurd declarations of Sydney Smith, the witty canon, in his *Plymley Letters*, were even yet not out of date. "When a country squire hears of an ape his first feeling is to give it nuts and apples; when he hears of a dissenter his immediate impulse is to commit it to the county jail, to shave its head, to alter its customary food, and to have it privately whipped." The country was getting beyond this, and civil and religious freedom went hand in hand with political and social reform, while earnest endeavours were also made to establish schools and advance education, though no truly national system was yet within measurable distance.

The clouds that had obscured the horizon were breaking—were, in fact, opening wide and disappearing before a light that was increasing in brilliancy and benign power, and the whole national atmosphere was stirring with a freer and purer air. This may be said of the physical atmosphere also. In the autumn of 1831, the storm and tumult of political strife was followed by the threatened subversion of law and order by those who incited to riot and rapine, and "the arrow that flieth by day" took greater terrors because the "pestilence that walketh in darkness," the cholera, was here.

At the time that the infuriated mob was assailing Apsley

House, and all London was in a ferment of heat, strife, and anger, the disease, against which the doctors seemed to strive in vain, was causing a terrible rise in the death-rate. There was scarcely a neighbourhood in which some of the poorer inhabitants were not stricken, and patients were borne along the streets to the hospitals in covered stretchers, on the approach of which the knots of people, gathered to discuss the news or to declaim about the Reform Bill and the duke, would hurry out of the way, many of them sniffing at camphor or holding handkerchiefs to their faces.

But even the cholera brought its lessons. Not only was there a decidedly perceptible increase in the attendance at churches and chapels, and a greater seriousness in relation to religious observances, but investigations and some practical improvements were made for the purpose of promoting better sanitary measures in streets and houses. Parts of London and other large towns continued to be undrained or badly drained, and the cesspool was not abolished for many years afterwards, but the subject of public health was receiving more attention.

These more prominent events of the time at which the Princess Victoria became the recognized heir to the throne demand to be briefly noted, that we may intelligently follow the course of the narrative of a life that had then become dearer to and more closely identified with the national interests and the national progress. Though, of course, neither the Duchess of Kent nor her young daughter could take any conspicuous part in public events, and there were obvious reasons for preserving that unostentatious manner of living which guarded them from an appearance of challenging public attention, the princess was, as we have seen, sufficiently "in evidence" to mark her new relationship to the court, though by no means sufficiently to satisfy the King.

We may note also that the birthday ball and the drawing-room were held at the time when a tremendous political conflict was going on in London, and the whole country was stirred with the question of the action of the Lords in relation to the Reform Bill. The princess must surely have witnessed symptoms of the general excitement; and, without doubt, the surging of the wave of popular commotion was heard at Kensington Palace, even if a dash of the spray was not felt in a place where a good deal of company was now occasionally seen, and which the Duke of Sussex had in some sense identified with "advanced" liberal opinions.

But when the Reform Bill had passed, and the King and Queen had retired to Windsor, the young princess with her mother went on that pleasant tour through some of the most attractive districts of England and Wales which has been already mentioned, an excursion which included visits to the mansions of many English noblemen, to those stately houses where the youthful princess was a welcome and a most distinguished guest.

It would be easy to fill the page with suggestions of the vivid sentiments and pleasant imaginings which were probably awakened by historical scenes and buildings, by ancient mansion and cathedral, by quaint and picturesque towns, by mouldering ruins, by busy scenes of industry, and sequestered woods and vales, where the very stones and trees had long been themes of song and story, or landmarks of the by-ways of historic lore. It would be easier still to follow the journey of the princess, and repeat the legend or the chronicle with which each place is associated; but it was neither a guide-book excursion nor a royal progress. The effect of such a tour on the quick and inquiring intelligence of the princess was doubtless emphasized by the reception that she met with, by some public signs of welcome, by ceremonies such as the opening of a bridge or a building, and by addresses presented to the Duchess of Kent; but it will be sufficient to indicate these without giving them a prominent place in the narrative.

The journey was first to North Wales, and there the princess enjoyed her first experience of mountain scenery, remaining for some time amidst the most charming localities of the country before proceeding through Coventry and Shrewsbury, and visiting Powis Castle, Wynnstay, and Beaumaris, where her royal highness was present at the national musical and bardic contest —the Eisteddfod—and presented the prizes to the successful competitors. At Anglesey the royal visitor and her mother were the guests of General the Marquis of Anglesey (Henry William Paget), who had led the final charge against the French guards at Waterloo, and had received a wound in the knee which cost him his leg. From his mansion at Plas Newydd the distinguished party went to spend a day at Eaton Hall, the seat of the Marquis of Westminster, and thence to Oakley Park, near Ludlow, the home of the Clive family, near relatives of the Duchess of Northumberland, the governess of the princess. Returning by Chester they stayed for two or three days at the quaint, picturesque old city, a place full of interest, where they were received by the bishop on their visit to the cathedral. In her reply to an address presented by his grace, the Duchess of Kent said: "I cannot better allude to your good feelings towards the princess than by joining fervently in the wish that she may set an example in her conduct of that piety towards God, and charity towards men, which is the only sure foundation either of individual happiness or national prosperity." The princess named a new bridge which was opened at Chester during her stay, but it was called the "Grosvenor" bridge, the duchess cautiously refraining from giving permission for it to be named the "Victoria."

A short stay was made at Chatsworth, the superb residence of the Cavendishes, Alton Abbey, the seat of Lord Shrewsbury, Hardwick Hall, Shugborough, the seat of the Earl of Lichfield, and the old city of Lichfield, with its fine cathedral where "The Sleeping Children," Chantrey's beautiful sculpture, delighted the princess, to whom, even while she was herself an infant, babies and little children had always been so great an attraction.

From Chatsworth a visit had been paid to Belper in Derbyshire, to the famous cotton mills of the Messrs. Strutt, and there Mr. James Strutt had explained to the princess by means of a model the various processes of cotton spinning. In this the young visitor took most intelligent interest, and it is not too much to say that the opportunity afforded by the journey, and those provincial tours which succeeded it, to make acquaintance with great industrial enterprises, and the occupations of mechanics and operatives, was the beginning of a new bond of interest between the future sovereign and the people, which afterwards enabled her to mix with more complete freedom and mutual good understanding with her subjects, and to take keen personal concern in the progress of those inventions and manufactures upon which the vast commercial prosperity of the country so much depends. Her royal highness was greatly pleased with the enthusiastic reception given her by the workpeople at Belper, and they were equally delighted, for this was the first royal visit ever paid to a cotton mill. It may be mentioned here that in 1856 the son of Mr. James Strutt received the dignity of a peerage with the title of Baron Belper.

It is recorded that the nailers and iron-workers of Bromsgrove were also visited while the princess was in Worcestershire, and that she was specially delighted with a present made to her by the workmen of a thousand minute examples of nails of various patterns inclosed in a quill contained in a small gold box.

Of course there were addresses, receptions, and various ceremonial signs of welcome, to all of which the duchess replied on behalf of the princess. There was a rare round of visits: the Earl of Plymouth, and the Earl of Liverpool, a good friend of the Duchess of Kent, from whose abode at Pitchford Hall they went to quaint old historical Shrewsbury, both received the welcome guests, who reached Woodstock on the 7th of November, and stayed till next day at Wytham with the Earl of Abingdon. On the following day they went over to Oxford, their entrance to the great university city being attended by an escort of yeomanry. The celebrities of the university, the professors, dons, and doctors, assembled in the Sheldonian Theatre to receive the princess with hearty enthusiasm, and there the vice-chancellor presented an address, to which in her reply the Duchess of Kent said: "We close a most interesting journey by a visit to this university that the princess may see, as far as her years will allow, all that is interesting in it. The history of our country has taught her to know its importance by the many distinguished persons who, by their character and talents, have been raised to eminence by the education they have received in it. Your loyalty to the King, and recollection of the favour you have enjoyed under the paternal sway of his house, could not fail, I was sure, to lead you to receive his niece with all the disposition you evince to make this visit agreeable and instructive to her. It is my object to ensure by all means in my power her being so educated as to meet the just expectation of all classes in this great and free country."

The present of a magnificent Bible from the university press, and an account of her visit printed on white satin, added to the pleasure she had experienced in seeing the beautiful halls and colleges, the churches, and the treasures of the Bodleian and Radclyffe libraries. It was a fitting termination to a remarkable and instructive tour On the 9th of November the faces of the travellers were set homewards, and they once more reached Kensington—after a journey which, we should remember, was made by road, for there were yet no railways, no special trains and royal saloon carriages.

The excursions in the following autumn (1833) were confined to places on the south coast, which were visited while the household were occupying Norris Castle, in the Isle of Wight. They even went as far as Plymouth and Torquay, where the princess evinced an unmistakable liking for the sea and an interest in everything relating to maritime affairs. At Norris Castle the old simple mode of life was renewed, and long walks, drives, and visits to the scenery of the island were among the pleasures that were most enjoyed: but trips were frequently made by sea in the yacht *Emerald*, which was retained for the princess. The Duchess of Kent was, as she said in reply to addresses at Plymouth and elsewhere, anxious that her daughter should visit the various places that were associated with the marine importance of the country; and it should be noticed that, in order to carry out this part of the education of the princess, as well as to give her what soon became a great pleasure, that of making sailing excursions to some distance, the careful mother had to exercise much self-denial, for she was by no means "a good sailor," and frequently had to suffer great inconvenience and discomfort that she might accompany the princess in these voyages.

It was while returning from the Eddystone on board the *Emerald* that an accident placed the princess in very serious danger, from which she was rescued by the presence of mind of the pilot, Mr. Saunders. It was rather brisk weather, and the princess was on deck when a mast was sprung and heard to crack. The pilot saw that the topmast was likely to come down near the spot where her royal highness was standing, and, as there was no time for ceremony, darted to the spot and carried her aft out of harm's way. The next moment the top-mast fell crashing on the deck at the spot from which she had been removed, and where she would in all probability have been killed but for the presence of mind of Mr. Saunders, to whom the princess with much emotion expressed her gratitude for his prompt and timely action. It need scarcely be added that the pilot and his family were not lost sight of after the accession of the princess to the throne.

There were many memorable visits paid to places of interest to which the voyage could be made on board the *Emerald*, but, perhaps the most important event of the pleasant holiday was the opening of the new landing pier at Southampton, a ceremony which the Duchess of Kent and the princess graced by their presence. The royal yacht, having been towed from Cowes to Southampton Water by a steam-tug, was met by a deputation from the corporation of the town, who came in a state barge, on board which one of the town serjeants attended bearing a silver oar. The deputation presented an address, to which the duchess replied that she wished her daughter to become attached at an early age to works of utility. The distinguished visitors entered the barge and were rowed ashore, where they were entertained at luncheon, and the pier having been declared open was, by permission, named the Royal pier.

It was while on their journey to Weymouth, the quiet and highly decorous watering-place where the Duke of Kent had stayed with George the Third, who made it his favourite seaside resort, that the duchess and her daughter stopped at Portsmouth to pay a visit to the young Queen Donna Maria da Gloria of Portugal, of whom mention has already been made. This youthful sovereign received much kindly and courteous attention from the English royal family, and in the *Greville Memoirs* we are told of a ball given by the King, who led the juvenile Queen of Portugal by the hand. She was magnificently attired, her dress and appearance offering a remarkable contrast to the simplicity of costume and the fresh, fair, sensible face of the Princess Victoria. The royal guest maintained most notable dignity of mien, though during the progress of the ball she accidentally fell and was somewhat hurt. We have already seen that Donna Maria became related by marriage to the Queen, and it may be mentioned here, before her disappearance from the narrative, that she was grand-niece to Amélie, Queen of Louis Philippe, King of the French. Amélie was the daughter of the King of Naples and Sicily, and married Louis Philippe (then Duke of Orleans) while he was at Palermo, where her father and his family were living under British protection. It was said that Louis Philippe had been intriguing to make a match between one of his sons and the young Queen Donna Maria when his intentions were frustrated by her marrying Prince Ferdinand of Coburg.

The next two years passed quietly enough, though some of the best society in England was occasionally entertained by the

Duchess of Kent at Kensington Palace. Sir Walter Scott, alas! would no more record a visit there, for the "Wizard of the North," who had enchanted a nation with his wondrous genius, had died at Abbotsford in 1832—died of a last vast effort to conquer the adversity of debt and difficulty which had overtaken him in his later years. We hear, however, of Lord Campbell dining at Kensington Palace in 1833, when the invited guests found the Princess Victoria in the drawing-room on their arrival and again on their return thither after dinner. This was not always the case, especially in the two succeeding years; but the mention of it shows with what care the childhood of the princess was preserved till she had reached an age when she could more properly participate in all the social pleasures that belong to a refined and intelligent circle. The duchess could not, of course, permit her young daughter to visit much at houses where "society" was always making itself conspicuous. The assemblies at Holland House and other places, which were attractive centres of famous people, would not have been suitable associations for the princess, even had she been two or three years older; but now that she was, by her knowledge, her studious disposition, and her marked intelligence, able to appreciate the company of those who were distinguished in science, art, or literature, or were known for their philanthropy and other marked qualities, there were frequent gatherings not only of those who held high rank or place in the state but of the aristocracy of culture. We hear of a visit of Southey, who appears to have called expressly to see the princess, and found not only that she was acquainted with his works, but that she could pay him a graceful and artless compliment by saying how she had read his life of Nelson half a dozen times over. We hear, too, of authors, artists, and a number of other people by whom the English "May-flower," now in sweetest bloom, was looked upon with loving, reverent, but not unfamiliar eyes. It is not to be supposed that no visits were ever paid other than those of ceremony, or when the duchess and the Princess Victoria were the guests at great mansions and historical houses, where the noble hosts welcomed them during their autumn journeys; but the visiting in London was necessarily restricted, and though the poet Moore speaks of being invited to meet these distinguished guests at the house of a private friend, the circle so honoured was necessarily select. But the Princess Victoria now began to appear more in public, at musical performances and picture-galleries, and Leslie, the Academician, recording her visit to the Royal Academy, says that she had all the charms of youth, health, and high spirits, adding she could have seen little of the exhibition as she was herself, from the moment of entering the room, the sole object of attraction, as there were so many people among the nobility present whom she knew, and everyone of whom had something to say to her. It is also recorded, as incidental to the visit, that she shook hands and chatted with Mr. Rogers, the banker and poet, and also that Mr. Charles Kemble, the famous actor, was presented to her.

In July, 1834, the princess, then fifteen years old, was confirmed by the Archbishop of Canterbury (Dr. Howley) in the Chapel Royal, St. James's. The rite of confirmation, for which she had been prepared according to the instructions ordained by the English Church, is understood to mark the personal acceptance of those spiritual obligations which at the time of baptism are represented by the promises of the sponsors who devote the infant to the service of the Most High in the Christian faith and life; and there is reason to believe that the infinitely serious meaning and the solemn responsibility of this obligation were deeply realized. The King and Queen were present with the Duchess of Kent, attended by some other members of the royal family; and when, after the confirmation, the archbishop tenderly but very earnestly addressed the princess, exhorting her to consider the great duties which her high position would require her to fulfil, and entreating her in every trial and difficulty to seek strength and guidance of Him who, being the King of Kings, can alone give to his children and subjects help in their utmost need, she was so deeply affected that every one present was moved to tears.

The current of the young life going peacefully on gives little to record during that year; but there are suggestions of kindly and benevolent deeds, indications that the perception of personal responsibility took a practical form. One anecdote, which seems, possibly because of some touching associations, to have been more distinctly repeated, records that at Tunbridge Wells, whither the Duchess of Kent and the princess went for the autumn, the husband of an actress who was engaged at the small theatre there had died, leaving the poor woman, who was soon to become a mother, in great want and distress. The princess on hearing of the sad case at once took ten pounds from her own allowance of pocket-money, and, after persuading the Duchess of Kent to contribute the same amount, carried the money to the poor widow, with whom she conversed for some time. It is not easy to imagine what was the gratitude of the sufferer, who seems, however, to have been a person both worthy of this timely and gracious help and capable of interesting her distinguished visitor, for we are told that further aid was given, and that on the accession of the princess to the throne an annuity of £40 a year was conferred on the woman for the remainder of her life.

It may be worth while to pause here for a moment to remember that among the numerous anecdotes and professed reminiscences relating to the Princess Victoria, as well before as after she became Queen, there are many which are not authentic, many that have no foundation in fact, and that at a comparatively recent date her Majesty has permitted a statement of a pretended incident in her early life to be contradicted. That none of those statements, which have about them even a remote air of probability, are in the least derogatory to the child who, as a princess, won the hearts of the people, who saw her so frequently, or to the Queen who has carried on that conquest in the stories of our lives from year to year, is in itself a marvellous testimony to her worth. It is obvious that authentic anecdotes such as those which we have been able to record as illustrations of the private or domestic life and the characteristic disposition of the Princess Victoria, could only be multiplied by a breach of confidence on the part of those who have been privileged to witness acts of personal beneficence or domestic incidents, which, however admirable, should be reserved from the public eye unless they are made known with the sanction of the august person who is directly interested.

The life of our sovereign Lady has been plain and clear to the respectful onlooking of her people. She herself has made it so, and has depicted its domestic no less than its regal conditions in words so simple and unaffected that even children can understand and appreciate them. The Queen has left little opportunity for the inventions or the pretended disclosures of prying gossip-mongers, either in or out of print, whose province it seems to be, at once to stimulate and profess to satisfy a mean curiosity which disregards the reticence that belongs to common courtesy. The visits of the Princess Victoria to the theatre or places of public amusement had not been numerous even at the time of her accession to the throne, though her delight in music had been gratified by her comparatively frequent presence at concerts and at the opera-house. Till 1835 she had not appeared in public in state as a member of the royal family and heir to the throne, except when she accompanied the King and Queen to the musical festival at Westminster Abbey in the previous year. In June, 1835, however, in presence of a brilliant assembly, and of a multitude who lined the race-course at Ascot on the gold-cup day, the royal cortége arrived preceded by the Life Guards. The Princess Victoria, her fresh, fair young face beaming with pleasure at the spectacle presented by the enthusiastic crowd and the aspect of the grand-stand, was recognized, and shared with the King and Queen the continuous and hearty applause, though she appeared to be more delighted with the welcome accorded to the King than with any direct manifestations of loyalty to herself. A description of her appearance on the occasion tells us that her hair was braided in "Clotilde" bands under a large bonnet of pink or pale-rose colour, and that over a rose-coloured satin dress "*broché*" she wore a "pelerine" trimmed with black lace.

The mention of these particulars carries us back to a time which only the elderly reader can remember: the time of large widely-spreading bonnets, of short waists and rather short skirts just reaching the ankles, of sandal shoes, and pelerines. Yet, who can tell! The wave of fashion may set that way again ere long; indeed it is a matter of surprise that the jubilee year has not witnessed a "revival" in this direction.

It happened that in the summer of 1835 Nathaniel Parker Willis, an American author and journalist of some reputation, was in England, and having introductions to various fashionable circles, made a good deal of literary capital out of his observations by describing, without much delicacy of reticence, people he had met, and repeating their remarks and conversations. He was at Ascot on the occasion of the royal visit, and subsequently included this among his rather random and personal pencillings: "In one of the intervals I walked under the King's stand and saw her Majesty the Queen and the young Princess Victoria very distinctly. They were leaning over the railing listening to a ballad singer, and seeming as much interested and amused as any simple country folk could be. The Queen is undoubtedly the plainest woman in her dominions, but the princess is much better looking than any picture of her in the shops, and for the heir to such a crown as that of England unnecessarily pretty and interesting. She will be sold, poor thing! bartered away by those great dealers in royal hearts, whose grand calculations will not be much consolation to her if she happens to have a taste of her own."

The *rawness* of these remarks seems peculiar to-day when we remember that in America Mr. Willis was regarded as a highly cultured writer, and had gained much distinction as a poet, or, at all events, as a writer of verses of sentiment; but the assumption of the critic and the moralist is immensely amusing. It is not on record that Mr. Willis was ever presented to the Princess Victoria, who, soon after the Ascot meeting, accompanied her mother on a journey northward as far as York, where they visited the Archbishop at Bishopsthorpe, and were greatly interested in the noble minster when they attended the York musical festival, at which the fine oratorio the *Messiah* was performed. It may not be inappropriate to quote the following lines which appeared in *Blackwood's Magazine*, addressed "To the Princess Victoria on seeing her in York Cathedral during the performance of the *Messiah*."-

> "Sweet princess! as I gaze upon thee *now*,
>   In the bright sunshine of thy youthful grace,
>   And in thy soft, blue eyes, and tranquil brow,
>   Would seek resemblance to thy lofty race.
>   I think how soon the whelming cares of state
>   May crush thy free, young spirit with their weight,
>   And change the guileless beauty of thy face;
>   Nor leave of that sweet, happy smile one trace:
>   Then earnestly I pray that thou mayst be
>   Through all thy life beloved, good and great;
>   And when from thy calm home, by Heaven's decree,
>   Thou art called to rule a mighty nation's fate,
>   Mayst thou throughout thy reign be just and wise,
>   And win at last a crown immortal in the skies."

On the homeward journey visits were made to the Earl of Harewood at Harewood House; to Wentworth, near Rotherham, where the duchess and the Princess Victoria were the guests of Earl Fitzwilliam; and to the Duke of Rutland at Belvoir, whence they went to stay with the Marquis of Exeter at Burghley House. "They arrived from Belvoir at three o'clock in a heavy rain," says Greville, the chronicler whose rather acrid and cynical humour has made his memoirs famous, and gives them something of the flavour of court scandal, which he occasionally reproduces— "they arrived from Belvoir at three o'clock in a heavy rain, the civic authorities having turned out at Stamford to escort them, and a procession of different people, all very loyal. When they had lunched, and the mayor and his brethren had got dry, the duchess received the address, which was read by Lord Exeter as recorder. It talked of the princess as 'destined to mount the throne of these realms.' Conroy handed the answer just as the prime-minister does to the King. They are splendidly lodged, and great preparations have been made for their reception. The dinner at Burghley was very handsome; hall well lit; and all went off well, except that a pail of ice was landed in the duchess's lap, which made a great bustle. Three hundred people at the ball, which was opened by Lord Exeter and the princess, who, after dancing one dance, went to bed. They appeared at breakfast next morning at nine o'clock, and at ten set off for Holkham." Greville of course was present; and on reading this and other descriptive touches in his memoirs one is led to wonder whether he and the American tourist Mr. Willis ever met, and if they did, what they thought of each other.

Among the visits made by the princess, probably one of the most interesting was that to the Duke of Wellington at Walmer Castle, near Deal, where, as warden of the Cinque Ports, his grace mostly resided for a part of each year. The fine bracing sea air and the outlook over the great roadstead of the "Downs," with its ever-changing fleet, suited him well, and though at sixty-seven years old he maintained the plain habits of living which, even as the commander in long campaigns, he had acquired, he could doubtless observe as splendid hospitality at the castle as he displayed at Apsley House. Personally—that is, for himself—the great captain had some disdain for luxuries and even for superfluities. Few people have been more simple in their requirements; and it was declared on good authority that, even at his great house in town, he slept upon a narrow camp bedstead in a room bare of all but actually indispensable furniture.

He was, however, punctilious, if not somewhat ceremonious, in observing those distinctions which society expected in a noble host, and what may be called his rule of manners was well expressed when, on one occasion, he resented what appeared to be disrespectful familiarity on the part of a great personage, and defended his anger by saying, "No man has any right to take a liberty with me, for I never take a liberty with any man."

In fact he was too really great a gentleman to think about condescension. His manners, though rather formal, were cheerful, and on ordinary occasions were as simple as his tastes; and it was well known that the children of houses where he visited were delighted to have the duke for a playmate, for he was neither formal nor austere with them, but jovially abetted them in their noisiest romps and even in some of their mischievous pranks.

Doubtless the visit of the Duchess of Kent and the Princess Victoria was one of some ceremony; but it is certain that "the duke" must already have been regarded as a faithful friend, and it is quite certain that he had a loyal and, so to speak, a paternal affection for the young princess to whom he would one day devote his allegiance. Already he must have felt that his duty was to protect her; for he had for some time past had his eagle eye upon the Duke of Cumberland, whom he neither liked nor respected, and whose clumsy machinations against the Duchess of Kent and the Princess Victoria were soon to be brought to public notice.

The stay at Walmer Castle was brief, but it was likely to be agreeably associated with a cherished and most pleasant event, for, during a sojourn at Ramsgate, the Duchess of Kent and the princess received a visit from the brother and uncle who had been guardian and counsellor. Prince Leopold was then firmly established on the throne of Belgium. He had in his opening address to the Belgian parliament declared that he would encourage industry, and rule according to the principles of civil and religious liberty; and this promise he had so well redeemed that his reign was secure while other sovereigns were watching, not without dismay, the changes wrought by revolution. Leopold had now a queen to share his throne. He would never lose the memory—a sad and abiding, though no longer a poignant memory of the wife who had died so soon, in the first blossom of wedded happiness. With that sorrow fresh in his heart he had been unable to look upon the face of the infant Victoria, who, in respect to the succession to the throne, was to take the place of his Princess Charlotte; but it was from no ignoble feeling of jealousy or base repining—only that the sight of the little babe in his sister's arms roused too keenly the recollection of that hour of anguish when his own wife and her babe lay dead at Claremont. In the hour of his sister's affliction, however, he was at hand, and not only looked upon, but loved her child, all the more, perhaps, that he saw in her some resemblance to her whom he had lost. Whether this was so or not, he bestowed a genuine affection on the little Victoria, and made her and her future well-being his especial care. Nor was that care to cease now that he had found a worthy queen and companion, the Princess Louise-Marie-Thérèse, eldest daughter of Louis Philippe, King of the French, and his Queen, the amiable Amélie. This princess, like all the daughters of Amélie, was a charming and most estimable woman. Everybody loved, everybody spoke well of her. Even Stockmar, who, in his admiration for his royal master, might have been expected to utter only undertones of praise, speaks of her as though she were a saint, and yet his words found true echo in the hearts of those who best knew Louise, Queen of the Belgians. In a few memorial words, written years after he had formed the highest opinion of her character and also of her clear insight and sound judgment, he said: " From the moment that the queen entered that circle in which I for so many years have had a place, I have revered her as a pattern of her sex. We say and believe that men can be noble and good: of her we know with certainty that she was so. We saw in her daily a truthfulness, a faithful fulfilment of duty, which makes us believe in the possible, though but seldom evident, nobleness of the human heart. In characters such as the queen's I see a guarantee of the perfection of the Being who has created human nature."

The Queen Louise accompanied her husband on that visit to Ramsgate, where she met the young princess, to whom she became a beloved and intimate friend, thenceforth to be held in closest regard.

The year 1836 was an important and an eventful one for the Princess Victoria, who then had attained the seventeenth year of her age. Until September the Duchess of Kent had remained at Kensington, where much company had been entertained and special visitors had been received. There had also been assemblies, state dinners, and state concerts, and the months from the birthday of the princess in May to late in August had been rather full of excitement and marked by peculiar interest.

The incidents were not all agreeable, however, and even some of the more important occurrences were calculated to be hostile to the peace of the princess. The King appears to have been under some jarring influence which increased the asperity of temper that he had on more than one occasion displayed towards the Duchess of Kent, whose determination to maintain the entire direction of her daughter's training and education seems to have aroused his resentment. The King, who was certainly liable to get into a passion, and when in it to use expressions which were neither dignified nor polite, had apparently been jealous of the independent position taken by the Duchess of Kent, and had not hesitated to say in as many words that he expected and desired to see the princess more frequently at Buckingham Palace or at Windsor. That he would have liked to have been more frequently consulted, and to have had a great deal more control over the appointment of her surroundings and the bestowal of her engagements, was obvious enough; and during the early part of this year the part taken by Prince Leopold as well as by the Duchess of Kent in directing her probable destinies had, perhaps, been more conspicuous. At anyrate, though his Majesty showed much kindness to his niece, and spoke both to her and of her in a manner that was affectionate, he was evidently much disturbed in temper: at first in somewhat of a sulky humour, that afterwards worked up to one of those rages in which he was sometimes known to "speak his mind," or what he thought was his mind, in a very disturbed and unceremonious manner.

Most of the court and other festivities were drawing to a close when, on the King's birthday, the 21st of August, the Duchess of Kent and the princess were at Windsor Castle on a visit, and there was a private dinner, at which, however, about a hundred persons were present. The Duchess of Kent sat on one side the King and the Princess Augusta on the other, and his majesty, having proposed, and joined in drinking, the health of his sister, said, "And now, having given the health of the oldest, I will give that of the youngest member of the royal family. I know the interest which the public feel about her, and although I have not seen so much of her as I could have wished I take no less interest in her, and the more I do see of her, both in public and in private, the greater pleasure it will give me." This is what the King was afterwards reported to have said; but we have been told in memoirs more recently published that he said more; that in answering to the drinking of his own health he referred in direct and angry terms to the seclusion of the princess from court, and to what he considered to be disrespect or insult on the part of the Duchess of Kent. Of the duchess he spoke with so much asperity and evidently uncontrolled temper that the Queen was much distressed, the princess in tears, and the whole company somewhat horrified; while the lady herself, too indignant or too prudent to make any reply to such an attack, rose to leave the table and asked for her carriage; but, on some kind of explanation or concession being made, was induced to remain till next day. It is not out of place to refer to this, even if it be only a piece of court scandal, for it indicates what was certainly the condition of temper exhibited by the King, and it is possible also that there may have been the same sinister influence at work as that which in that very year was exposed in Parliament —the influence of the Duke of Cumberland, who, though he was not likely to succeed in setting the King against the Princess Victoria, might without much difficulty arouse his existing jealousy of the duchess of Kent and excite his suspicions with regard to the regency which she was to exercise in case of the death of the King before the princess came of age.

The report of this unseemly speech of the King and of his marked attack on the duchess was, however, only taken from hearsay: said to be from a repetition of what took place by Adolphus Fitzclarence. This piece of scandal, however, appears to have been made known at second hand by the Princess Lieven, the wife of the Russian ambassador, a dangerous, and apparently a malicious intriguante, who, it is known, was plotting with Cumberland in political matters at an earlier date, and of whom it is perhaps only necessary to give Stockmar's word-portrait to indicate her character. " A disagreeable, stiff, proud, and haughty manner. It is true she is full of talent, plays the pianoforte admirably, speaks English, French, and German perfectly; but then, she is well aware of it. Her face is certainly handsome, though too thin, and the pointed nose as well as the mouth, which can be contracted into various folds, show, even outwardly, the small inclination she has to consider others as her equals. Her neck is like a skeleton's."

This personage seems to have had something of the same kind of spite against the Duchess of Kent which was shown by the Duke of Cumberland. After the coronation we learn from Greville's memoirs that she told him (Greville) of an interview she had had with the duchess, in which the animus with which she repeats and interprets very natural and simple remarks suggests at once that she had been biassed by dislike or by some previous interest which was inimical to the duchess and to the Queen herself.

It is not difficult to fancy what this influence was by the light of other events which occurred in 1836. The Duke of Cumberland was violent and overbearing, and of course, as an extreme Tory, had been opposed to Catholic emancipation and other concessions. This would not have mattered so much had he not been, in spite of his arrogant assumptions of high-mindedness and religious principle, a coarse and sometimes almost brutal man, with ungovernable pride, not many scruples where his own advantages were concerned, and with an almost fatal knack of acting in such a way as to alienate those who might have inclined to be friendly to him. He seemed to care very little who was unfriendly, and was ready to trample or to gallop over anybody who stood in his way, and to treat anybody with almost ogreish insult. It would not be accurate to say that everybody detested him, for he continued to be on good terms with a few people, and kept up a correspondence with them, and especially with one of them (Lord Strangford) for some years after he had left

England; but he was heartily disliked by nearly everybody with whom he came in contact, and the people of England, for the most part, held him in positive abhorrence.

It is pretty certain that any personage in such a high position, if he be disliked, will have accusations brought against him for which there may be little or no foundation, and it is not necessary to recount other charges that were made against the Duke of Cumberland. It is only that of conspiring to set aside the succession to the crown that need be even briefly referred to in these pages. That the duke was a Tory of an extreme type, was of less consequence because of the general break-up and disappearance of that section of political parties; indeed, what had been known as the Tory party was seemingly destroyed; and the tactics of Sir Robert Peel had organized against the Whig or Liberal government a steady though small opposition, who assumed the name of "Conservatives." The weakening of the Whig government by the secession of some of the cabinet on the Irish Church question, causing the resignation of Earl Grey in July, 1834, had been followed by the formation of a feeble ministry by Lord Melbourne, and its dismissal by the King in the following November, when Sir Robert Peel was sent for from Rome and undertook the government on " Liberal-Conservative" principles, a declaration which led to his being distrusted by both parties, and to his defeat and resignation in April, 1835, when Lord Melbourne returned to office.

The Duke of Cumberland had been so violent at the time of the passing of the Catholic Emancipation Bill that the King (George the Fourth) had been positively afraid of him, and the Duke of Wellington had to show that *he* was not the man to be frightened by anybody. The headstrong, abusive brother of the King was so generally suspected and disliked that, though he was grand-master or president of the Orange lodges, and the Brunswick lodges which represented Protestant ascendency, Peel wrote to the Duke of Wellington, "The Duke of Cumberland has no sort of influence over public opinion in this country, or over any party that is worth consideration. I do not believe that the most violent Brunswickers have the slightest respect for him or slightest confidence in him." The plan that the Duke of Cumberland then took was to haunt the sick and dying King (George the Fourth), and to use every opportunity to malign the Duke of Wellington and the ministry. Greville calls his conduct "atrocious—a mixture of narrow-mindedness, selfishness, truckling, blustering, and duplicity, with no object but self—his own ease and the gratification of his own fancies and prejudices." The King would have given a good deal to get rid of him, but he would not go abroad as he was entreated to do. William the Fourth, however, was not so easily frightened, and, when his brother began to trouble and worry him, showed that he would neither be bullied nor cajoled. "The land we live in, and let those who don't like it leave it," was the significant toast given by the bluff sailor King at one of his dinners when the Duke of Cumberland was present.

It was the public distrust of this fierce, unscrupulous "grand-master" which produced the feeling that the Princess Victoria would not be safe in case of the King's death without the appointment of a regency, and in 1835 there had been some disclosures which sufficiently justified the suspicions that had been entertained. Several of the Liberal members, including Mr. Sheil, a famous parliamentary orator, and Mr. Hume, had unearthed a portentous secret, and pressed for an answer to the question whether it was true that 182 addresses from Orange societies had been presented to the King, and whether answers had not been returned to the parties, stating that the addresses had been most graciously received. The question was evidently intended to lead up to something else. Sir Robert Peel and ministers were taken by surprise, and could only say in defence of returning such answers to Protestant societies alleged to be illegal, that the illegality of Orange lodges had never been judicially declared, and that the addresses had been received and answered only according to usual form. Mr. Sheil moved for the production of copies of the addresses and of a letter by Lord Manners when he was Chancellor of Ireland relative to the illegality of Orange societies, and also for the opinions of the Irish law officers. This was resisted and finally withdrawn; but Mr. Hume obtained a committee to investigate the matter of the Orange lodges and their designs, and the evidence taken was startling enough, and was regarded as proof of the existence of a powerful conspiracy of Orange clubs, having for its object to set aside the Princess Victoria as next in succession.

The chiefs of the Orange movement pretended or professed to suspect the Duke of Wellington of an intention to seize the crown, a notion for which they were perhaps indebted to Napoleon Bonaparte, and they proposed to declare William IV. to be insane, to set aside the princess as a woman and a minor, and to place the Duke of Cumberland on the throne. There could at all events be no doubt that there was in existence an extensive Orange confederation, and that the duke as grand-master, and the Bishop of Salisbury as grand-chaplain, with several Tory peers among the Orange leaders, must have been aware of it. In England there were 145,000 members, in Ireland 175,000, and there were branches in nearly every regiment of the army at home and abroad. Naturally enough the "dreary duke" and Lord Kenyon, who was implicated along with him, denied having any guilty knowledge of the proceedings, and declared that they did not know of the existence of Orange clubs in the army. This was so improbable that the committee could do no other than report that they could not reconcile the statement with the evidence. Lord John Russell induced the House to suspend judgment, and this was to give the duke time to withdraw from the association and make the best of his shameful situation; but as he took no such steps, and bullied and protested as usual, he was censured by vote. Then it came about that in 1836 the Radicals with a fine irony determined to indict the Duke of Cumberland, the Bishop of Salisbury, and Lord Kenyon under an act which had become almost obsolete (the act making the extra-judicial administration of oaths a criminal offence). The irony was this, that not long before, numbers of operatives who were members of trades-unions had been holding meetings, and their example seemed likely to be followed by some agricultural labourers, who thought they might unite to secure some improvement of their condition. This filled land-owners and farmers with alarm, and the question was asked what could be done to stop such dangerous demonstrations. The question was answered when six Dorchester peasants were caught administering unionist oaths to some of their poor companions, and, under the Extra-judicial Administration of Oaths Act, were indicted, found guilty, and sentenced to seven years transportation. Of course they were ignorant of the law, and though they were not excused on that account they knew quite well that they were being punished, not for the oaths, but for meeting to agitate the questions that most affected them. There were tremendous demonstrations of the actual trades-unions; a deputation of 30,000 waited on Lord Melbourne, who sent word to them that they could not be attended to unless they sent in a memorial in a proper manner: consequently the memorial was sent, and after a time the Dorchester labourers received a free pardon.

Under the same act against administering illegal oaths the indictments against the Duke of Cumberland and his confederates were drawn; and the prosecution was about to commence, but the death of an important witness delayed it; and when the House of Commons again met, Mr. Hume proposed an address to the crown. The duke was then obliged to do what he had the opportunity of doing at first, and, apparently without any shame or a feeling of humiliation, he proceeded to break up the confederation.

There was one very obvious cause of King William's ill-temper, which had been smouldering ever since he had heard that the principal birthday guests at Kensington Palace would be the Duke of Coburg and his two sons, the Princes Ernest and Albert. Even if the secret had been kept from the princess, he probably knew that it had always been the desire of King Leopold, and perhaps of the Duchess of Kent, that the younger of the two princes should win his way to the affection of the little " May-flower," of whom the court and family circle at Coburg were ever speaking lovingly, and of whom even the nurse of the prince used to talk to him as though some twin destiny had been appointed for him and his little cousin in England.

The King, however, was altogether opposed to the young Prince of Coburg becoming a suitor to the Princess Victoria, and he went so far as to endeavour to prevent the duke's visit with his two sons to England. William the Fourth doubtless considered that, as his niece could not be supposed to have any preference, even if at her early age the subject had been presented to her, he ought to claim precedence in providing a suitable bridegroom, and he was greatly in favour of Prince Alexander of the Netherlands, brother of the King of Holland. He had never mentioned this to the Princess Victoria, nor does it appear that at that time she had heard any distinct references to the claims or qualifications of other apparently eligible suitors; but not unnaturally the King may have thought that his candidate should have the earliest opportunity.

It says something for the King's good-nature, however, that he invited the visitors to be present at all the court festivities. More than this, the Queen has made known that in later years Queen Adelaide said to her, that if she had told the King it was her own earnest wish to marry her cousin, and that her happiness depended on it, he would at once have given up his opposition to it, as he was very fond of, and always very kind to his niece. We have it on the Queen's authority that she certainly would never have married anyone else, though several other candidates for her hand were seriously thought of. Among these, it might be supposed, were her cousins in England, Prince George of Cambridge and Prince George of Cumberland; but the attitude assumed by the Duke of Cumberland towards his niece must at all events have prevented any such expectations on the part of his son, even if the unfortunate youth had not passed, by an accident, from partial to almost total blindness. Duke Ernest of Wurtemberg, in whose favour some interest was being made, was the brother of Prince Albert's step-mother; and among later requests for permission to seek the hand of the Princess Victoria was that on behalf of Prince Adalbert, the son of Prince William of Prussia.

It was evident to those who had carefully and anxiously watched the habits and education of Prince Albert, that he

showed promise of soon becoming eminently suitable for the position, at once delicate and arduous, of consort to the future queen of this country. In personal appearance he was singularly and even strikingly handsome, and, though not so tall and apparently not so strong as his brother, who was a year older, bore an expression of higher refinement. This expression, together with remarkable faculties of observation and reflection, increased during the completion of his education, which after that time was principally conducted under the advice of Baron Stockmar. In accordance with his opinion the princes, who from infancy had been inseparable, went to Brussels to pursue their studies partly under the eye of their uncle Leopold, who would himself be able to instruct them on political and international questions and the principles of constitutional government. From Brussels they went to the university at Bonn, where they remained from April, 1837, to the end of 1838, during which period Stockmar, at the earnest request of King Leopold, came to reside in England as the trusted helper and adviser of the Princess Victoria.

The young Prince Albert must have been endowed with a rare mental and moral temperament to have escaped, without being spoiled, from the open admiration and "petting" which attended his childhood; but it was not only the remarkable personal beauty of the fair-haired, blue-eyed infant, nor even his childlike gentleness combined with unusual vivacity, that made him a favourite. The same equable good sense which seemed to preserve him from the deteriorating influence of admiration, was itself a chief reason for the undeviating affection and esteem entertained for him by his early friends, companions, and play-fellows, no less than by those who were his later associates. Fellow-students and companions on educational tours or at college—men distinguished in statesmanship, science, or art, professors, tutors—all were attracted and interested by the same characteristics, which deepened as infancy passed to boy-hood and youth to manhood.

"Every grace had been showered by nature on this charming boy," wrote Herr Florschütz, the "Rath" or tutor chosen to in-struct the children while they were yet infants (Albert being not five years old), and who remained with them till they went to college. "Every eye rested on him with delight, and his look won the hearts of all." Herr Florschütz was a man eminently suited for his position. He loved the boys, and they learned to love him, and this affection grew with their learning and the knowledge that he imparted; but he was not too indulgent, and as they had plenty of play and lived much in the open air, the good Rath, both then and later, lamented—almost resented — the time spent in breakfasting with their father in one or other of the gardens belonging to the palaces, a practice which, he considered, wasted the whole of the forenoons during the spring and summer months in the year. Still they made good progress with their studies, and as both were very precocious children, and Albert especially so, it may have been as well that the tutorial instincts were not to have all their own way.

The little Albert, *so* little that he was glad for Herr Florschütz to carry him up stairs, was not "let off" much during school time.

"I cried at my lesson to-day because I could not find a verb, and the Rath pinched me to show me what a verb was. And I cried about it," wrote the little prince in a journal which he kept in 1825 before he was six years old, and while the Duke of Coburg was much away from Rosenau, where the children remained. "I wrote a letter at home. But because

I had made so many mistakes in it the Rath tore it up and threw it into the fire. I cried about it." This was on the 26th of March, a month after the former entry; but the next day the entry was, " I finished writing my letter, then I played;" and on the 4th of April came the pleasant announcement that the duke had returned. "After dinner we went with dear papa to Ketschendorf. There I drank beer, and ate bread and butter and cheese." It may be remarked that the consumption of beer or of wine did not become a habit, for Prince Albert could, or at all events seldom did, drink little else than water at dinner, and was more than indifferent to what are called the "pleasures of the table."

This journal, kept with much regularity, was singularly truthful. It recounted events and recorded faults without palliation. " I got up well and happy; afterwards I had a fight with my brother. . . . After dinner we went to the play. It was 'Wallenstein's Lager,' and they carried out a monk" This is on April 9th. On the 10th: "I had another fight with my brother: that was not right." A previous entry records . . . " I was to recite something, but I did not wish to do so· that was not right: naughty!"

There is, of course, nothing extraordinary in these childish records, though even to keep a journal at all at so early an age is unusual; but there are indications of character even here, and as the entries go on—for it was continued for some years—the development of the education and disposition of the prince is apparent, and especially the maintenance of that strict truthfulness which is equally observed in his letters to his father, his grandmothers, and his young friends.

There can be no doubt that the childhood of the princes was a happy one, and though Albert in infancy was in some respects not robust and suffered from attacks of croup, their habits were simple, active, and healthy. There was much exercise, much change in visiting various friends and taking part in sports and entertainments, and, along with eager and well-ordered study, a good deal of recreation and numerous playfellows to join in games of the sturdy Saxon fashion.

The duke appears to have had a very genuine affection for his sons: but they had, even at the earlier age of which we have been speaking, lost the care of their mother, the Princess Louise, daughter by his first wife (a princess of Mecklenburg-Schwerin) of Augustus, last reigning duke but one of Saxe-Gotha-Altenburg. She was a beautiful little woman, fair with blue eyes, and was full of cleverness and talent, but, according to Herr Florschütz, she showed too much partiality in the treatment of her children "She made no attempt to conceal that Prince Albert was her favourite child. He was handsome and bore a strong resemblance to herself. He was, in fact, her pride and glory. The influence of this partiality upon the minds of the children might have been most injurious; and to this was added the unfortunate differences which soon followed, and by which the peace of the family was disturbed, differences that, gradually increasing, led to a separation between the duke and duchess in 1824, and a divorce in 1826."

The children must, of course, have been affected by this, for when the duchess finally left Coburg they never saw her again. The marriage had not been a happy one. Incompatibility of temper, and views that were irreconcilable, appear to have ended in the necessity for this separation, which, though it must for some time have been the occasion of wonder and grief to the two children, did not permanently interfere with their happiness, nor did they lose a loving and respectful memory of the mother whom they did not see.

The Queen has recorded that the prince (Albert) "never forgot her, and spoke with much tenderness and sorrow of his poor mother. . . . One of the first gifts he made to the Queen was a little pin he had received from her when a little child. Princess Louise (the prince's fourth daughter, and named after her grandmother) is said to be like her in face."

The father of the duchess had been long married a second time, and her stepmother, the Duchess Dowager of Gotha, appears to have been a sincere friend to her, to the time of her death, after a long and painful illness, at St. Wendel in Switzerland in 1831, when she was in her thirty-second year.

It was then that the amiable Duchess, her stepmother,[1] wrote to the Duke of Coburg:—"My dear Duke,—This also I have to endure, that the child whom I watched over with such love should go before me. May God now allow me to be reunited to all my loved ones! . . . It is a most bitter feeling that the dear, dear House of Gotha is now extinct."[2]

The little princes at the Rosenau were still the objects of a constant care and solicitude which was next to maternal. There was a loving competition between the old Dowager Duchess of Coburg, their paternal grandmother, and the other maternal step-grandmother at Gotha, who had them always near her heart, and, as often as she could, would have them to stay with her as visitors, taking care to make that visit a holiday, from which they returned improved in health and spirits.

The education of the princes was of the broad general character best suited to their position. It included history, geography, mathematics, philosophy, religion, Latin, and the

---

[1] She was the Princess Caroline of Hesse Cassel (born in 1768), daughter of William, Elector of Hesse, and Wilhelmina of Denmark.

[2] See p. 64.

modern European languages, relieved by the study of music and drawing, for both of which the prince early showed a marked inclination. He was also from childhood fond of natural history.

In the autumn of 1833 the duke remarried, the new duchess being the Princess Mary of Wurtemberg, the daughter of his sister Princess Antoinette and Duke Alexander of Wurtemberg. She was a year older than the first wife of the duke would have been had she lived, and the two lads, who accompanied their father to the Castle of Thalwitz in Saxony, there to await the arrival of the princess from Petersburg and to escort her to Coburg, appear to have afterwards treated her with genine loyalty, and the letters written to her by Prince Albert during his travels are expressive of confidence and affection.

Up to the year 1835, with the exception of a short visit to their uncle, King Leopold, at Brussels, in 1832, the princes had not left home. In that year, after their confirmation in the Protestant faith in the chapel of the palace at Coburg, they went to Mecklenburg to congratulate the Grand-duke of Mecklenburg-Schwerin, their great-grandfather by the mother's side, on the fiftieth anniversary of his accession, and, after a few days spent there, they travelled on to Berlin. At both places they were well received, and produced a most favourable impression. "It requires, however," writes the prince from Berlin (9th May, 1835), to his stepmother, the Duchess of Coburg, "a giant's strength to bear all the fatigue we have had to undergo. Visits, parades, rides, déjeuners, dinners, suppers, balls, and concerts follow each other in rapid succession, and we have not been allowed to miss anyone of the festivities." From Berlin the princes went to Dresden, Prague, Vienna, Pesth, and Ofen, returning towards the end of May to Coburg to resume their studies, with which

Prince Albert, at all events, was well pleased. Their simple habits of early rising, plain living, open-air exercise, daily lessons, and regular amusements made him indifferent to fashionable assemblies and conventional "gaieties," which bored and fatigued him, and he had an invincible tendency to fall asleep when the hour grew late. This feeling of drowsiness was constitutional; his tutor had known him when quite a child to slumber so profoundly as to fall off his chair, and, unhurt, to remain still asleep upon the floor; and he was frequently compelled after a long day, if engaged at a late hour in any festive gathering, to steal away to some recess or bay of a window, and there have, at least, a few minutes' repose. The tendency never left him, but he never suffered it to interfere with the duties of courtesy, and, however fatigued, would stand or move about for a whole evening watchful for the comfort and enjoyment of others.

For some time before the seventeenth birthday of the Princess Victoria, in May, 1836, rumours of proposed matrimonial alliances for her may have reached the ears of the King of the Belgians. In the following year she would attain her majority, and her accession to the throne could not be far distant, he therefore seriously considered how a meeting of the prince and princess might best be proposed, with a view to awakening a spontaneous but undeclared interest, the first half-conscious and yet unembarrassed advances of mutual admiration and regard. If these lines were part of a novel, and that part of it over which we might linger with a touch of fancy, subtle and delicate, something might be said of tender thoughts, unexpressed questions, gentle resolves, wistful hopes or fears that had vibrated at intervals in two young hearts—the heart of the princely youth in the old palace of the Rosenau, amidst the beautiful peaceful scenery

of the Thüringerwald;—the heart of the maiden, in the rather
dowdy old palace at Kensington or the more delightful seclusion
of Claremont. Messages and tokens of cousinly good-will had
passed during these years of childhood. Something of the
semblance of each was probably known to the other so far as
portraits went, though the sun had not then risen upon photo-
graphs. One might almost take a simile from photography
itself, and say that in these young souls the sensitive plates were
all this time being prepared, and that they needed for their
development only the illumination of the eyes that would look
love to eyes that looked again.

Thus far we may speculate without being indebted to
imagination. No novel that was ever written, no poem that
was ever sung or said, has more in it of a true love story than
arose from the first meeting of this prince and princess, of
whose wooing it probably was declared, that it was "cut and
dried—arranged beforehand, as all royal wooings or betrothals
are."

It had been "cut and dried"—arranged beforehand—no
doubt in the minds, the hopes, the ardent wishes of those who
held these children dearest, but who, because they held them
so dear, were for hearing the voice of their hearts before even
the fondest of these wishes should be formed into fetters however golden. If the youth and maiden had, as children, been
accustomed to some half dawning of the relation which they
might one day sustain to each other, they were not to be
reminded of it at the time of the first approach.

Stockmar, who had been taken into the counsels of the King
of the Belgians, and at once began critically to diagnose the
character of the prince and to suggest plans for his education,
that he might be worthy to fulfil the trust that should be reposed

in him, advised the acceptance of the invitation to the birthday
of the Princess Victoria. On the 16th of April (1836) he wrote,
" Now is the right moment for the first appearance in England.
If the first favourable impression is now made the foundation-
stone is laid for the future edifice. But it must be a *conditio
sine quâ non*, that the real intention of the visit should be kept
secret from the princess as well as the prince, that they may
be perfectly at their ease with each other."

There seems to be little—though in significance there must
have been much—to record of that four weeks' visit to Kensington
Palace. We are not informed how inquiring eyes met the light
each in each, or whether the flicker of a tell-tale blush went out
for a moment as signal amidst the greetings. These are matters
into which none need pry. Enough for us to remember, that
both youth and maiden were of self-possessed, because not weakly
self-conscious temperament,—that there was a noble simplicity
in both, and a modesty that consists with the true dignity that
can bide its time. They were kindred in pursuits, tastes, and
acquirements, and it has been distinctly declared that there was
a marvellous likeness observed between them as the prince came
into the hall. There is no need to repeat the list of entertainments and assemblies which the princes and their father
attended. Only one descriptive note need be added, and it
occurs in the words of the Queen herself. " The prince was
at that time much shorter than his brother, already very handsome, but very stout, which he entirely grew out of afterwards.
He was most amiable, natural, unaffected, and merry; full of
interest in everything, playing on the piano with the princess,
his cousin, drawing; in short, constantly occupied. He always
paid the greatest attention to all he saw, and the Queen
remembers well how intently he listened to the sermon preached

in Saint Paul's, when he and his father and brother accompanied the Duchess of Kent and the princess there on the occasion of the service attended by the children of the different charity schools. It is, indeed, rare to see a prince not yet seventeen years of age bestowing such earnest attention on a sermon."

The Princess Victoria had been left to form her own estimate of the young prince, and though it is scarcely probable that she was unaware of the wishes of the family that there should be a mutual regard between her and her cousin, the young people were left to form an unbiassed opinion of each other. That the mutual impression was favourable was to be seen in the letters which the princess sent to her uncle after the departure of the visitors. The language of love needs no words, and even the first advances thitherward are known to those most interested by tokens too subtle and delicate for direct speech. There had been nothing said, nothing hinted between them, unless it may have been by such signs as the giving of a flower, the glance of an eye, the momentary pressure of a hand; but yet from the time of this visit there was not only an understanding on the part of all concerned, but a very general belief among the public that this young couple would be married. King Leopold now spoke more distinctly to his niece of his hope that the wishes which had been entertained were likely to be promoted by her knowledge of the prince, whose society had been so agreeable to her, and the replies of the princess were sufficiently decided to show that she had become deeply interested and that her affection had been engaged. The letter in which she responded to these inquiries concluded by saying: "I have only now to beg you, my dearest uncle, to take care of the health of one now so dear to me, and to take him under your special protection. I hope and trust that all will go on prosperously and well on this subject, now of so much importance to me."

This was written on the 7th of June, 1836, and though the modest avowal of the princess gave much satisfaction to her uncle Leopold, it appears not to have been thought advisable at once to acquaint the prince with the favourable light in which he was regarded. That is to say, there was no formal engagement; but the advice of Stockmar was adopted, and the education of the prince was directed into such channels as would best fit him for the position to which he might be called. He and his brother went at once to Brussels, calling at Paris on the way, to make the acquaintance of the Orleans family, one of the most cultivated, amiable, and agreeable in Europe. At Brussels the youths entered at once upon a serious course of study of history, modern languages, and the higher mathematics, Prince Albert being an ardent pupil of M. Quetelet, the famous statist. From Brussels, in April, 1837, they went to Bonn, where they studied under the most eminent professors of that university, and Prince Albert distinguished himself by his attainments in the natural sciences, political economy, and philosophy, at the same time that he won the affectionate regard and esteem of his companions, one of the most intimate of whom was Prince William of Löwenstein. Meantime the princes, and particularly Prince Albert, maintained a simple, affectionate, and cousinly correspondence with the Duchess of Kent and the Princess Victoria at Kensington. The young people were biding their time, each perhaps with the consciousness of a secret which possibly each thought might be not quite known to the other.

In 1837 the princess would be eighteen years of age and would therefore attain her majority. Preparations were made suitably to celebrate the event. As the birthday approached, however, the condition of the King was such as to preclude him from taking any active or prominent part in the forthcoming festivities. His Majesty, who was seventy-one years of age, had mostly been liable to attacks of hay-fever in the spring of the year, and at this time he was suffering severely not only from that disorder, but from other infirmities and from the weakness which followed the attacks. He strove manfully to fulfil his duties, and on the 21st of May held a levee and drawing-room, but was obliged to remain seated while receiving the company. On the 24th, the birthday of the princess, he could not quit his apartments, and the Queen could not leave him; but he sent affectionate messages to his niece, along with a very elegant present of a superb grand-piano, and made arrangements for a grand ball to be held in her honour at Saint James's Palace. It is said that he had some time previously offered to allow her a considerable additional income if she would, on coming of age, commence with a household of his appointment, but that the offer was declined. Even if this had been the case, it seems to have made little difference in the kindness with which his Majesty had prepared to celebrate the birthday; and when he and the Queen found that they could not be present, they would not allow their absence to interfere with any of the rejoicings or to mar the festivities, the day being observed as a general holiday in London, and both Houses of Parliament suspending their sittings on the occasion.

Early in the morning—at seven o'clock (the hour of the birth of the princess)—a band of vocal and instrumental musicians performed a serenade in Kensington Gardens close to the palace. The princess, always an early riser, listened to this concert from a window, and requested the repetition of one of the pieces. The concert ended with the national anthem, in which the public, who had been admitted to the gardens, joined very heartily. Kensington was *en fête*: flags were flying, bells ringing, and everywhere there were signs of holiday gladness; while, during the day, a succession of carriages brought friends to express their warm congratulations, and, of course, there was a long succession of receptions and of the interchange of good wishes, which were more than merely ceremonial. The presents were numerous and valuable, and doubtless the loving mementos from Coburg held a place and had a value of their own apart from their intrinsic worth. In the letters from the young prince at Bonn there are naturally few allusions to which reference can be made; but we can easily imagine the simple, manly, unaffected way in which the prince would write to his cousin on her birthday. He was no flatterer, and was far too much his own master to think he ought to be constantly reminding of his absence her to whom he stood in so peculiar a relation; but his messages, if brief, were tender and true. The circumstances did not admit of so-called love-letters, but the words used were such as to display and to evoke a serene confidence. "A few days ago," he wrote to his father, soon after the birthday of the princess, "I received a letter from Aunt Kent, inclosing one from our cousin. She told me I was to communicate its contents to you, so I send it on with a translation of the English. The day before yesterday I received a second and still kinder letter from my cousin, in which she thanks me for my good wishes on her birthday. You may easily imagine that both these letters gave me the greatest pleasure."

The state-ball at St. James's Palace was very magnificent, and though the absence of the King, in consequence of the severity of his illness, during which the Queen found it necessary to remain near him, caused much disappointment, it was, perhaps, felt that the duties which therefore devolved on the youthful princess were all the more significant. This was, of course, the first occasion on which her royal highness took precedence of the Duchess of Kent and, indeed, of every person present, occupying the central chair of state supported by the duchess and the Princess Augusta.

The illumination of the streets of the metropolis, and the various demonstrations of popular rejoicing throughout the country, were followed by successive addresses of congratulation, the earliest being those of the corporation of the city of London, which were presented by the lord-mayor, aldermen, and representatives of the common council. The Duchess of Kent replied with great tact and good sense to these addresses, and the princess also occasionally responded briefly, but with much grace and self-possession, to some of those specially intended for herself.

The position of the princess, so young, so liable to become the object of political intrigue, so certain, amidst the jealousies and rancours of parties, to be placed in a position of great difficulty, needed a faithful, independent, and disinterested adviser, possessed of consummate ability, and yet able to keep in the background, and to give no reason for suspicion that any advice given or assistance rendered would have any other motive than that of dutiful regard and willing service. Such a faithful adviser and assistant King Leopold had found in Stockmar, and, turning to Stockmar once more to help him in the task that was dear to his heart, that self-sacrificing servant and affectionate philosopher responded without delay. On the 25th of May, the day following the eighteenth birthday of the princess, he arrived in England.

Perhaps no other man could have fulfilled the precise

position occupied by Stockmar, for he was in some sense the friend and guardian of the personal interests of the princess, and this continued for some months after she came to the throne; while on the other hand—though there were, of course, accusations of "German" influence and undue interposition— he carefully refrained from interfering in any affairs of state. Stockmar was trusted and his integrity was thoroughly acknowledged by ministers and by leading men of both parties, who gave voluntary testimony to his ability as well as his worth and disinterested motives. From love for those whom he served, he consented to long and frequent separations from the wife and children for whom he had an ardent affection. He had, by force of circumstances, been so placed as to be able, by his personal qualifications, to do much to influence the conditions of some of the reigning families of Europe, and his loyalty to Leopold of Belgium, to the Princess Victoria, and to the House of Coburg, especially so far as Prince Albert was concerned, was undoubted, though it is worthy of record that with regard to the proposal for the marriage of the prince with the future Queen of England, Stockmar spoke with his usual plainness in reference to the qualifications which the prince must be able to attain to fit him for so responsible and arduous a position. Even in his later correspondence with Prince Albert, his letters, though full of affection and sympathetic praise and encouragement, never lost the tone of serious exhortation.

The health of the King continued so seriously to decline that before the end of the month of May it was feared that he would not recover. He was too ill to be removed to Brighton, as had been intended, and there was a general feeling of grief throughout the country, for William the Fourth was deservedly popular, his faults of hasty temper and of self-will having always been redeemed by real good-nature, a kind and forgiving disposition, and a generous regard for all who had any claims on his good-will. In his last days, too, all the asperities and infirmities of temper seemed to fall away from him. His mind was serene, his manner placid, his whole demeanour that of a man who has sought and found in the blessed consolations of religion that gentle fortitude and loving consideration for others which combine to make the Christian character. To the last he continued to transact the official business of the country which required his personal attention.

His good and faithful Queen was with him constantly. He had anxiously desired to live over the anniversary of the battle of Waterloo—Sunday the 18th of June. At twelve minutes past two on the morning of Monday, the 19th of June, he passed away, and the Archbishop of Canterbury (Dr. Howley), Lord Conyngham (the lord chamberlain), the Earl of Albemarle (master of the horse), and Sir Henry Halford, the late King's physician, started at once to ride from Windsor to Kensington through the pearl-gray twilight before the dawn of that summer's day.

Everything was still as they neared London, for, though it was known that the King was in all probability sick unto death, his immediate dissolution was not anticipated, and no intelligence of it could have reached the metropolis before the arrival of the distinguished messengers at Kensington Palace. The event had been so little anticipated in that quiet household that, when they arrived at about five o'clock, they found nobody stirring, and had considerable difficulty in making their presence known. According to the account afterwards received, they knocked, thumped, and rang for a long time before they could rouse the porter at the gate; they were again kept waiting in the court-yard, then turned into one of the lower rooms, where they seemed to be forgotten by everybody. They rang the bell, and desired that the attendant of the Princess Victoria might be sent to inform her royal highness that they requested an audience on business of importance. After another delay, and another ringing to inquire the cause, the attendant was summoned, and, with an apparently complete inability to understand that anything could be of more importance than her own special charge, stated that the princess was in such a sweet sleep she could not venture to disturb her. The archbishop and the lord chamberlain must have been lost in admiration at such an example of single regard to immediate and specific duty, but they had to explain that they had come to the Queen on business of state, and that even her sleep must give way to that. The word "Queen," perhaps, impressed the attendant with a sense that she might venture to wake her young mistress, who was so concerned at the probable news, and at her two visitors having been kept waiting on such an occasion, that, without causing a further delay of more than a few minutes, she came into the room attired in a shawl over a loose white night-gown, "her night-cap thrown off, and her hair falling upon her shoulders, her feet in slippers, tears in her eyes, but perfectly collected and dignified."

This is in effect the account given by Miss Wynn in the *Diary of a Lady of Quality* and there is reason for believing it to be substantially accurate. The intelligence was sudden and the occasion a very solemn one, but there was little time for reflection, as it was necessary at once to communicate with Lord Melbourne, that he might summon the privy-council without delay.

The archbishop and the lord chamberlain hastened to London: the message went forth, the privy-council was summoned

to attend at Kensington at eleven o'clock, and at that hour
the youthful Queen, with the Duchess of Kent, entered the
council chamber. Probably the best and most authentic account
of the scene, and of the effect produced on the assembly
by the appearance and conduct of the young princess thus
suddenly placed in such an exalted situation, is that of the
diarist who, even though his official position may be supposed
to have influenced him in speaking of the occasion, his
published journals show to have been an unsparing, if not a
cynical and bitter, recorder of the scenes and events of which
he was for so many years a witness. Greville, who was the clerk
of the council, says in his journal:—" Never was anything like
the first impression she produced, or the chorus of praise and
admiration which is raised about her manner and behaviour, and
certainly not without justice. It was very extraordinary, and
something far beyond what was looked for. Her extreme
youth and inexperience, and the ignorance of the world concern-
ing her, naturally excited intense curiosity to see how she would
act on this trying occasion; and there was a considerable assemblage at the palace notwithstanding the short notice which was
given. The first thing to be done was to teach her her lesson,
which, for this purpose, Melbourne had himself to learn. I gave
him the council papers, and explained all that was to be done,
and he went and explained all this to her. He asked her if she
would enter the room accompanied by the great officers of state,
but she said she would come in alone. When the Lords were
assembled the lord-president informed them of the King's death,
and suggested, as they were so numerous, that a few of them
should repair to the presence of the Queen and inform her of
the event, and that their lordships were assembled in consequence;
and accordingly the two royal dukes (Cumberland and Sussex,

the Duke of Cambridge being at Hanover), the two archbishops, the chancellor, and Melbourne went with him. The Queen received them in the adjoining room alone. As soon as they had returned the proclamation was read, the doors were thrown open, and the Queen entered accompanied by her two uncles, who advanced to meet her. She bowed to the Lords, took her seat, and then, in a clear, distinct, and audible voice, and without any appearance of fear or embarrassment, read the following declaration: 'The severe and afflicting loss which the nation has sustained by the death of his Majesty, my beloved uncle, has devolved upon me the duty of administering the government of this empire. This awful responsibility is imposed upon me so suddenly, and at so early a period of my life, that I should feel myself utterly oppressed by the burden, were I not sustained by the hope that Divine Providence, which has called me to this work, will give me strength for the performance of it, and that I shall find in the purity of my intentions, and in my zeal for the public welfare, that support and those resources which usually belong to a more mature age and to longer experience. I place my firm reliance upon the wisdom of Parliament and upon the loyalty and affection of my people. I esteem it also a peculiar advantage that I succeed a sovereign whose constant regard for the rights and liberties of his subjects, and whose desire to promote the amelioration of the laws and institutions of the country, have rendered his name the object of general attachment and veneration. Educated in England under the tender and enlightened care of a most affectionate mother, I have learned from my infancy to respect and love the constitution of my native country. It will be my unceasing study to maintain the reformed religion as by law established, securing at the same time, to all, the full enjoyment of religious liberty; and I shall steadily protect the rights and promote to the utmost of my power the happiness and welfare of all classes of my subjects.' She was quite plainly dressed, and in mourning. After she had read her speech and taken and signed the oath for the security of the Church of Scotland, the privy-councillors were sworn, the two dukes first by themselves, and as these two old men, her uncles, knelt before her, swearing allegiance and kissing her hand, I saw her blush up to the eyes, as if she felt the contrast between their civil and natural relations, and this was the only sign of emotion which she evinced. Her manner to them was very graceful and engaging: she kissed them both, and rose from her chair and moved towards the Duke of Sussex, who was furthest from her and too infirm to reach her."

The meeting of the council concluded by the cabinet ministers tendering to the Queen their seals of office, which she was graciously pleased to return, and they were then permitted to "kiss hands" on their reappointment. Arrangements had then to be made for the public proclamation, and the Queen appointed ten o'clock the next morning, June 21st, for the ceremony, which was to be at St. James's Palace.

On the following day, therefore, the young Queen, plainly dressed in deep mourning, with white tippet and cuffs, and a border of white lace under a small black bonnet, went thither, accompanied by her mother and ladies in attendance and with an escort of cavalry, and was there met by members of the royal family, cabinet ministers, and officers of the household. It must indeed have been a trying occasion, and one likely to flutter even steady nerves, so that there is little to wonder at in finding it recorded that when Lord Melbourne and Lord Lansdowne led her to the window of the presence-chamber overlooking

the court-yard, which was filled with heralds, pursuivants, robed officials, and "civic dignitaries," she looked fatigued and pale. There was an immense concourse of people, and on her appearance the cheering and acclamations were most enthusiastic.

The scene in the court-yard was very imposing, and as the sonorous tones of the herald gave emphasis to the solemn wishes that closed the proclamation, and the trumpets blared out, the assembly cheered, and the stirring notes of the band playing the national anthem burst forth, the young heart was too full. A sense of the great position, the solemn responsibility, smote upon the sovereign who was yet a child, and tears were on the youthful face as she turned with a pathetic look to the mother who thenceforth would have a difficult and sometimes a painful task to observe. Her daughter, as sovereign, must now be, in a certain sense, separated from her—no longer to obey, but officially, at anyrate, to command—while the duchess must avoid all that might seem to bear the appearance of undue influence, or could be construed into an assumption of power or authority in the counsels of her daughter. But the tears were there, for nothing ever could or did make Victoria other than truthful and natural, and it was a time when emotion stirred every breast. Those who were present saw and deeply sympathized; the sight of the weeping Queen caused other tears to flow in renewed springs of loyalty and love.

There was but one sentiment throughout the country with regard to the personal admiration and affection with which the young Queen was welcomed; and her abandonment of the name Alexandrina for her second name Victoria in assuming the royal title met with general approval, though it necessitated a change in the rolls documents of the House of Lords, and in the printed form of the oath to be presented to the members of the

House of Commons. It is true that apprehensions, which were not altogether without reason, existed among the older members of the Tory party. The Melbourne ministry was not likely to be subjected to such vicissitudes as it had suffered from the disaffection of the late sovereign, and as the Queen had, it was believed, been taught to look upon the Whigs as her friends, and had even been educated in Whig principles, the opposition could scarcely look forward to a return to power. Indeed, the Duke of Wellington is reported to have regarded the accession of the young Queen as a distinct disablement of himself and his colleagues, and he was represented to have said, " I have no small-talk, and Peel has no manners," a remark which we can only infer, from the gallantry of the speaker and his admiration for Peel, was made in a half jesting or satirical manner, for Wellington, like the rest of the world, looked with interested admiration on the girl sovereign.

The succession of a female to the throne severed the connection between the kingdoms of Britain and Hanover, which had been maintained ever since George I. reigned over both countries. Probably nobody in this country was sorry for the separation, for Hanover was of little advantage to us, and yet entailed considerable expenses, which had been paid out of English taxation. If any sentimental regret yet lingered in the minds of any, it may have been dispersed by the reflection that, by the death of William IV., it was the Duke of Cumberland who became King of Hanover, and that this country would be well rid of the man who had been accused, and not acquitted, of having conspired to set aside the succession of a queen, to the oath of allegiance to whom he was now the first to attach his signature.

On the 22d of June a royal message was laid on the table of

both houses of parliament, stating that in the judgment of her Majesty it was inexpedient that any new measures should be recommended for adoption beyond such as might be requisite for carrying on the public service from the close of the session to the meeting of the new parliament on the 15th of November; and the address was unanimously agreed to. Sir Robert Peel, in a speech of great eloquence, expressed the general sentiments of all parties when he said: "I will venture to say that there is no man who was present when her Majesty, at the age of eighteen years, first stepped from the privacy of domestic life to the discharge of the high functions which, on Tuesday last, she was called on to perform, without entertaining a confident expectation that she who could so demean herself was destined to a reign of happiness for her people and glory for herself. There is something which art cannot emulate and lessons cannot teach; and there was something in that demeanour which could only have been suggested by a high and generous nature. There was an expression of deep regret at the domestic calamity with which she had been visited, and of a deep and awful sense of the duties she was called upon to fulfil; there was a becoming and dignified modesty in all her actions, which could, as I have already observed, only have been dictated by a high and generous nature, brought up, no doubt, under the guidance of one to whose affection, care, and solicitude she is, and ought to be, deeply grateful. I trust I have said enough to convince the house that all persons, without reference to party distinctions, and in the oblivion, on this day, of all party differences, join in the expression of cordial condolence with her Majesty on the loss which she and the country have sustained, and in the most heart-felt wish that we are now at the commencement of a long, a prosperous, and a happy reign."

There was something peculiarly charming in the presence of this young and innocent girl—something perhaps almost bewildering in the notion that with her an entirely new relation would be established between the ministry and the crown. "If she had been my own daughter I could not have desired to see her perform her part better," said the Duke of Wellington bluntly, and probably forgetting in his paternal admiration his rather bitter impression that neither he nor Peel would be among her counsellors. Even Greville himself, the unsparing critic and recorder of the doings of his contemporaries, was under the same influence, for he says, "she appears to act with every sort of good taste and good feeling, as well as good sense; and so far as it has gone, nothing can be more favourable than the impression she has made, and nothing can promise better than her manner and conduct do."

A letter written, on the 26th of June, 1837, to the young Queen by her cousin, was as simple as it was judiciously unassuming. There is no suggestion in it of any expectation or mutual understanding.

"My dearest Cousin,—I must write you a few lines, to present you my sincerest felicitations on that great change which has taken place in your life.

"Now you are Queen of the mightiest land of Europe, in your hand lies the happiness of millions. May Heaven assist you, and strengthen you with its strength in that high but difficult task.

"I hope that your reign may be long, happy, and glorious, and that your efforts may be rewarded by the thankfulness and love of your subjects.

"May I pray you to think likewise sometimes of your cousins in Bonn, and to continue to them that kindness you favoured them with till now. Be assured that our minds are always with you. I will not be indiscreet and abuse your time. Believe me always, your Majesty's most obedient and faithful servant, ALBERT."

In Brussels, where the princes had been staying, the report that a marriage was contemplated between the young Queen of England and Prince Albert had been considerably talked about, and it was therefore desirable, as no definite proposals of the kind had been made, or were likely to be made for some time to come, that the princes should withdraw from public notice by making a quiet tour in Switzerland and Italy. This was quite in accordance with Prince Albert's views, and accordingly the vacation from college at Bonn was spent in a delightful journey, which ended by crossing the Simplon into Italy, and visits to the Italian lakes, Milan, and Venice.

At this time there had been no understanding whatever with regard to the relations between the Prince and the Queen. There was no engagement, no words of "courtship" had passed, and by the etiquette which rules sovereigns no actual proposal of marriage could be first directly made except by the Queen herself. It requires a moment's thought to enable youths and maidens not of royal rank to realize the difficulties of such a situation. Such communications as passed between the cousins were necessarily a little guarded, simple as they may have been. Amidst all the excitement of her accession to the throne and her approaching coronation, and even afterwards when she was learning to realize the privileges and responsibilities of royalty, the young Queen may secretly, and perhaps half unconsciously, have cherished the thought that among the distinguished students at the old university of Bonn, or on the route to some scene famous in history, or for natural beauty, or treasures of art, a young prince—who by nobility, personal beauty, high aims and attainments, and manly purity of life, was peer to any sovereign or potentate—bore her image in his heart and memory, but she could at present make no sign. Nor could he do more than remember that his fair young cousin, from an eminence almost perilous, might be looking forward to the day when it would be required of her to say whether the whispered hopes and anticipations of those who had been their best friends in infancy and childhood, should be realized. Both his position and his personal independence of character forbade his taking for granted that he would be regarded even as a suitor for the Queen's hand, but at the same time his loyal simplicity, his manly patience, and tranquillity of soul, enabled him to observe the sweet courtesies of cousinly regard without for a moment overstepping the bounds of princely etiquette. An alpine rose from the summit of the Rigi, a scrap of the writing of Voltaire obtained from an old servant of the philosopher when a visit was paid from Geneva to the house at Ferney, a book containing views of nearly all the places visited on the journey in Switzerland and Italy, and forming a small album, with the dates at which each place was visited in the prince's handwriting,[1] were tokens sent to show that in the midst of his travels he often thought of his young cousin.

The old palace of Kensington was no longer to be the home of the Duchess of Kent and the youthful sovereign; but their departure has been associated with a very happy reminiscence of the kindness of heart which has always characterized our sovereign Lady. The old soldier who had once been a servant of the Duke of Kent still lived in a cottage not far from the palace, and he and his family had been cared for and visited

[1] This album the Queen has always considered to be one of her greatest treasures.

by the princess. Two of that family, a boy and girl, had always been weak and ailing, and the boy had died, but the girl lived and was made happy by the visits of the princess. A few days after the Queen had quitted Kensington the clergyman of the parish called to see the invalid, and found her radiant with delight. When he inquired the reason she drew a little book from under her pillow, with smiles lighting the tears which filled her eyes, saying: "Look what the new Queen has sent me to-day;" and went on to explain that it was a book of Psalms, and that one of the Queen's ladies had brought it, with the message that though obliged to leave Kensington, the young Queen of England did not forget her: that the lines and figures in the margins of the book marked the dates of the days on which the Queen herself had been accustomed to read those particular psalms, and that the "book marker," with a little peacock worked on it, had been made by the Queen's own hands while she was still the Princess Victoria.

It has been recorded that on the death of William the Fourth the widowed Queen Adelaide had written to her niece saying that she desired to remain for a time at Windsor Castle, and that the young Queen immediately replied by a letter of condolence, in which she asked her to remain as long as she pleased and to consult only her own convenience. This reply was addressed to "the Queen of England," and a lady in attendance calling the attention of the young sovereign to this, said: "Your Majesty is now Queen of England;" to which the answer was, " I am aware of it, but the widowed Queen is not to be reminded of it by me." Whether this is to be regarded as an actual incident or not, it is to some extent supported by the fact that the queen-dowager was afterwards properly enough spoken of by her niece as "the Queen," and "our dear Queen Adelaide."

The suffering widowed queen had been present in the royal closet of the chapel of St. George's, Windsor, on the occasion of the funeral of the King, which took place on the evening of the 8th of July, attended by members of the royal family, the Duke of Sussex being the chief mourner. On the 13th, the Duchess of Kent and the young Queen took up their abode at Buckingham Palace, in which several alterations had now been made, and some new buildings added on the south.

The last drawing-room of the former reign had been held at St. James's Palace early in June; the first under the new régime was almost immediately after the arrival of her Majesty at Buckingham Palace. Of course the court was in deep mourning, the young sovereign wearing black crape with jet embroidery over black silk, the star of the order of the Garter alone relieving it; but the royal bearing and striking appearance of the *petite* but graceful figure, and the fair young face elicited the genuine admiration of those who attended in very large numbers to witness the girl Queen presiding over her court, and to introduce the *débutantes* who were in a flutter of excitement to be presented. But even more important duties had to be fulfilled.

On the 17th of July the Queen went in state to the House of Lords to dissolve parliament. The streets were crowded, and an enormous concourse of persons assembled to welcome the young sovereign with shouts and acclamations. On this her first appearance before her parliament her Majesty was superbly attired in a robe of white satin, the ribbon of the Garter across her shoulder. She wore a tiara of magnificent diamonds and a necklace of brilliants, the front of the dress being also adorned with brilliants of great lustre. She, of course, assumed the crimson robe of state on entering the

house. At the sound of the trumpets peers and peeresses rose
and remained standing till her Majesty ascended the throne, Lord
Melbourne standing near her and ready to instruct her in the
usual formalities, the first of which was to request those present
to be seated, which was done in a low but audible tone and with
courteous gesture. In addressing the assembly, including, of
course, members of the House of Commons present, her Majesty
said: "I have been anxious to seize the first opportunity of
meeting you, in order that I might repeat in person my cordial
thanks for your condolence upon the death of his late Majesty,
and for the expression of attachment and affection with which
you congratulated me upon my accession to the throne. I am
very desirous of renewing the assurances of my determination
to maintain the Protestant religion as established by law; to
secure to all the free exercise of the rights of conscience; to
protect the liberties and to promote the welfare of all classes of
the community. I rejoice that in ascending the throne I find
the country in amity with all foreign powers; and while I faithfully perform the engagements of the crown, and carefully watch
over the interests of my subjects, it will be the constant object
of my solicitude to maintain the blessings of peace." The
manner in which the young Queen read her speech—the perfect
self-possession, the clear and musical accents of a voice which,
though not loud, was of a quality that caused every syllable to
be heard throughout the assembly—caused admiration amount-
ing to enthusiasm. No less competent a judge than Miss
Fanny Kemble afterwards wrote: "The serene serious sweetness of the candid brow and clear soft eyes gave dignity to the
girlish countenance; while the want of height only added to the
effect of extreme youth of the round but slender person and
gracefully moulded hands and arms. The Queen's voice was

exquisite, nor have I ever heard any spoken words more musical in their gentle distinctness than ' My Lords and Gentlemen,' which broke the breathless silence of the illustrious assembly, whose gaze was rivetted on that fair flower of royalty. The enunciation was as perfect as the intonation was melodious."

The court had returned to Buckingham Palace on the first days of November, and the Queen had accepted an invitation to dine with the lord-mayor and corporation of the city of London at the Guildhall on the 9th. This was the first visit of her Majesty to the city, and preparations were made for a magnificent reception. In spite of inclement weather and the murky atmosphere of a November day, a great crowd lined the route from Buckingham Palace to Cheapside. The Queen, who rode in the state carriage attended by the mistress of the robes and the master of the horse (Lord Albemarle, was greeted with continued acclamation, and her appearance elicited hearty admiration. She was attired in a very beautiful dress of pink satin shot with silver, and her fair hair shone beneath the wreath-shaped tiara which became her so well. The bells of the churches pealed forth, and the flags and banners that decorated the streets, the crimson hangings, green boughs, and flowers that adorned many balconies and windows, together with the coloured lamps formed into devices for an illumination at night, gave an aspect of warmth and freshness even on that November day. Conspicuous, because of his well-known face and figure, and made more noticeable by the repeated bursts of cheering that greeted his appearance, was the Duke of Wellington, who received these thunders of applause with his customary salute of two fingers to the brim of his hat. His usual calm imperturbable smile and a twinkle of the eye showed a certain sense of humour as well as of pleasure as he recognized the change of front presented to him by the public since he was hissed during the Reform Bill days.

At Temple Bar, which then stood with its massy gates marking the boundary between the City and the Strand, the lord-mayor, sheriffs, and aldermen had mounted horses brought from the artillery barracks at Woolwich, each horse being led by the soldier to which it belonged. On the approach of the Queen the lord-mayor dismounted, and, holding the civic sword of state, awaited her Majesty on the south side of the gate. The royal carriage stopped at the gateway in the rain while the chief magistrate delivered the keys to her Majesty, who at once graciously returned them amidst the cheers of the people, who filled the streets and the windows, from attic to basement, and the seats and scaffoldings erected for the occasion. The lord-mayor then took his place immediately before the royal carriage, the other civic authorities formed in procession, and went on to the Guildhall, where they arrived at about five o'clock. The lord-mayor assisted her Majesty to alight at the gate, and the lady-mayoress and the attendant civic maids of honour stood to receive her. The council chamber, converted into a drawing-room, and the royal boudoir, were sumptuously decorated in crimson, gold, and white satin. The Queen was attended by her mother the Duchess of Kent, the Duchess of Cambridge, and the Duchess of Gloucester.

In the drawing-room a loyal address from the city of London was read by the recorder, and fitly responded to by the youthful Queen, who, on dinner being announced, was conducted to the grand old hall by the lord-mayor and lady-mayoress—Sir John and Lady Cowan—who stood on either side of her Majesty as she took her seat at the royal table, till she requested them to be seated at their own table, where they were to preside over the

company, which included cabinet ministers, foreign ambassadors, and many of the nobility, as well as city dignitaries and
members of the common council.   All eyes, all hearts were
directed to that small, slight figure in the central chair of state—
the child that so many remembered not long before, riding or
running in the gardens at Kensington—now the girl Queen of
a vast empire, and resplendent in the sheen of the diamonds
that flashed on her brow and neck, and the jewel and "George"
that sparkled from her shoulder.   The Duchesses of Kent,
Cambridge, Gloucester, and Sutherland (mistress of the robes),
the Dukes of Sussex and Cambridge, and her Majesty's two
cousins Prince George and Princess Augusta of Cambridge, sat
on either side of her at the royal table.   The banquet was as
profuse as civic banquets are, but there was an air of mingled
state and sentiment pervading the assembly, and not till after
the "*Non nobis, Domine*" was sung, and a flourish of trumpets
had heralded the announcement that the lord-mayor gave the
toast of "Our most gracious Sovereign Queen Victoria," did
the enthusiasm of the company find voice.   The national
anthem was sung with vehement emphasis, and the Queen
rose and bowed with evident gratification.   Then the trumpets
blared again and the common crier announced that her most
gracious Majesty the Queen gave the toast of "The Lord-mayor
and Prosperity to the City of London."   A selection of music
followed, and then the final toast by the lord-mayor, "The
Royal Family."   At half-past eight, after partaking of tea in the
drawing-room, the Queen left the hall, accompanied to her
carriage by the lord-mayor, to whom she said, shaking hands
with him as he stood at the step, "I assure you, my lord-
mayor, that I have been most highly gratified."   At the end
of Cheapside, amidst a strange gleamy mist, composed partly of

fog and partly of the beams of the illuminations, the cortége stopped for a few minutes to listen to the national anthem sung by the Harmonic Society accompanied by a band of wind-instruments, and followed by multitudinous cheers the royal party returned to Buckingham Palace. The value of the plate used at the Guildhall on the occasion of this banquet was valued at from £300,000 to £400,000.

On the lord-mayor, Sir John Cowan, a baronetcy was conferred, and on the sheriffs, Mr. John Carroll and Mr. Moses Montefiore, the honour of knighthood, the latter gentleman being the first member of the Jewish community who had received that distinction.

At the general election, which quickly followed the dissolution of parliament, the Whigs said a great deal too much of the influence which their party exercised in the councils of the young Queen, and this had the effect not only of weakening their cause, but of discrediting the ministry and even the Queen herself, by the charge of political favouritism and undue authority conceded to Lord Melbourne as the adviser of the sovereign. It was undoubtedly true that the prime-minister had from the time of her accession been the trusted adviser and instructor of the Queen, and there was perhaps no man more capable of imparting a knowledge of political and state affairs in a manner at once unprejudiced and disinterested,—no man who, to the experience which comes of age and long acquaintance with statesmanship, united more of that ease and grace of manner which takes from serious counsel the appearance of dictation, and from important instruction the air of authoritative teaching. He was no strenuous politician, and therefore many solemn doctrinaires abused him for being indifferent to what they regarded as the best interests of the country. He hated "humbug" and pretence, and therefore fell into what was, if not pretence, an affectation of *laisser faire*. The man who, while receiving a deputation, would balance a sofa-cushion in his hands, or blow at the feather of a quill pen, though diligently listening all the time, would not be likely to be credited with profound political convictions. Even his shrewd common-sense would be very liable to be misinterpreted, when, after considering some question which his colleagues thought demanded immediate attention, but which he regarded as unnecessary or premature, he would say: "Can't we leave it alone?" If there was one thing about which he was really indifferent it was his own exaltation. He had little of the pride of place or power, and simply laughed away the Queen's proposal to bestow upon him the blue ribbon of the Garter as a mark of her gratitude. "A garter may attach to us somebody of consequence whom nothing else would reach," he replied; "but what would be the use of my taking it? I cannot bribe myself!" Acute observers like Sydney Smith and Lord Lansdowne saw and said that his appearance of indifference was only assumed, that he was really a man with a capacity for hard work, but one who offered, by his pretence of levity, a kind of practical sarcasm on the solemnity of Peel and the volcanic energy of Brougham. Even in his accomplishments—and he was a man not only of elegant and courtly manners but of great culture—he assumed a dilettante air, while those who knew him best were aware that he was a hard reader, his studies extending to an unusual knowledge of the works of the fathers of the Church.

Before Lord Melbourne had, at fifty-eight years of age, given up the greater part of the time left him for rest or leisure from his duties as prime-minister to the instruction and friendly guardianship of his young sovereign, there had been constant complaints and suspicions about the supposed influence of the Baroness Lehzen, who for a short time acted as private secretary as well as lady in attendance on the Queen. After she had retired from that position, there were mutterings which grew into open accusations of the interference and authority of Baron Stockmar, and of the influence which, it was hinted, he exercised not only on the Queen, but on Melbourne and the government. That this charge was without foundation Melbourne knew well enough, and he sometimes said so in unmistakable terms; but the declaration that " German " influence and Whig monopoly had joined to ruin the country, made a strong party cry at the time of the election. It must be granted, also, that the opposition had much reason for the animosity which they displayed, in the conduct of some of the ministerialists, who went to the hustings with the swagger of being supported by the favour of the young Queen, and, as their opponents said, "placarded with her Majesty's name, as though they expected the Whig ministry, with Melbourne as premier, to be maintained in perpetual authority."

At this time, however, though there were inimical influences at work, and her uncle the King of Hanover was already writing to his correspondents in England letters that were offensive, and were soon to be followed by others that were malignant, there was little or no diminution of the exuberant loyalty which was manifested for the Queen. It may be said, too, that whatever may have been the influence of Melbourne's kindly and unselfish devotion, it would have been futile even for him to have endeavoured to reduce the young sovereign to a cipher. From the very first she set herself assiduously, not only as far as possible to control her own household and to establish the order of the daily observances and recreations, but

to the business of state, and to the understanding of all that
was required from her, so that she would refuse to sign a
state document or a paper of any importance until she understood not only its meaning and intention, but its probable consequences. It is even said that on one occasion she insisted
on delaying to place her name to a paper that was considered
to be immediately important because Lord Melbourne had
represented that it was "expedient;" her reply being that she
had been taught that anything might be right or wrong, but
she could not understand expediency in such a serious matter,
and must first, as far as possible, thoroughly acquaint herself
with the meaning of what she was asked to sign.

The results of the election were that the former government
returned to power with a small majority and considerably
weakened in reputation. This, however, did not affect the
loyalty of the opposition, and when parliament had reassembled
and on the 12th of December the Queen asked the House
of Commons for an addition to the provision made for the
Duchess of Kent, the income of the duchess was increased
from £22,000 to £30,000 a year. There was some debate
over the proposals made for the civil list. The Queen had
placed unreservedly in the hands of parliament the hereditary
revenues transferred to the public by the late King, and it was
pointed out, while former sovereigns had inherited considerable
property, Victoria had not even the revenues of Hanover, which
had now become a separate kingdom. Eventually the sum of
£385,000 was voted as the annual income of the sovereign, of
which £60,000 was the amount for the privy-purse.

It may be said of the Queen, that the healthy tone of mind
and body which had resulted from her previous education preserved her from many mistakes which might have been serious.

Her position was a very difficult one, and only a strong conscientious desire to do right, and to fulfil even the most trying obligations of the high station to which she had been called, would have enabled her to enter so thoroughly into the business of the state. Yet she retained that simple buoyancy and love of fun which belonged to her youth. She had the happy faculty of working when she worked and playing when she played; and though some slight records of the ordinary daily life of the royal household seem to point to the fact that the routine was rather formal and sometimes a little dreary, there is a certain pathetic interest in imagining the girl Queen arranging the proprieties and the amusements, the duties and recreations of the royal establishment.

One paramount duty was not forgotten. Directly the civil list was settled and her Majesty knew how much money she had to spend, she had said to Lord Melbourne, "My father's debts must be paid;" and so heartily did the daughter mean what she said, that within the following year she had paid them. In the next twelvemonths the obligations incurred by the Duchess of Kent during the years that she had held an onerous and difficult position were also discharged.

The opening of parliament—her first parliament- by the Queen had been the occasion of another great demonstration of loyalty and attachment as she went in state through the streets, and the concourse of people assembled at and near the approaches to Westminster was as great as that which had awaited the prorogation. Again her Majesty performed with admirable self-possession the formal duties of royalty, and in a clear and audible voice repeated after the lord-chancellor the declaration which involves a solemn denial of those tenets of the Church of Rome which are opposed to the belief of English Protestants.

There were many topics of importance to engage the attention of the legislature, for there was much distress in the manufacturing districts and many signs of political agitation, which took the form of what was called Chartism, and a demand for the repeal of the taxes on food imported from abroad. There were symptoms of serious troubles in Lower Canada, where disturbances had arisen from the opposition offered by the Canadian legislature to resolutions carried in the House of Commons in March, 1836, declining to make the council of Lower Canada elective, continuing the charter of the Land Company, and authorizing the provincial government, independent of the legislature, to appropriate the money in the treasury for the administration of justice and the support of the civil government. Early in the year Lord John Russell had pointed out that since October, 1832, no provision had been made by the legislators of Lower Canada for defraying the charges of the administration of justice or for the support of civil government in the province. The arrears amounted to a very large sum, which the House of Assembly refused to vote, and at the same time demanded an elective legislative council and entire control over all branches of the government.

Thus the political and social atmosphere was less serene than might have been desired at a time when the youth and inexperience of the sovereign needed the support of a stronger ministry than that which was accused of clinging to office by virtue of the prime-minister having become mentor to the throne; but the popularity of the Queen herself continued both in parliament and in the country. The royal speech had concluded with the words: " In meeting this parliament, the first that has been elected under my authority, I am anxious to declare my confidence in your loyalty and wisdom. The early age at which

I am called to the sovereignty of this kingdom renders it a more imperative duty that under Divine Providence I should place my reliance upon your cordial co-operation and upon the love and affection of all my people."

That reliance was not misplaced. Notwithstanding the seething of public opinion and the signs of coming political conflict, the whole nation was more immediately concerned with the preparations for the coronation, which was to take place on the 28th of June in the following year. It was not only that the ceremony was to be gorgeous and imposing, and the signs of rejoicing splendid and appropriate; but the national sentiment, which had been deeply moved at the accession of a young and innocent girl to the throne, was maintained and even increased by all that was known of her. The expenses of the coronation were to be limited to £70,000, a considerable portion of which sum was expended on preparations and appointments for the ceremony at Westminster Abbey, to which, with the other most important ceremony in the life of her Majesty—her marriage— we may well devote a separate if a brief chapter.

<h1 style="text-align:center">CHAPTER III.</h1>

For many weeks before the day fixed for the coronation all kinds of preparations were being made to celebrate the occasion. Coronation jewelry, ribbons, and ornaments of every kind were manufactured, medals were struck, portraits were engraved, pictures painted, concerts rehearsed, festivities organized. A new issue of coin with the Queen's image and superscription was to be made from the Mint, and in every town and shire there was to be feasting of rich and poor. On every cliff around the coast, on every hill where a beacon had flashed in olden time, a signal was to flame; in the London parks and on provincial fields and commons there were to be displays of fireworks; and in the streets of the metropolis, of old historic cities, or of modern towns that had grown round mills and factories, the windows of shops and houses were to be illuminated with wreaths and crowns and mottoes formed of coloured lamps or jets of gas with the letters V. R. ablaze at every corner, and even in quiet thoroughfares or sequestered by-ways a candle in every window-pane.

In place of the royal banquet in Westminster Hall, which had formed a feature of previous coronation observances, there was to be a grander and more imposing procession for the gratification of the people who would assemble to see the maiden Queen and her splendid cortége going to and returning from the Abbey. The banquet for the few was to give place to the spectacle for the many; and Dymocke, the hereditary royal champion, was no more to fling down his gauntlet on the floor of the great hall and challenge all the world to gainsay the right of the royal claimant of the crown.

It is difficult to convey any adequate impression of the magnificence of the spectacle in Westminster Abbey on the occasion. The superb and ancient pile is in the form of a cross, the aisles from the royal entrance running west and east and the transepts north and south. The royal entrance led beneath the organ gallery to a "theatre" or raised platform twenty-four feet wide, and with a smaller platform on either side for those who were to take part in the ceremony. In the centre of the building immediately under the lantern was a raised dais or platform ascended by four steps covered with claret-coloured drapery and embroidered in gold. On this facing the altar stood the throne, or rather chair of state, on which her Majesty was to receive the homage of the vast assembly. It was a richly carved and gilded chair covered with crimson velvet and gold embroidery and emblazoned with the royal arms, and in front of it was a footstool similarly decorated. The galleries were so arranged that, rising like a vast amphitheatre, a view could be obtained of the general effect even from the loftiest of them, and that general effect was magnificent beyond description, for the decorations, sumptuous as they were, accorded well with the architectural character of the grand old building, which, it should be remembered, was not at that time crowded with the incongruous monuments and the aggressively prominent sculpture that has of late years tended to depreciate its matchless proportions and to distract the eye from its exquisite architectural beauty.

If the scene in the Abbey was designed to be grand and

impressive, the pageant of the state procession was well calculated to delight the vast multitude of people who by daybreak began to wend their way towards the parks, and to occupy the line of route from Buckingham Palace, up Constitution Hill, and along Piccadilly, St. James' Street, Pall Mall, Cockspur Street, Whitehall, and Parliament Street. It was computed that to the London population were to be added 400,000 persons who had come from the provinces and foreign countries to witness the spectacle. At seventeen minutes past three in the morning a salute of twenty-one guns, fired from the Tower of London, had heralded the dawn of that auspicious day, and though for some hours the skies looked threatening, and rain occasionally fell, nothing seemed to damp the ardour of the crowds that thronged the streets on foot or in every variety of vehicle. By six o'clock the thoroughfares mentioned were closely lined by expectant crowds, and every window, balcony, and platform was soon packed with those who had secured places; while at many private mansions, banks, and public buildings, and at the principal club-houses, great preparations had been made, not only for seeing the pageant, but for dispensing hospitality to invited guests. The Green Park, the Mall, and the inclosure of St. James' Park were thronged. At eight o'clock the band of the Life Guards played the national anthem, and soon afterwards the first carriages of the procession prepared to take their places. Equerries, trumpeters, and a squadron of Life Guards led the way, followed first by the carriages of the foreign ambassadors resident in this country, and next by those of the ambassadors and ministers-extraordinary who had come to represent foreign powers on the august occasion. They took precedence according to the date at which they had made known their arrival in England; and first was the ambassador from the Sultan—next being the famous old warrior, Marshal Soult, Duke of Dalmatia, who had come to represent France. As the front of the pageant moved on through the closely-packed ranks of the people, a great shout arose and continued—a shout of hearty applause and generous welcome of the soldier who had come to visit us, no longer as a foe, but as a comrade of our own victorious duke. The white head bowed repeatedly in courteous recognition of these greetings, the rugged war-worn face was bright with smiles, and thereafter Marshal Soult was a firm friend of French and English alliance.

After the ambassadors came the elder members of the royal family. They were but few now, and the Princess Augusta, who was seventy years of age, was unable to be present, while the Princess Sophia was in such weak health that she feared the exertion and excitement of the occasion. The King and Queen of Hanover (Duke and Duchess of Cumberland) and the Princess Elizabeth of Hesse-Homburg were also absent. The carriages of the royal family and their attendants were drawn each by six horses, and accompanied by an escort of Life Guards. That of the Duchess of Kent came first, and the mother of the Queen was received with unbounded enthusiasm and applause, the police and troops having at some points to restrain the front ranks of the crowd from surging round the carriage in an attempt to shake hands with the duchess. The Duchess of Gloucester came next, and was followed by the Duke and Duchess of Cambridge and the Duke of Sussex, who was received with abundant manifestations of popular favour. Then came a procession of twelve royal carriages, each drawn by six horses, and conveying ladies of the bed-chamber, maids of honour, principal officers of the household, and her Majesty's suite, preceded by equerries, a regiment of the household brigade, the Queen's bargemaster and forty-eight watermen, and followed by a squadron of Life Guards, the mounted band of the household brigade, and the brilliant military staff and officers, royal huntsmen and foresters, horses from the royal stables, decked in gay trappings, and led by grooms; the knight marshal, with his marshals, and yeomen mounted and on foot. The state coach was drawn by eight cream-coloured horses, and a yeoman of the guard walked at each wheel, and two footmen at each door; Viscount Combermere (gold stick) and the Earl of Ilchester, captain of the yeomen, riding on either side. With the Queen were the Duchess of Sutherland, mistress of the robes; the Earl of Albemarle, master of the horse; and the Duke of Buccleugh, captain-general of the Archer Guard. The pageant closed with an escort of six squadrons of Life Guards.

It was ten o'clock when the Queen entered her state carriage at Buckingham Palace, and two robust-looking sailors, who had charge of the flagstaff on the top of the Marble Arch at the entrance, set the royal ensign flying in the clear summer air as a mighty shout went up from the dense multitude. The clouds had dispersed, the sun shone out as with jubilant welcome, and the day became an example of what has since come to be known as "Queen's weather."

Amidst continuous outburst of cheering and acclamation the state carriage reached the west door of Westminster Abbey at half-past eleven o'clock. The great officers of state, the noblemen bearing the regalia, the Archbishops of Canterbury and York, the Bishops of Bangor, Lincoln, and Winchester, carrying the patina, the chalice, and the Bible, and the Bishops of Bath and Wells and of Durham, were there to receive her Majesty as she entered, all the bands playing the national anthem as she alighted, and her arrival being signalled by

the firing of a gun. The ambassadors and other distinguished
personages had already been conducted to their seats before
the Queen appeared from the robing-room, and the whole
scene presented by that great and brilliant assembly amidst the
superb decorations, which, with all their wealth of colour, were
subordinated, toned, and harmonized by the "dim religious light"
and the marvellous architecture of the gray old Abbey, was so
magnificent that even oriental visitors and others, who were
accustomed to witness the most splendid spectacles, paused to
gaze around them with solemn wonder and admiration before
they were conducted to their seats. The dais of cloth of gold
bearing the throne; the altar, with its grand communion service
of gold plate; and the chair of Saint Edward, or King Edward's
chair,[1] which stood within the altar rails, were objects of the
greatest interest.

At a little after twelve o'clock the gorgeous procession
entered the choir amidst a profound silence which had
succeeded to a burst of acclamation. First came the dean
and prebendaries of Westminster, and then followed officers
at arms,—the chief officers of the royal household, the
lord privy-seal, the lord-president, and the lord-chancellor
of Ireland. An officer from the Jewel Office bore upon a
velvet cushion a sword for the offering at the altar, and the
ruby ring which was to be used in the ceremony. Next
came the Archbishops of Canterbury, York, and Armagh, with
the lord-chancellor; and then the princesses of the blood
royal, the Duchess of Cambridge, the Duchess of Kent, and
the Duchess of Gloucester, in robes of state of purple velvet,
and wearing circlets of gold on their heads, their coronets

[1] The chair in which the Scottish kings had been crowned before Edward I. brought it from
Scotland in 1296.

carried by viscounts, their trains borne by noble ladies-in-waiting. Then came the bearers of the regalia: St. Edward's staff carried by the Duke of Roxburgh, the golden spurs by Lord Byron, the sceptre royal by the Duke of Cleveland, the sword of justice or temporality by the Marquis of Westminster, the sword of mercy by the Duke of Devonshire, another sword by the Duke of Sutherland. The lord great chamberlain of England — Lord Willoughby d'Eresby — preceded the royal Dukes of Cambridge and Sussex, — whose coronets and trains were borne by gentlemen of title, — the Duke of Norfolk, earl marshal of England, with his staff of office, and on either side Viscount Melbourne bearing the sword of state, and the Duke of Wellington, high constable of England, with staff and field-marshal's baton. The Duke of Richmond bearing the sceptre and dove, lord high steward the Duke of Hamilton bearing the crown — which has been named St. Edward's crown after the ancient one — and the Duke of Somerset bearing the orb, were followed by the bishops with the patina, Bible, and chalice. Then the Queen entered the choir wearing a royal robe of crimson velvet and ermine bordered with gold lace, the collars of the orders of the Garter, Bath, Thistle, and St. Patrick, and on her head a circlet of gold. Between the two bishops, who walked at either side, and the accompanying gentlemen-at-arms, she moved slowly but with graceful and dignified mien, and her face was animated and radiant.

Her Majesty's train was borne by eight ladies who even in that assembly were distinguished for grace and beauty: Lady Adelaide Paget, Lady Frances Cowper, Lady Anne Wentworth Fitzwilliam, Lady Mary Grimston, Lady Caroline Gordon Lennox, Lady Mary Talbot, Lady Catherine Stanhope, and Lady Louisa Jenkinson. The Duchess of Sutherland as mistress of the robes, followed by Lady Lansdowne first lady of the bed-chamber, and the other ladies of the bed-chamber, and a bevy of maids of honour, came next. The brilliant procession, in which noble ladies, youthful pages, and gentlemen-at-arms attended to bear trains and carry coronets, and were many of them attired in gorgeous and picturesque costume, closed with the captain-general of the Royal Scottish Archer Guard and a following of officers of the yeomen of the guard and gentlemen-at-arms and their attendants.

During the procession, when every eye had been fixed on the Queen, the anthem " I was glad " was performed, and then the Westminster boys chanted *Vivat Victoria Regina.* The peers, peeresses, lords, and ladies who were not further engaged in the ceremony took their seats, and her Majesty moved towards the space between the throne of homage and the altar, where a faldstool had been placed before a chair. She then knelt down and after a few moments of silent prayer took her seat in the chair.

The rather intricate ceremonial commenced with " The Recognition." The Archbishop of Canterbury advanced to the Queen with the lord-chancellor, the lord-chamberlain, the lord high constable, and the earl marshal, preceded by the deputy garter, and said: " Sirs, I here present unto you Queen Victoria the undoubted Queen of this realm, therefore all you who are come this day to do homage, are you willing to do the same?" This was answered by the vast assembly with a loud cry of " God save Queen Victoria!" The archbishop, turning to the north, south, and west, repeated " God save Queen Victoria!" the Queen turning at the same time.

The patina, chalice, and Bible were placed on the altar

by the bishops who carried them in the procession. The Archbishop of Canterbury and the bishops who were to read the litany put on their copes. The Queen, attended by the Bishops of Bath and Wells and Durham, and the great officers of state, and noblemen carrying the regalia, advanced to the altar, knelt upon the crimson velvet cushion, and made her first offering of an altar-cloth of gold, which had been brought by an officer of the wardrobe and was handed to her Majesty by the great chamberlain. The archbishop placed it upon the altar, and the Queen then handed to him an ingot of gold of one pound weight, which had been brought by the treasurer of the household. This the archbishop placed in the oblation basin.

After prayer by the archbishop the regalia, except the sword, were laid on the altar, the great officers of state, except the lord-chamberlain, took up their respective places on the dais near the chair of state.

After the singing of the Sanctus the communion service was read by the Archbishop of Canterbury, the Bishop of Rochester reading the epistle, and the Bishop of Carlisle the gospel. The sermon was preached by the Bishop of London from the 31st verse of the 34th chapter of the 2d Book of Chronicles, "And the king stood in his place, and made a covenant before the Lord, to walk after the Lord, and to keep his commandments, and his testimonies, and his statutes, with all his heart, and with all his soul, to perform the words of the covenant which are written in this book."

Next came the administration of the coronation oath by the Archbishop of Canterbury, who advanced, and, standing before the Queen, asked, "Madam, is your Majesty willing to take the oath?" to which the Queen replied "I am willing."

Her Majesty then solemnly promised to govern the people of the United Kingdom and the dominions belonging to it according to the statutes in Parliament agreed on and the respective laws and customs of the same; to her power to cause law and justice, in mercy, to be executed in all her judgments; to the utmost of her power to maintain the laws of God, the true profession of the gospel, and the Protestant reformed religion established by law; and to maintain and preserve the settlement of the united Church of England and Ireland, and its doctrine, worship, discipline, and government as by law established within England and Ireland and the territories thereunto belonging, and to preserve to the bishops and clergy of England and Ireland, and the churches there committed to their charge, such rights and privileges as by law do or shall appertain to them.

Her Majesty, attended by her supporters and the lord great chamberlain, the sword of state being carried before her, went to the altar, and kneeling, laid her right hand upon the Gospels tendered to her by the archbishop, kissed the book, and signed a transcript of the oath. She then kneeling upon the faldstool, the choir sang the *Veni, Creator, Spiritus.* After preparatory prayer and the anthem "Zadok the Priest," &c., there followed the anointing. The Queen, having been disrobed of her crimson robe by the mistress of the robes, sat in the ancient chair of King Edward, four knights of the Garter, the Dukes of Buccleugh and Rutland, and the Marquesses of Anglesea and Exeter, holding a pall of cloth of gold. The Dean of Westminster poured some oil from the ampulla into the anointing spoon, and the archbishop anointed her Majesty on the head and hands, marking them in the form of a cross, saying, "Be thou anointed with holy oil as kings, priests, and prophets were anointed, and as Solomon was anointed king by Zadok the priest and Nathan the prophet, so be you anointed, blessed, and consecrated Queen over this people, whom the Lord your God hath given you to rule and govern." After the invocation, the Queen knelt during the prayer and blessing. When she had resumed her seat, the golden spurs were taken from the altar by the dean and handed to the lord-chamberlain, and by him presented to her Majesty, who returned them to be laid again on the altar. Viscount Melbourne next delivered the sword of state to be laid on the altar by the archbishop, who repeated the prayer, " Hear our prayers, O Lord, we beseech thee, and so direct and support thy servant Victoria," &c. Then, accompanied by the other bishops, he gave the sword into the Queen's right hand, saying, " Receive this kingly sword, brought now from the altar of God and delivered to you by the hands of us, the servants and bishops of God, though unworthy." Then followed an exordium, and the sword having been restored to the altar, Lord Melbourne, according to ancient custom, redeemed it for a hundred shillings, and carried it unsheathed during the rest of the ceremony.

The Queen, when standing, was invested by the dean with the imperial mantle or declaration robe of cloth of gold, the Lord Great Chamberlain fastening the clasps. When she was again seated, the archbishop handed to her the orb with a suitable exordium before its return to the altar. Then followed the " investiture *per annulum et baculum*, by the ring and sceptre, the archbishop receiving the ruby ring and placing it on the fourth finger of the Queen's right hand. The dean then brought the sceptre with the cross and that with the dove and delivered them to the archbishop; and the Duke of Norfolk as Lord of the Manor of Worksop, left his seat to perform his ancient suit and service of presenting to her Majesty a glove, embroidered with the arms of Howard, for her right hand. This her Majesty put on, and the duke stood by her to support her right arm and to hold the sceptre. The archbishop first delivered the sceptre of the cross, or royal sceptre, and then the sceptre of the dove, or rod of equity.

The actual "Coronation" followed, and this was really the grandest part of the ceremonial. The archbishop, placing the crown upon the altar, offered up a prayer to Almighty God on behalf of the Queen, that she might be crowned with all princely virtues—then, accompanied by the other prelates, he advanced towards the Queen, and receiving the crown from the Dean of Westminster, placed it reverently upon her head. At this moment, from every part of the grand edifice arose the cry "God save the Queen!"—a multitudinous shout accompanied by acclamations, the waving of hats and handkerchiefs;—trumpets blared out, drums beat, the peers and peeresses put on their coronets, the bishops their hats, the kings-at-arms their crowns, and the guns at the park and the Tower boomed out their signals. It would be difficult to imagine any scene more grand and imposing. Almost at the moment of the crown being placed on the head of the Queen a broad brilliant stream or ray of sunlight from one of the windows fell upon her and lighted up the jewels of the imperial diadem and the fair young face beneath it. Earlier in the ceremony, that one apparently small figure, made to look smaller by the long-trained robe, the surrounding pageantry, and the accompanying attendants, had been greeted with acclamations, not unmingled with tears. "She looked almost like a child," said one spectator, who noticed that those near him were affected as he was. But at the moment when the crown was placed upon her head, and that great burst of sound proclaimed her Queen indeed, amidst shouts and fanfares and psalms of rejoicing, the princess herself was visibly weeping,

and had to summon all her courage—or may we say the recollection of the sustaining goodness of God—to preserve her self-
control. For a few seconds, it is said, she looked wistfully at
her mother, who was herself so overcome with emotion as to be
sobbing audibly, but in a few moments the young Queen had
regained composure, perhaps because she could see expressions
of sympathy, admiration, and affection in every face.

The Bible was next taken from the altar and presented to
the Queen by the archbishop, to whom she restored it, that he
might place it on the altar again. His grace then pronounced
the benediction, the other bishops and the peers responding,
and then, turning to the people, pronounced the invocation,
"And the same Lord God Almighty grant," &c., after which the
"*Te Deum*" was sung by the choir, and her Majesty removed to
the chair of recognition, the two bishops (her supporters), the
great officers of state, and the noblemen who had borne the
regalia, attending her. The Queen then ascended the dais for
the enthronement, the archbishop, bishops, and peers around her
lifting her into the throne of state. After the exhortation
"Stand firm and hold fast," &c., and having delivered the sceptre
to the Lord of the Manor of Worksop and the Duke of Richmond, her Majesty received the homage of the peers, which was
an imposing and interesting part of the august ceremony, having
something of a feudal character. The Archbishop of Canterbury
himself first knelt and did homage for himself and the other
lords spiritual, who knelt around him, repeated the words after
him, and succeeded him in kissing hands. The Dukes of Sussex
and Cambridge followed, the Duke of Sussex saying the words,
which were repeated by the Duke of Cambridge as follows:—
"I do become your liegeman of life and limb and of earthly
worship: and faith and truth I will bear unto you, to live and die,

against all manner of folks. So help me God." The royal dukes each touched the crown upon the Queen's head and kissed her on the left cheek, and it was afterwards said that the Duke of Sussex, a man of very impressionable nature and then in infirm health, was so much affected that he could not control his emotion, and was assisted from the dais by peers in attendance. The other peers made their homage kneeling, the senior peer in each degree pronouncing the words, saying after him, and each of the same degree touching the crown and kissing her Majesty's hand. The Duke of Wellington, Earl Grey, and Lord Melbourne were loudly cheered as they ascended to the dais to perform the homage. While this ceremony was going on, the anthem, "This is the day," was sung, and the Earl of Surrey, treasurer of the household, threw silver coronation medals about the choir and lower galleries, and a decided scramble ensued, in which some of those present, including noble ladies, maids of honour, and pages, joined with such eagerness that some of the more sedate and punctilious onlookers were a little scandalized. This, however, was not the only incongruous incident of this part of the ceremony. Among those barons who came to pay homage was Lord Rolle, an old nobleman who had received George III., the Queen's grandfather, at his house in Devonshire, and had made that occasion one of great display. He was now more than eighty years of age, but though physically infirm, full of courage and loyalty, so that he made a brave attempt to mount the steps of the throne, supported by two noblemen to assist him, for he was a large heavy man. He had nearly reached the royal footstool when, either stumbling or missing his footing, he slipped through the hands of his supporters and fell, rolling over and over to the bottom step, where he lay coiled up in his robes till he was lifted up, when he tried again and again to mount the steps. Meantime the Queen was much concerned at his efforts, and was seen to speak to Lord Melbourne, who stood at her shoulder, and on his bowing an affirmative she rose, and with a gentle smile held out her hand to the brave old man, who was excused from touching the crown. He was not hurt, and took his misadventure with the utmost good-humour, which was perhaps the reason that some foreigners present took for fact the representation of some unscrupulous jester, who said that the noble lord had only been observing a custom relating to feudal tenure, by which he held his title of Lord *Rolle*. Another version of the story attributed this jest to his lordship's own daughter, who was present.

The "homage" having been completed, the Queen prepared to receive the communion, and removing her crown, which was held by the Lord Chamberlain, knelt at the altar, and after returning to the archbishop the chalice and patina to be placed there, made the second offering of a purse of gold. Her Majesty, after receiving the sacrament, at once returned to the throne, where she again held the sceptre, remaining there till the end of the communion service, the anthem " Hallelujah! the Lord God omnipotent reigneth," the final prayers, and the blessing. Then attended, as before, with the swords carried before her, she went through the south door into St. Edward's Chapel, amidst the music of the organ and the orchestra. She delivered the sceptre with the dove to the archbishop, who laid it on the altar. She was then disrobed of her imperial robe of state and arrayed in her royal robe of purple velvet. With the swords carried before her the Queen went to the west door of the Abbey, the sceptre with the cross in her right hand, the orb in her left. Near the door the swords and the portions of the regalia which had not been again placed on the altar were received by the officers of the Jewel Office, and her Majesty, wearing her crown, and the princes and princesses, peers and peeresses, wearing their coronets, returned to the palace in the same order as they had left it. Thus this splendid ceremony came to a close; it had lasted three hours, and the majority of those who occupied seats in the Abbey had been there some hours longer.

A state banquet at Buckingham Palace, where a hundred royal and noble guests were entertained, and afterwards, from windows and roofs, witnessed the fireworks in the park, closed the day, which, throughout the country, and among British communities in foreign lands and in distant colonies, was devoted to festivity and rejoicing. In London the holiday-making lasted all the week. On Friday, Saturday, and the following Monday a fair in Hyde Park was succeeded by a review, at which the Queen and some of her distinguished guests were present, and where old Marshal Soult again came in for popular applause, which he shared with the Duke of Wellington. Her Majesty appeared in an open barouche, with her aides-de-camp in full uniform.

There was a short season of repose at Windsor in the autumn and winter of 1838, when Leslie, the painter, went thither to obtain sittings of the Queen and the principal personages in her train for the coronation picture; but early in the year 1839, when the Queen had returned to London, an occurrence of a very painful nature threw a temporary shadow upon the social and domestic life of the court; and though her Majesty had no personal part in the circumstances that led to it, political jealousy and party calumny turned it to account in associating her ministry, and, by implication, the Duchess of Kent and the Queen herself, with what was a very sad and distressing mistake, and had been represented as a palace plot on the part of certain Whig ladies of the court.

It is not necessary to repeat all the details of the too-often-told story of Lady Flora Hastings, the lady who had borne the train of the Duchess of Kent at the coronation, and was in attendance on her royal highness at court. This lady was the daughter of Flora, Countess of Loudoun, and of Earl Moira, a distinguished soldier and statesman, who had been Governor-general of India, was created Marquis of Hastings, and died at Malta while he was governor-general there. She was dearly beloved by her relations, highly accomplished, and with reputation unblemished; and though her family had become "Conservative" in politics, she occupied a position of confidence at the court. Early in the year Lord Melbourne informed Sir James Clarke, the court physician, of a communication made by Lady Tavistock, one of the ladies of the Duchess of Kent's household, that the personal appearance of Lady Flora Hastings had given rise to the suspicion that she might have been privately married. This was a most serious imputation, and the more painful because it seemed to be somewhat justified by the appearance referred to, which had been noticed by the physician, who also attributed it to the cause that had been suggested. The Duchess of Kent expressed her entire disbelief in any imputation against the character of the lady, and in the conclusions which had been stated; but the imputation had been made, and farther inquiry was therefore deemed necessary. Lady Flora, after firmly and indignantly denying that there were any grounds for such a suspicion, submitted to an examination, which proved that the peculiarity referred to was caused by an internal disorder, and that there were no reasons for the insinuation that had been made. The Marchioness of Hastings, naturally indignant at the proceedings, and at the clumsy and blundering manner in which her daughter had been made a victim to suspicions, magnified into accusations by Whig ladies of the court, demanded further inquiry into the origin of the slander, and called for the dismissal of Sir James Clarke as physician to her Majesty. These demands were not complied with, as Lord Melbourne considered that they were not reasonable, and the letter to the Queen, in which they were made, did not make them appear so. Lady Tavistock, on the other hand, declared that what had been said and done was for the honour of her Majesty and the character of the household, that the suspicion entertained should not be permitted to grow and spread. In writing an account of what was called "the Palace Conspiracy" to her uncle at Brussels, the unfortunate Lady Flora mentioned the tenderness of the Duchess of Kent, of whom she said that a mother could not have been kinder to her, while the Queen not only endeavoured to show her regret by her civility to her, but "expressed it handsomely with tears in her eyes." Whether the disease from which the poor lady was suffering had been increased by the anxiety and agitation cannot be declared, but she died four months afterwards at the palace, at the age of thirty-three.

The Tories, however, soon had another party cry of "Whig conspiracy," which immediate events gave them the opportunity of using with more or less effect.

On the 5th of February parliament was opened by the Queen, and the royal speech referred to events in Afghanistan which might make military operations necessary. Lower Canada was still in a disturbed condition, and hostile incursions had been made into Upper Canada by some lawless inhabitants of the United States of America. The Chartist agitation was also referred to, as its leaders in some parts of the country endeavoured to excite large assemblies to disobedience and resistance to the law, and to recommend dangerous and illegal practices, for the counteraction of which the efficiency of the law, the good sense and right disposition of the people, and their attachment to the principles of justice and their abhorrence of violence and disorder would be depended on. The affairs of Ireland were still a cause of considerable agitation, and Daniel O'Connell was constantly maintaining it by addressing vast meetings, and using expressions of profuse loyalty to the Queen, while denouncing the Tories and the Orange societies, among whom there were speakers as violent and abusive against the Queen and her government. A measure relating to Irish municipal corporations was promised in the speech from the throne, and reference was made to further measures of law reform.

On the 6th of April there was a debate on the ministerial proposal temporarily to suspend the constitution of the Jamaica government, because of the alleged excesses and lawlessness of the planters. This was opposed by the Radicals, because of its alleged violation of Liberal principles, and their influence added to Conservative opposition left the government with only a majority of five. The ministers, who had contemplated a similar measure for Canada, therefore resigned, and Lord Melbourne advised her Majesty to send for the Duke of Wellington, who referred her to Sir Robert Peel. For two years the Queen had been in almost daily communication and in the most friendly relation to Lord Melbourne, in whom she had implicit confidence, and most of the ladies who were her friends and attendants in her household were, of course, included in her favourable estimate of the only ministry she had known. It probably did not much mitigate the somewhat constrained and reserved manner of Peel to be told by the Queen that she much regretted having to part with her late minister, in whom she had confidence, but it was frankly said, and Peel was a man who appreciated frankness and that personal loyalty which gave sentiment to the Queen's regret. He lived to acquire the same confidence and the same high estimation, and it may be assumed that his already strong loyalty was not diminished by the young sovereign's outspoken expressions of favour to his opponents. Unfortunately for his immediate chance of a similar distinction, when he undertook to form a ministry, and sent to her Majesty a list of those who would be invited to become his colleagues, he also required that some of the first ladies of the royal household should resign their position, because of their relationship to members of the previous cabinet. The reason for this was that Ireland was becoming, or had become, the chief difficulty of the government, and indeed of any probable Conservative government, for the Whigs only held office by a kind of hollow alliance with O'Connell; and the wife of Lord Normanby, who had been Lord-lieutenant of Ireland, and the sister of Lord Morpeth, who had been Irish secretary under the Whig government, were in close attendance and companionship with the Queen.

It ought to have been made clear that the demand for the dismissal of the ladies of the bed-chamber meant only the chief ladies, for probably the Queen understood that she was to be separated from all those ladies, members of her household, with whom she had long been on terms of intimate companionship. In a personal interview, however, Sir Robert had intimated that it would be of great importance as an indication of her Majesty's confidence if certain offices of the household of the higher rank, which might not be voluntarily relinquished by the ladies holding them, were subject to some change; and he afterwards told his proposed colleagues that he meant only those of the rank of ladies of the bed-chamber. The Queen stated in reply that she must reserve the whole of these appointments to herself. There was a slight touch of imperious temper here, and a touch of strong will, for her Majesty felt strongly on the subject, and was perhaps ruffled by a request which seemed, almost in the form of a demand, to aim at her private friendships. At all events she wrote next day: "The Queen, having considered the proposal made to her yesterday by Sir Robert Peel, to remove the ladies of the bed-chamber, cannot consent to a course which she conceives to be contrary to usage, and is repugnant to her feeling." To this Sir Robert replied that he was reluctantly compelled by a sense of public duty and the interest of her Majesty's service to adhere to his opinion, and gratefully thanking her Majesty for the distinction conferred on him of requiring his advice and assistance to form an administration, it was his earnest prayer that whatever arrangements her Majesty might be enabled to make for that purpose might be most conducive to her personal comfort and happiness and to the promotion of the public welfare. So there was dignity on both sides, and the Melbourne ministry was recalled, a minute being adopted at a cabinet meeting to the effect that though the great offices of court and situations in the household held by members of parliament should be included in the political arrangements made on a change of administration, a similar principle should not apply to the offices held by ladies in her Majesty's household. It may be mentioned, however, that it has since been the custom for the ladies holding the higher offices to retire on a change of ministry.

It may be understood that the return of the Whig administration—not, as Melbourne declared, because he sought office, but because he would not hold back from assisting the sovereign when his services were required—gave new occasion for political denunciation. O'Connell and others represented that the Queen, by refusing the demands of the Tories that she should dismiss her friends, had knowingly defeated Tory machinations and fully purposed keeping the Whigs in power. Thus she was becoming more and more identified with what was already a feeble, and, in some respects, an incompetent government. The excitement in London was very great, especially at the clubs and elsewhere, where it was reported that at the Queen's ball on the 10th of May her Majesty "had danced with Lady Normanby's son, and the Tories had looked foolish."

Court entertainments and festivities had necessarily become more frequent and more splendid since the coronation, and the addresses of congratulation, the bestowal of peerages and honours, and the royal receptions, assemblies, and visits that followed. Even at Windsor—though the ordinary domestic life, the morning's attention to the business of the state, the afternoon rides or drives, the music and singing, the rather formal but yet pleasantly friendly dinners, and the evening's conversation or listening to the music of the band were resumed—there were receptions of distinguished guests and pleasant quadrille parties, in which the Queen took part. For a short time after the political crisis just referred to there was some diminution in the expressions of loyalty that greeted her when she appeared in public. Some hostile hisses were heard amidst the acclamations on one or two occasions, especially when she visited Ascot; but they were to be attributed to violent partisans of the opposition, who sought to discredit the Queen that they might injure the ministry. The more ignorant of the public had expected that the influence of the youthful and amiable sovereign would lead to an immediate redress of all kinds of grievances.

There was, therefore, some disappointment, which was increased to a passing feeling of disloyalty by the representations of unscrupulous partisans and scurrilous prints filled with shameful insinuations against the Queen. But the loyalty of the nation had been too personal and real a sentiment to be perverted; the truthful character no less than the simple confiding manner of Victoria appealed to the mass of the people, as it did to those by whom she was immediately surrounded. The charm which wrought on the hearts of all was no false spell, but was well described by a writer whose somewhat cynical and critical disposition had succumbed to it. " It is, in fact, the remarkable union of *naïveté*, kindness, and native good-nature with propriety and dignity which makes her so admirable and so endearing to those about her as she certainly is. I have been repeatedly told that they are all warmly attached to her, but that all feel the impossibility of for a moment losing sight of the respect which they owe her. She never ceases to be a Queen, but is always the most charming, cheerful, obliging, unaffected Queen in the world." At the same time her position was one of increasing difficulty, if not of danger—danger to the simplicity and truthfulness which were her happy characteristics —danger also to that freshness of spirit which enables its possessor to enjoy, because it forbids satiety. A court, be it never so pure, is full of large or small anxieties and wearing responsibilities for the mistress of it, and especially if she be young and with a forthright conscientiousness of soul. Its round of observances too may be deadening, and with a sense of solitude amidst all the splendour, till the very amusements and festivities become formalized into somewhat dreary and heartless observances. The Queen herself has said, " A worse school for a young girl, or one more detrimental to all natural feelings and affections, cannot well be imagined, than the position of a Queen at eighteen, without experience and without a husband to guide and support her. This the Queen can state from painful experience, and she thanks God that none of her dear daughters are exposed to such danger."

The prince, who had with manly modest independence only occasionally sent his royal cousin a souvenir of his travels, was not forgotten, but after her accession the Queen had not kept up her correspondence with him as she had done before it, and this she much regretted at a later time. He was, so to speak, a figure with the halo of sincere and loving interest around it, but at present seen through the mist of indefinite time and space. The sudden change from the secluded life at Kensington to the independence of her position as Queen Regnant at so early an age had, the Queen tells us, put all ideas of marriage out of her mind.

It was not greatly to be wondered at, and we may surmise that there existed that indefinable desire common to all youthful maidens whose choice is made, and who know that the response is waiting, before binding engagement or betrothal, to take a short flight of liberty without relinquishing the sweet sense that there will soon come a time when a word shall be spoken that will be a signal for voluntary return and happy self-bestowal. Moreover, the Queen had had reasons for deferring an engagement that must have meant early betrothal and marriage. Her clear common-sense was concerned in the perception that Prince Albert spoke English imperfectly, that he needed to learn more of the language and the ways of the country which would be the land of his adoption. Also, young as she herself was to marry, he was two or three months younger, and though he was for his age manly, accomplished, and with a serene self-possession that became him well, he yet was not old enough to be husband to a queen. But many months had passed, and the youth who had gone to complete his studies and to acquire more of princely knowledge, as well as to exercise princely virtues and strengthen princely character, had been earnestly devoting himself to these ends, and had become an able, self-reliant young man, far-seeing, and with clear views of life, and above all with the power of patience and a nobility above self-seeking. These qualities were inseparable from a manly independence, which required to be satisfied that so far as his relations to the Queen were concerned, his waiting would not be in vain. In the early part of 1838 the King of the Belgians had written to the Queen, and probably had then definitely referred to the subject of the proposed marriage. In March the king must have had some sanction from his niece to communicate with Prince Albert on the same subject, and this communication was made while the young princes were at Brussels before going on their Swiss tour. Prince Albert looked at the question from its most elevated and honourable point of view, and when told that his youth would make it necessary to postpone the marriage for a few years, he replied that he was ready to submit to that delay if he had some certain assurance to go upon; but if after waiting perhaps three years he should find that the Queen no longer desired the marriage, it would place him in a very ridiculous position, and would to a certain extent ruin all the prospects of his future life.

The king was greatly impressed with the character, attainments, and manners of the prince, who had already so manly an appearance that though he was not then nineteen he might have been taken for two or three and twenty.

The opinion expressed by the prince was endorsed by his father the Duke of Coburg, who pointed out that should he wait till he was twenty-two or twenty-three, he would be unable to begin any new career, and his whole life would be marred if the Queen should change her mind. Of this, however, the Queen herself has said she never entertained any idea, and she afterwards informed the prince that she would never have married anyone else, a declaration emphasized years afterwards by the admission that she could not even then think without indignation against herself of her wish to keep the prince waiting, at the risk of ruining all his prospects for life, until she might feel inclined to marry.

In the month of June, 1839, Ernest, the hereditary prince of Coburg, came of age, and Prince Albert had, by special act of the legislature, been declared to be of age at the same time. "Now," he wrote, "I am my own master, as I hope always to be, and under all circumstances." In July the majority of the princes had been celebrated at Coburg. Prince Albert and his brother had parted with mutual grief, for the latter had gone to pursue his military studies by taking service with the King of Saxony at Dresden, and Prince Albert had, as we have seen, been making a journey in Italy, where he had the advantage of being accompanied by Baron Stockmar, and, at Florence, by Lieutenant (afterwards Major-general) Seymour, who read English with him, and whose refinement of manners and character so well suited the prince that they became firm friends. The days spent in Italy were to good purpose, and the prince lived in his accustomed simple manner. Early rising, study from six to noon, a simple mid-day meal, a visit to some gallery of art or public building, a long walk or ride into the country, or two or three hours devoted to playing the organ in the church

of the Badia, where the passing monks would stay to listen to
the music of the foreign prince, whose performance equalled that
of their own organ-master—such were the usual occupations,
with occasional attendance at a ball or some assembly, invitations
to which could not be refused. When the pleasant working
holiday was over the prince was about to settle down at
Rosenau to complete his English studies, but his father called
upon him to accompany him to Carlsbad. At the beginning
of October we find him with his brother at Brussels, whence
they were to pay another visit to England, the prince intending
to tell the Queen that if she could not now make up her
mind she must understand that he could no longer wait for
a decision, as he had done at a former period when the marriage was first talked about. They brought with them a
guarded letter from King Leopold, who recommended them to
the "*bienveillance*" of his dearest Victoria, saying, "They are
good, honest creatures, deserving your kindness, and not
pedantic, but really sensible and trustworthy. I have told them
that your great wish is that they should be quite at their ease
with you. I am sure that if you have anything to recommend
to them they will be most happy to learn it from you." The
king probably had made a shrewd guess that matters would be
brought to a happy crisis, though the prince went under the
impression "that the Queen wished the marriage to be broken
off, and that for four years she could think of no marriage." To
this effect he had written to his old and intimate friend Prince
von Löwenstein, and he perhaps had good reason for it in the
representations made by King Leopold, as repeating those
of the Queen herself; but a good many changes had taken place
since the cousins had last met. The mutual distrust of political
parties was increasing, and it was more and more difficult for

the sovereign to hold a position of neutrality. There were many reasons in favour of the young Queen having a suitable protector, with the right to be constantly near her. Other alliances had already been proposed, and might soon be pressed upon her attention. The change that had taken place in the young princes themselves was remarkable, and Albert's appearance was so striking for its manly beauty and for the expression of self-control, gentleness, and high intelligence, that doubts founded on his youth and inexperience were not likely to last.

On the 12th of October, the second day after their arrival, it was evident that whatever reasons the Queen may have had for demanding delay were destined to give way before the personal influence of the prince. "Albert's beauty is most striking, and he is most amiable and unaffected," her Majesty wrote to her uncle, "in short very *fascinating*. The young men are very amiable, delightful companions, and I am very happy to have them here." To this the king replied, "Albert is a very agreeable companion. His manners are so gentle and harmonious that one likes to have him near oneself. . . . May Albert be able to strew roses without thorns on the pathway of life of our good Victoria! He is well qualified to do so."

Before this letter reached her, however, "our good Victoria" had wisely acted according to her new impulse. Lord Melbourne, Lord Clanricarde, Lord and Lady Granville, Baron Brunnow, and Lord Normanby were staying at the castle, and the daily routine was for the princes to pay the Queen a visit in her own room after breakfast, and at two o'clock to take luncheon with her and the Duchess of Kent. In the afternoon nearly everybody went out riding, forming a large cavalcade; and every evening there was a great dinner, with a dance afterwards, on three evenings a week.

It is on record that Lord Melbourne had sometime previously spoken to the Queen on the subject of her probable marriage, but whether this was so or not, on the 14th of October her Majesty told him that she had made up her mind. Such an acute observer—and one too who watched with loving and guarding eyes—was probably not much surprised, and he certainly received the news with great satisfaction. "I think it will be very well received," he said, "for I hear that there is an anxiety now that it should be, and I am very glad of it;" adding in a paternal tone. "You will be much more comfortable, for a woman cannot stand alone for any time in whatever position she may be."

An intimation had next to be given to the prince, for royal etiquette debarred him from speaking; and Baron Alvensleben, the master of the horse to the Duke of Coburg, who had accompanied the prince to England, was charged with a message that the Queen wished to speak to him next day.

The prince, with his brother, was out early the next morning, for it was a hunting day; but he returned at noon, and half-an-hour afterwards obeyed the summons to the Queen's room, where she was alone. The first few words of the interview must have been the prelude to other words—spoken, perhaps, with hesitation, certainly with modest emotion, but as certainly without affectation. The Queen's frank, truthful nature, and the delicacy that belonged to her purely womanly character, would have made her lovely, even if she had not been already loved. It is, of course, chiefly from letters that we have any of these side-lights which show us what took place at this happy time. In one written to his beloved grandmother at Gotha the prince said: "The Queen declared to me, in a genuine outburst of love and affection, that I had gained her whole heart, and would make her intensely happy if I would make her the sacrifice of sharing her life with her, for she said she looked on it as a sacrifice; the only thing which troubled her was that she did not think she was worthy of me. The joyous openness of manner in which she told me this quite enchanted me, and I was quite carried away by it."

That the prince received the sweet intimation as a lover should, with the warmest demonstration of kindness and affection, is known on the best authority. "How I will strive to make him feel as little as possible the great sacrifice he has made! I told him it *was* a great sacrifice on his part, but he would not allow it," the Queen wrote in her journal. "I then told him to fetch Ernest, which he did, who congratulated us both, and seemed very happy."

"I write to you," says the prince in a letter to Baron Stockmar, "on one of the happiest days of my life, to give you the most welcome news possible. Victoria is so good and kind to me that I am often at a loss to believe that such affection should be shown to me. I know the great interest you take in my happiness, and therefore pour out my heart to you. . . . More or more seriously I cannot write to you, for at this moment I am too bewildered.

> "Das Auge sieht den Himmel offen
> Es schwelgt das Herz in Seligkeit."[1]

To this dear old confidential friend of them both the Queen had already written: "I do feel so guilty, I know not how to begin my letter, but I think the news it will contain will be sufficient to ensure your forgiveness. Albert has completely

[1] "Heaven opens on the raptured eye,
And flooded is the heart with bliss."
Schiller's *Song of the Bell.*

won my heart, and all was settled between us this morning.
. . . I feel certain he will make me very happy. I wish
I could say I feel as certain of *my* making him happy, but I
shall do my best."

To her uncle Leopold the Queen had also written on the
same day, telling of her happiness, speaking of the kindness and
encouragement shown by Lord Melbourne, and saying that it
had been thought better that the marriage should take place
soon after the meeting of parliament, about the beginning of
February. The letter concluded by saying: " I wish to keep
the dear young gentlemen here till the end of next month.
Ernest's sincere pleasure gives me great delight. He does so
adore dearest Albert."

The king replied: " Nothing could have given me greater
pleasure than your dear letter. I had, when I learnt your
decision, almost the feeling of old Simeon, ' Now, lettest thou
thy servant depart in peace.' . . . You say most amiably
that you consider it a sacrifice on the part of Albert. This is
true in many points, because his position will be a difficult one,
but much, I may say *all*, will depend on your affection for him.
If *you* love him, and are kind to him, he will easily bear the
bothers of his position, and there is a steadiness, and at the same
time a cheerfulness in his character which will facilitate this."
It was afterwards determined that, instead of waiting to make
the announcement first to parliament, the Queen should, after
the departure of her cousins, assemble the privy-council, and
make the announcement to them.

The princes were to leave Windsor on the 14th of November,
and the intervening days were very happy; the young lovers
talking over future arrangements, among which it was settled
that Prince Albert should not take any title, but that he should

naturally have precedence of everyone else after the Queen. It was a brief but happy wooing, and there is a tone of joy in the young Queen's brief records of it—a pervading sense of the sweetness of mutual affection, of the heart-glow and comfort of belonging to somebody who is dearest.

A battalion of the Rifle Brigade was quartered at Windsor, under the command of General, afterwards Sir, George Brown, and so there was a review in the Home Park by the Queen, in her Windsor uniform, a jacket with deep tabs, a black silk neck-cloth covering the shapely neck, and a cap, with a big peak, almost concealing the fair hair; the prince cantering by her side in the green uniform of the Coburg troops, and taking care to wrap the dear little fiancée in her cape, the weather being stormy, wet, and cold.

They were delightful days—days to be remembered with tears in time of after sorrows, but yet with a blessed hope of reunion. There was much letter-writing and letter-reading, and from Stockmar comes a long epistle to the prince full of good advice, exacting reminders, and deep affection; letters from Coburg and from Gotha reminding the prince that he would have to leave his old home, his country, his relatives, his life of freedom and leisure, and devote himself to the onerous duties of a great position, and to the continuous effort to secure the confidence and promote the welfare of a people who for some time to come would regard him as a foreigner. But he had set his heart to the fulfilment of the duties that would fall to him, and he shared the opinion expressed by King Leopold: if the Queen loved him he could face all the difficulties of his position.

On the 14th of November the prince left Windsor for Coburg, where the rejoicings on the announcement of the coming marriage were most enthusiastic. The prince himself was evidently happy in the love of the bride who awaited him, and he appeared mostly to be in the best of spirits; but he was necessarily subjected to many conflicting emotions.

"I think I shall be very happy, for Victoria possesses all the qualities which make a home happy," he wrote to his friend Löwenstein. To the Duchess of Kent, who had from the first taken the prince to her heart as a son, he wrote in reply to a letter from her: "What you say about my poor little bride sitting all alone in her room, silent and sad, has touched me to the heart. Oh that I might fly to her side and cheer her!" The duchess appears to have asked him to send her as a souvenir something that he had worn, and the prince says: "I send you the ring which you gave me at Kensington on Victoria's birthday in 1836. From that time it has never left my finger. Its very shape proclaims that it has been squeezed in the grasp of many a manly hand; but the name is Victoria's too, and I beg you to wear it in remembrance of her and of myself." And at a later date, during the excitement at Coburg, he also earnestly referred to the multitude of emotions which overwhelmed him: "Hope, love for dear Victoria, the pain of leaving home, the parting from very dear kindred, the entrance into a new circle of relations all meeting me with the utmost kindness, prospects the most brilliant, the dread of being unequal to my position, the demonstrations of so much attachment on the part of the loyal Coburgers, English enthusiasm on the tiptoe of expectation, the multiplicity of duties to be fulfilled, and, to crown all, so much laudation on every side, that I could sink to the earth for very shame." "Love letters" now travelled between London and Coburg, and had even anticipated his arrival at Coburg, for from Wiesbaden, when he was on the way home, he had written: "That I am the object of so much love and devotion often comes over me as something I can hardly realize. My prevailing feeling is, What am I that such happiness should be mine? For excess of happiness it is for me to know that I am so dear to you." And again, from Coburg on the 7th of December: "I cannot even yet clearly picture to myself that I am to be indeed so happy as to be always near you, always your protector." From the elder brother, Ernest, the Queen had also received a charming manly letter, full of tender homage and of unstinted praise for the brother whom he held so dear, and to part from whom he felt would be a great grief.

The Queen had now to perform the trying duty of making a declaration of her intended marriage. On the 23d of November eighty members of the privy-council assembled in the "Bow-room" at Buckingham Palace. Precisely at two o'clock the Queen went in. "The room was full," she records in her journal; "but I hardly knew who was there. Lord Melbourne I saw looking kindly at me with tears in his eyes, but he was not near me. I then read my short declaration. I felt my hands shook, but I did not make one mistake. I felt most happy and thankful when it was over. Lord Lansdowne then rose, and in the name of the privy-council asked that this most gracious and most welcome communication might be printed! I then left the room. The Duke of Cambridge came into the small library where I was standing and wished me joy." The Queen wore a bracelet with the Prince's picture, and this she says "seemed to give me courage at the council."

If any doubts existed as to the manner in which the intelligence of the approaching marriage would be received by the country they were soon dissipated. The announcement was received with cordial congratulations on all sides, and with demonstrations of rejoicing, which showed that the people were animated by heart-felt wishes for the happiness of their sovereign sentiments which were not diminished by the reflection that we should now finally get rid of Hanover, where the king (the still detested Duke of Cumberland) was indulging in abusive comments on men and affairs in England.

The anxieties of the Queen, however, were not half over. On the 16th of January, 1840, she went to open parliament, and not only the House of Lords but the streets leading to it were crowded, while there was a revival of the enthusiastic welcome which her Majesty had been wont to receive. This augured well for the national interest in the intended marriage which was now to be announced to parliament; and the occasion was one which may well have moved the hearts of the people, as the sovereign, now only in her twenty-first year, went to say with modest mien, and with a thrill of emotion, but with no uncertain or inaudible voice, "Since you were last assembled I have declared my intention of allying myself in marriage with the Prince Albert of Saxe-Coburg and Gotha. I humbly implore that the divine blessing may prosper this union, and render it conducive to the interests of my people as well as to my own domestic happiness; and it will be to me a source of the most lively satisfaction to find the resolution I have taken approved by my parliament."

As Lord Melbourne had prognosticated, the marriage was popular because it was well understood to be "a love match," and not an alliance for merely dynastic or political reasons, and it soon became the subject of exuberant congratulation and sympathy; nor were there any other expressions than those of the expectation of domestic happiness and public advantage in the addresses that followed the royal speech in both houses of parliament.

Sir Robert Peel, as representing the opposition, claimed the right of joining most warmly in the congratulations offered to her Majesty, and his speech was remarkably felicitous. But there were still important matters to be debated, in relation to the prince who was to occupy so distinguished a position, and these were made unnecessarily painful to the Queen, not only because of opposition or contention, but in consequence of some inexcusable blundering.

In the declaration of the marriage made to the privy-council the statement that Prince Albert was a Protestant had been omitted, and this was taken hold of, in spite of the fact that the prince and all his house were well known to be Protestants. The prince pointed out in a letter to the Queen, that to the house of Saxony, Protestantism, in a measure, owed its existence; that there had not been a Catholic or Papistical princess introduced into the family since the appearance of Luther in 1521, and that the Elector Frederick the Wise was the very first Protestant that ever lived. That his future wife and queen, at all events, might know and judge for herself what his creed and religious principles were, the prince sent her the confession of faith which he had worked out for himself in 1835, and had then publicly avowed in the High Church at Coburg. The Duke of Wellington, as well as others, argued that the word "Protestant" should be inserted; and though it was represented that the addition was superfluous, and Brougham pointed out that though an English sovereign was not forbidden by law to marry a Catholic, such a marriage meant simply the forfeiture of the crown: the addition was made. The calumny then changed sides, following perhaps the malignant assertion of the Duke of Cumberland; and the prince was spoken of as a sectarian, as a freethinker, as a man destitute of religious principles. All these suggestions died the death of lies that cannot bear the light.

When the settlement of the prince's annuity was brought to the vote of parliament, a proposal of £50,000 was met by an amendment from Mr. Hume that it should be reduced to £21,000; but this being negatived, Colonel Sibthorp, supported by Sir Robert Peel, several leaders of the opposition, and the economical Whigs, who had sided with some of the Radicals, proposed another amendment, making the amount £30,000, which was carried after considerable asperity of debate. Next came the question of the position the prince was to hold, with regard to his precedence as husband of the Queen. No provision existed in the constitution for the husband of a queen regnant, though the wife of a king stood next her husband in dignity; and instead of dealing with the exceptional circumstances at once, the ministry only introduced a bill for the naturalization of the prince, and this left the whole question of the prince's rank or position to be dealt with by letters-patent, a royal prerogative which enabled the Queen to give him precedence only in England.

Lord Torrington and Colonel (afterwards General) Grey had gone to Gotha to escort Prince Albert to England for the marriage, taking three of the Queen's carriages with them. On the 23d the prince was invested with the order of the Garter by command of the Queen, the duke, his father (himself a knight of the order), having been authorized to invest, assisted by Prince Leiningen. There were great festivities afterwards, and then came the farewells and the journey to England, whither Prince Albert was to be accompanied by the duke and Prince Ernest, attended by the ducal master of the horse and other noblemen and gentlemen, as well as by Lord Torrington, Colonel Grey, and

Mr. Seymour, a party of twelve occupying six travelling carriages, and followed by two *fourgons*. At Aix-la-Chapelle the prince heard of the proceedings in parliament. Stockmar, who had returned to England to assist in making some arrangements for the royal household, wrote to him explaining the effects of parties in England in relation to the vote on the annuity. The prince understood the conditions pretty well, and though he was provoked that there should have been contention, and what seemed like squabbling on the subject, which he thought made it personally degrading to him, he was not angry with any particular party, and only expressed regret that the diminution of the amount would leave him less to spend on the promotion of art and literature. He had begun to face the troubles and responsibilities of his position, and to face them with calmness and cool judgment. He wrote to the Queen that the news had had an unpleasant effect upon him when it reached him on his journey, and that people in parliament seemed to have made themselves unnecessarily disagreeable, but concluded with, "All I have to say is that while I possess your love they cannot make me unhappy."

He had been under the depressing doubt, whether the opposition in parliament and the calumnies directed against him were not indications of popular objection to the marriage, but the moment he arrived at Dover this doubt was dispelled. He and his party had been suffering considerably from a rough passage, but there was a great crowd of people at Dover, and with determined energy he shook off his malady and stood on the deck to respond to their genuine and hearty English welcome. These greetings attended him, and even increased in ardour during his journey, till, on the 8th of February, he reached Buckingham Palace, from Canterbury, where the party had stayed on the previous night, and whence the prince had despatched a loving message to her Majesty, and sent on as avant-couriers his faithful valet Cart, and his favourite greyhound "Eös," which had been with him in England in 1836, and had then become an attached retainer of the Queen.

The marriage of her Majesty Victoria, Queen of the United Kingdom of Great Britain and Ireland, to (Francis) Albert Augustus Charles Emmanuel, Prince of Coburg and Gotha, was to be solemnized on Monday, the 10th of February. It was half-past four in the afternoon of Saturday that the duke and the princes had arrived at Buckingham Palace, where they were received at the hall door by the Queen and the Duchess of Kent, attended by the whole household. At five, the lord chancellor administered the oaths of naturalization to the prince, and there was a state dinner in the evening. On the next day (Sunday) divine service was held in the palace by the Bishop of London, and there was an exchange of the wedding gifts. The prince had brought for his bride a beautiful sapphire and diamond brooch, and he received from her the star and badge of the Garter and the Garter itself set in diamonds. In the afternoon the prince went out to pay the usual formal visits to members of the royal family, and the crowds that filled all the approaches to the palace at once manifested by their acclamations that they at all events approved of his personal appearance.

In a very few days Stockmar, who had been anxiously observing events, was able to say, "The prince is liked. Those who are not carried away by party feelings like him greatly." The appreciation of his high and noble qualities grew rapidly, from the hour that he stood with calm and princely mien and thoughtful happy face before the altar, to place the wedding-ring upon the hand of her he loved. The general sorrow shown by the people of Gotha on the departure of their young prince had manifested how deeply he was beloved by all around him there, and the grief of the grandmother who held him so dear was acute. Even on the morning of his wedding he remembered that a message from him at that time would give her comfort, and he wrote: "In less than three hours I shall stand before the altar with my dear bride! In these solemn moments I must once more ask your blessing, which I am well assured I shall receive, and which will be my safeguard and my future joy. I must end. God be my stay!"

The marriage was to take place at the Chapel Royal, St. James's Palace, at one o'clock, and at half-past twelve the Queen left Buckingham Palace, with her mother and the Duchess of Sutherland in the same carriage. Her Majesty wore a rich white satin dress trimmed with orange blossoms, with a wreath of orange blossoms, over which a beautiful veil of Honiton lace hung down on each shoulder, but did not conceal her face. She wore the collar of the Garter and a diamond necklace and ear-rings. The Queen on leaving her apartment went to her carriage leaning on the arm of the Earl of Uxbridge, the lord chamberlain, supported by the Duchess of Kent, and followed by a page of honour, and was preceded by the Earls of Belfort, Surrey, and Albemarle, Lord Torrington, and other officers of the household. There were seven carriages, that of the Queen coming last, and the preceding ones conveying gentlemen-ushers, equerries, and grooms-in-waiting, great officers of the household, bed-chamber women, maids of honour, and ladies-in-waiting. The cortége was attended by a full guard of honour, but the carriages were drawn by only two horses each, and without the usual rich caparisons used on state occasions. It moved slowly with its cavalry escort, and shortly before one o'clock reached St. James's Palace. The Queen was conducted to her apartment behind the throne-room, the maids of honour and train-bearers being in attendance. The princely bridegroom, with his attendant train, had of course reached the palace some time before, attended by the suite from Saxe-Coburg, and accompanied by his father and brother. He wore the uniform of a British field-marshal, and had no other decoration than the collar and jewel of the Garter, with the star of the order and the Garter itself (the presents from the Queen) set in diamonds. The Duke of Saxe-Coburg-Gotha wore a dark-green uniform with red facings, high boots, and besides the collar and star of the order of the Garter, the star of his own order of Coburg. Prince Ernest was in light-blue cavalry uniform with silver ornaments, and carried a light helmet. He wore the grand cross of a foreign order. The lord-chamberlain and other great officers of the household, with Lord Torrington, who wore the grand cross of the order of Saxe-Coburg, had conducted Prince Albert and his suite from Buckingham Palace before the Queen left it; and on descending the grand staircase the prince was received with acclamations by the select few who stood behind the yeomen of the guard. Trumpets sounded, colours were lowered, and the escort presented arms as the prince entered his carriage with his father and brother, the attendants following in two other carriages, and a squadron of Life Guards accompanying them to St. James's Palace. The carriages were closed and the journey was a short one, so that only a few among the vast crowd which had assembled recognized the prince, or knew that the bridegroom was on his way to await the royal bride. The lord-chamberlain had then the prince at St. James's Palace, and returned to conduct her Majesty thither, amidst the vast multitude which had assembled in St.

James's Park, and in the vicinities of both palaces; while people were still thronging in great numbers towards Carlton Terrace and the foot of Constitution Hill that they might see the royal procession on the return from St. James's. But the crowd was orderly and good-humoured, and the police performed their duties with equal good temper and discretion, and though the crush was tremendous there were only some casualties of a somewhat ludicrous character, chiefly caused by the futile efforts of a few people to obtain a view of the procession by climbing the trees. The enthusiasm with which the Queen was received brought a smile and a look of grateful recognition to her face, which was paler than usual, and naturally wore a serious and somewhat anxious expression.

While her Majesty remained within her private apartment, the procession which was to accompany her to the chapel was marshalled in the throne-room, and the principal persons who were to compose the respective processions then assembled in the presence-chamber, that they might fall into their places, and pass in proper order through Queen Anne's drawing-room, and the guard or armoury room, into the vestibule, down the grand staircase, and along the colonnade to the chapel.

A fanfare of trumpets and a roll of drums, at twenty-five minutes past twelve, heralded the approach of the bridegroom, who, preceded by gentlemen of honour and heralds, supported by his father and brother, and attended by the officers of their suite, entered the chapel amidst great acclamations, which were chiefly directed to the prince himself, whose appearance elicited general admiration. His royal highness, bowing to the peers in acknowledgment of their salutations, was conducted to the chair provided for him. He walked up the aisle carrying a book in his right hand, and having reached the *haut pas*, kissed the hand of the queen-dowager, and bowed to the archbishops and the dean. An organ voluntary was performed by Sir George Smart, until a fresh blare of trumpets and beating of drums announced that her Majesty was approaching, and the lord-chamberlain and the lord-steward having conducted the prince to the altar, prepared to conduct the Queen. The royal procession entered the chapel, preceded by the knight-marshal, pursuivants, heralds, and pages of honour. Lord Melbourne carried the sword of state before her Majesty, whose train was borne by twelve bridesmaids, most of them the ladies who had attended her at the coronation.

Though acclamations greeted some members of the royal family, all interest was naturally centred first on the Queen, and, secondly, on the company of beautiful maidens, who, attired in white, with wreaths of roses, kept their attention fixed on their royal mistress, who walked up the aisle without returning any salutations, and knelt on her footstool in private prayer before taking her seat. After a few seconds her Majesty rose and advanced with Prince Albert to the communion-table, when the Archbishop of Canterbury at once commenced the marriage service, which was strictly according to the rubric, the Queen promising, as a wife, to love, honour, and obey; and the prince to love, comfort, honour, and keep her as a husband should; both bride and bridegroom speaking the " I will" in tones that could be heard, and the Duke of Sussex giving away the bride in the good old fashion. After the ring had been placed on the Queen's finger, and the concluding prayer had been offered by the archbishop, the park and Tower guns fired a royal salute, in answer to a semaphore signal, and the service concluded with the *Deus misereatur* performed by the organ and choir, and the remainder of the service as prescribed in the Book of Common Prayer.

The members of the royal family near the altar then paid their congratulations to the royal bride, the Duke of Sussex kissing her with paternal affection. The Queen then hastily crossed to where the queen-dowager was standing and kissed her. The processions returned in much the same order as that in which they had entered the chapel, with the important exception that her Majesty walked with his royal highness her husband, who held her hand in his in such a way as to display the wedding-ring.

The cheering, clapping of hands, and waving of handkerchiefs, as the royal bride and bridegroom and their brilliant retinue entered the colonnade of the palace, was vehement and continuous, and it broke out with great vigour as the Duke of Wellington appeared, though he had no personal part in the procession. In the throne-room the attestation was made and the marriage register was signed, and the brilliant company then returned to Buckingham Palace, amidst the cheering of a vast assemblage of the people who awaited the royal pair. On reaching Buckingham Palace the prince led in his bride with graceful pride, and the number of privileged spectators within the hall received them with a ringing welcome. The Queen, no longer pale, but with a blush that heightened the happy and radiant expression of her face, acknowledged the greeting with bows and smiles, and the royal and noble party, which had been joined by Viscount Palmerston and Lord John Russell, with some other invited guests, partook of the wedding breakfast, after which, at a quarter to four o'clock, the Queen and the Prince departed for Windsor amidst the vociferous acclamation of the dense masses of people who still waited to give expression to their loyal good wishes. The early part of the February day had been wet, murky, and lowering, but as the royal bride left Buckingham Palace the sun shone out, the mist cleared, and amidst cheerful brightness and the continuous sounds of rejoicing the royal pair, with their attendants, reached Eton. The college welcome was expressed, not only by jubilant shouts, but by a great triumphal arch in form of a Grecian portico, bedecked with flags, illuminated at night with 5000 coloured lamps, and bearing on its pediment the royal arms and the legend "Gratulatio Victoriæ et Alberto." Eton scholars shouted themselves hoarse, the college and town were illuminated, and festivities were the order of the evening. At Windsor the bride and bridegroom were awaited by throngs of people, and the streets were decorated with flags, wreaths, and transparencies. At twenty minutes before seven the royal carriage and its escort arrived in the High Street. A flight of rockets had announced their approach, and by that time the town was brilliant with illuminations. The royal carriage slowly passed through the assembled crowds, and amidst overwhelming demonstrations of loyalty and rejoicing, and when the last acknowledgments of the Queen and the Prince were made, and the royal pair had entered the castle, the people of Windsor continued to celebrate the happy occasion, several dinners being given at the principal taverns and at private houses, and generous provision having been made for a good substantial meal for the poorer inhabitants.

On the 12th of February the Duchess of Kent, the Duke and the hereditary Prince of Coburg, and the whole court followed to Windsor. There were two days of festivity, with dancing in the evening; and on the 14th it was time to return to London to receive addresses from parliament and almost every public body in England, to pay state visits to the theatres, and to commence a series of receptions, assemblies, and entertainments which were regarded as necessary celebrations of the royal marriage.

On the 19th the Queen held a levée, and was led in by the Prince, who then took the place on her Majesty's left hand which he always afterwards occupied at state ceremonials.

The great dinners, state balls, concerts, and receptions of royal and distinguished visitors continued, not only during the time immediately following the royal wedding festivities, but for successive seasons, and the round of splendid hospitality was in some quarters made the subject of bitter censure; the lavish expenditure for these entertainments being contrasted with the distress and want arising from depression of trade and the need of broader measures of political economy and popular representation. The country was agitated, the public mind excited, and the "extravagance and luxury of the court" was a text ready to the hand of the disaffected and the uninformed. It was thought that cries for "the cheap loaf," for the relief of factory hands, for the amelioration of the suffering poor, were to be emphasized by pointing to the magnificence of royal assemblies. When it was discovered that the cost incurred for these splendours was not sent in as a bill for parliament to pay, and that the Queen sacrificed much of the rest and peace which she would have desired—especially after she was engaged in maternal duties as well as the duties of state,—for the purpose of stimulating trade by a succession of state festivities, the adverse feeling subsided. It was known at last that the object of the Queen and the Prince was to encourage the spending of money on British productions, and this was particularly manifested on several occasions. One grand ball given at Covent Garden Theatre in May, 1842, for the relief of the Spitalfields weavers, was attended in state by the Queen and Prince Albert.

and the Queen had almost invariably set the example of wearing silk, satin, and other materials of British manufacture. A fortnight before the "Spitalfields" ball, however, there had been given at Buckingham Palace a *Bal Costumé* of such magnificence that it became historical as the most superb entertainment known in modern times.

The "Queen's Plantagenet Ball," as it came to be called, was organized by her Majesty and Prince Albert for the express purpose of helping trade in London, which was greatly depressed; and the large sums of money expended by those who were privileged to attend it must, at least, have had some effect in temporarily reviving some of the suffering industries.

Her Majesty was to represent Queen Philippa; and Prince Albert, Edward the Third; and the court was to appear in the court dress of that period. The preparations were on a great and sumptuous scale. Buckingham Palace had undergone some alterations, which were also great improvements. The library leading across the sculpture-gallery to the hall, the grand staircase of white marble, the lofty green drawing room occupying the centre of the eastern front, opening on the upper story of the portico and decorated in green satin with gold, and mirrored panels; and the throne-room, with its richly emblazoned coved ceiling, its sculptured frieze of white marble, and its hangings of crimson satin, were furnished and redecorated in accordance with the period to be represented. A throne of purple velvet with crowns, shields, and arms wrought in gold stood in an alcove in the throne-room. A great richly adorned tent, formerly belonging to Tippoo Saib, was raised beneath the Corinthian portico adjoining the green drawing-room. The windows were removed, and the tent was lit by an "Indian sun" eight feet in diameter set round a chandelier.

In this tent refreshments were to be served, and it was appointed with exquisite art and taste.

The whole scheme of this great entertainment was wrought out with the utmost care to make it a magnificent historical picture—an event to be remembered, and everybody with any pretensions to rank and fashion, especially everybody having the remotest chance of an invitation, became enthusiastic. There was, of course, a rage for securing accurate Plantagenet costumes, which, however, gave way in the main to more easily attainable habiliments of various historical periods and nationalities, since only the members of the court were expected to appear in the style of the reign of Edward the Third.

It would be useless to repeat the rumours that kept the town in a lively commotion. Enormous sums were said to have been expended on individual dresses by many among the noble guests, of whom a great company had been invited. The members of great and ancient families of high title, as well as of ample wealth, prepared to do honour to the occasion, and many of the rich and costly dresses were adorned with diamonds and jewels of almost fabulous value.

The leading feature of the ball, and that which gave it a distinctively historical character, was the assemblage and meeting of the court of Edward III. and Philippa and that of Anne of Brittany, who was represented by the Duchess of Cambridge; and this, as well as the other proceedings, was admirably accomplished. Arriving by a separate entrance, the Duchess of Cambridge and her court of Brittany assembled in one of the lower rooms of the palace, while the Queen and Prince Albert with a brilliant and gorgeous entourage awaited them in the throne-room.

Her Majesty's costume, which was entirely composed of the

manufactures of Spitalfields, consisted of a surcoat of blue and gold brocade lined with miniver over a skirt with demi-train of *ponceau* velvet, edged with fur. A mantle of gold and silver brocade lined with miniver was fastened with a jewelled band, which, traversing another band of jewels in gold tissue descending from the stomacher, gave the appearance of a great jewelled cross. Her Majesty's hair was taken up in the proper fashion of the period represented, and was surmounted by a light crown of gold, bearing but a single diamond of great size and brilliancy said to be worth £10,000.

Prince Albert was attired in a robe of blue and gold brocade slashed with blue velvet, over which was a scarlet velvet cloak lined with ermine and trimmed with gold lace in a pattern of oak leaves and acorns, and edged with pearls. The band of his cloak, the collar of his robe, and the shoes worn with scarlet silk hose were richly studded with jewels; and his gold coronet was set with precious stones.

The immediate suite were in correct costumes of the period, the maids of honour wearing dresses and surcoats decorated with gold and silver trimmings, the bed-chamber women with quarterings of lions and fleurs-de-lys, the Duke of Buccleugh, master of the horse, as one of the first Knights of the Garter, the Countess of Rosslyn as the Countess of Salisbury.

At half-past ten, marshalled by heralds, the procession ascended the white marble staircase and by the green drawing-room to the throne-room. The suites of apartments were thrown open, and were ablaze with light.

Many of the noble guests must have looked as though they were the old family pictures, from which their costumes had been copied, come out from the frames; but they had less to do with the actual spectacle of the ball than those visitors who were to take part in the series of brilliant state quadrilles that were to be the vivid episode of the occasion. There were quadrilles of various nationalities, French, German, Spanish, Italian, Greek, Scotch, Russian, a Waverley Quadrille led by Countess De la Warr, and a Crusaders Quadrille led by the Marchioness of Londonderry, who shone with brilliants even to her gloves and shoes. The great ceremony was the passing of the quadrilles before the Queen, who with the prince had headed the procession as it passed to the ball-room, where the general company was assembled. Taking their places on a *haut pas* under a canopy of amber satin they awaited each quadrille as it was danced in their presence. There were famous beauties, lovely dames, and fair maidens, knights and nobles of renown. The state quadrilles lasted for an hour, the Scottish sets taking the form of reels; and the court then returned to the throne-room to watch the Russian mazurkas; led by the Baroness Brunnow in a Cossack costume of Catherine II., a tunic of scarlet velvet over full loose trousers of white silk, gold-embroidered white satin boots, and a cap of scarlet velvet with heron's feathers. The scene in the throne-room during this dance was very striking and magnificent.

At one o'clock an ancient seneschal (Lord Liverpool, the lord high steward) conducted her Majesty to the dining-room, where supper was magnificently served at a long double table covered with grand and massy gold plate and beautifully decked with elegant services of china and glass. Opposite the centre of the cross tables, where the Queen sat, a splendid buffet rising almost to the lofty ceiling was covered with plate, which gleamed amidst a profusion of choice flowers. After supper her Majesty danced one quadrille with Prince George of Cambridge for a partner, and the Duke of Beaufort and the Duchess of Buccleugh as their *vis-à-vis.* At a quarter to three the Queen retired from the ball-room, and an hour afterwards the brilliant assembly dispersed.

Though this "Plantagenet Ball" was held, as we have seen, at a later date than the royal marriage, to which our main narrative has been brought, it properly belongs to the present page, for it may be said to have been the most remarkable of that series of splendid entertainments which began after the return of the royal pair from Windsor to London.

In the meantime other important social and political events had happened, and the Queen had entered upon a new phase of life. The tender cares and solicitudes of maternity had added a fresh grace to her youth. The birth of a princess royal and of a prince who would be heir to the throne had given a sweet but solemn intensity to all other responsibilities.

END OF VOL. I.